BOOKS BY ELLY GRIFFITHS

The Crossing Places
The Janus Stone
The House at Sea's End
A Room Full of Bones

A ROOM FULL of BONES

A ROOM FULL of BONES

A RUTH GALLOWAY MYSTERY

Elly Griffiths

HOUGHTON MIFFLIN HARCOURT
BOSTON · NEW YORK
2012

First U.S. edition

Copyright © 2012 by Elly Griffiths

For information about permission to reproduce selections from this
book, write to Permissions, Houghton Mifflin Harcourt Publishing
Company, 215 Park Avenue South, New York, New York 10003.

www.hmhbooks.com

First published in Great Britain in 2012 by Quercus

Library of Congress Cataloging-in-Publication Data
Griffiths, Elly.
A room full of bones : a Ruth Galloway mystery / Elly Griffiths.
—1st U.S. ed.
p. cm.
ISBN 978-0-547-27120-0
1. Galloway, Ruth (Fictitious character)—Fiction.
2. Women forensic anthropologists—Fiction. I. Title.
PR6107.R534R66 2012
823'.92—dc23
2012014833

Printed in the United States of America
DOC 10 9 8 7 6 5 4 3 2 1

For Nancy and Anita

PROLOGUE

31 October 2009

The coffin is definitely a health and safety hazard. It fills the entrance hall, impeding the view of the stuffed Auk, a map of King's Lynn in the 1800s and a rather dirty oil painting of Lord Percival Smith, the founder of the museum. The coffin's wooden sides are swollen and rotten and look likely to disgorge their contents in a singularly gruesome manner. Any visitors would find its presence unhelpful, not to say distressing. But today, as on most days, there are no visitors to the Smith Museum. The curator, Neil Topham, stands alone at the far end of the hall looking rather helplessly at the ominously shaped box on the floor. The two policemen who have carried it this far look disinclined to go further. They stand, sweating and mutinous in their protective clothing, under the dusty chandelier donated by Lady Caroline Smith (1884–1960).

'You can't leave it here,' says Neil.

'We were told "take it to the Smith museum,"' says the younger of the two men, PC Roy 'Rocky' Taylor.

'But you can't just leave it in the hall,' protests Neil. 'I want it in the Local History Room.'

'Is that upstairs?' asks the older man, Sergeant Tom Henty.

'No.'

'Good, because we don't do upstairs. Our union won't allow it.'

Neil doesn't know if they are joking or not. Do policemen have unions? But he stands aside as the two men shoulder their burden again and carry it, watched by myriad glass eyes, through the Natural History Room and into a smaller room decorated with a mural of Norfolk Through The Ages. There is a trestle table waiting in the centre of the room and, on this, the policemen lower the coffin.

'It's all yours,' says Taylor, breathing heavily.

'But don't open it, mind,' warns Henty. 'Not until the Big Guns get here.'

'I won't,' says Neil, although he looks with fascination, almost hunger, at the box, whose cracked lid offers a coy glimpse of the horrors within.

'Superintendent Whitcliffe's on his way.'

'Is the boss coming?' asks Taylor. Whitcliffe may be the most senior policeman in Norfolk, but for Taylor and others like him the boss will always be Detective Inspector Harry Nelson.

'Nah,' says Henty. 'Not his type of thing, is it? There'll be journalists, the works. You know how the boss hates journos.'

'Someone's coming from the university,' puts in Neil.

'Doctor Ruth Galloway, head of Forensic Archaeology. She's going to supervise the opening.'

'I've met her,' says Henty. 'She knows her stuff.'

'It's very exciting,' says Neil. Again he gives the coffin a furtive, almost greedy, look.

'I'll take your word for it,' says Henty. 'Come on, Rocky. Back to work. No peace for the wicked.'

1
———

Doctor Ruth Galloway, Head of Forensic Archaeology at the University of North Norfolk, is not thinking about coffins or journalists or even about whether she will encounter DCI Harry Nelson at the Smith Museum. Instead, she is racing through the King's Lynn branch of Somerfield wondering whether chocolate fingers count as bad mothering and how much wine four mothers and assorted partners can be expected to drink. Tomorrow is Ruth's daughter's first birthday and, much against Ruth's better judgement, she has been persuaded to have a party for her. 'But she won't remember it,' Ruth wailed to her best friend Shona, herself five months pregnant and glowing with impending maternity. 'You will though,' said Shona. 'It'll be a lovely occasion. Kate's first birthday. Having a cake, opening her presents, playing with all her little friends.'

'Kate doesn't play with her friends,' Ruth had protested. 'She hits them over the head with stickle bricks mostly.' But she had allowed herself to be convinced. And part of her does think that it will be a lovely occasion, a rare chance for her to sit back and watch Kate tearing off wrapping paper and shoving E-numbers in her mouth and think: I haven't done such a bad job of being a mother, after all.

As Ruth races past the soft drinks aisle, she becomes aware for the first time that the supermarket has been taken over by the forces of darkness. Broomsticks and cauldrons jostle for shelf space with plastic pumpkins and glow-in-the-dark vampire fangs. Bats hang from the ceiling and, as Ruth rounds the last bend, she comes face to face with a life-size figure wearing a witch's cloak and hat and a mask – based (rather convincingly, it must be said) on Munch's *The Scream*. Ruth stifles her own scream. Of course, it's Halloween. Kate only just escaped being born on 31 October, which, when combined with having a Pagan godfather, might have been one augury too far. Instead, her daughter was born on 1 November, All Saints' Day according to a Catholic priest who, to Ruth's surprise, is almost a friend. Ruth doesn't believe in God or the Devil but, she reflects, as she piles her shopping onto the conveyor belt, it's always useful to have a few saints on your side. Funny how the Day of the Dead is followed by the Day of the Saints. Or maybe not so funny. What *are* saints, after all, if not dead people? And Ruth knows to her cost that the path between saint and sinner is not always well defined.

She packs her shopping into her trusty, rusty car. Two o'clock. She has to be at the museum at three so there's not enough time to go home first. She hopes the choco-late fingers won't melt in the boot. Still, the day, though mild for October, is not exactly hot. Ruth is wearing black trousers and a black jacket. She winds a long green scarf round her neck and hopes for the best. She knows there'll be photographers at the museum, but with any luck she can hide behind Superintendent Whitcliffe. She'd never normally get to go to an event like this. Her boss, Phil, adores the limelight so is always first in line for anything involving the press. Two years ago, when *Time Team* came to a nearby Roman dig, Phil muscled his way in front of the cameras while Ruth lurked in a trench. 'It wasn't fair,' said Shona who, despite being in a relationship with Phil, knows his faults. 'You were the expert, not him.' But Ruth hadn't minded. She hates being the centre of attention; she prefers the research, the backroom stuff, the careful sifting of evidence. Besides, the camera is meant to put ten pounds on you, which Ruth, at nearly thirteen stone, can well do without.

But Phil is away at a conference so it's Ruth who is to be present at the grand opening of the coffin. It's the sort of thing she would normally avoid like the plague. She dislikes appearing in public and she feels distinctly queasy about opening a coffin live on Prime Time TV (well, *Look East* anyhow). 'Beware of disturbing the dead,' that's what Erik used to say. Erik Anderssen, Erik the Viking, Ruth's tutor at university and for many years afterwards her mentor and role model. Now her feelings about Erik are rather more complicated, but that doesn't stop his voice popping into her head at alarmingly regular intervals. Of course, disturbing the dead is an occupational hazard for archaeologists, but Ruth makes sure that no matter how long-dead the bones are, she always treats them with respect. For one nightmarish summer she excavated war graves in Bosnia, places where the bodies, sometimes killed only months earlier, were flung into pits to fester in the sun. She has dug up the bones of a girl who died over two thousand years ago, an Iron Age girl whose perfectly preserved arm still wore its bracelet of dried grass. She has found Roman bodies buried under walls, offerings to Janus, the two-faced God, and she has unearthed the bones of soldiers killed only seventy years ago. But she never lets herself forget that she is dealing with people who once lived and were once loved. Ruth doesn't believe in an afterlife which, in her opinion, is all the more reason to treat human relics with respect. They are all we have left.

The wooden coffin, believed to be that of Bishop Augustine Smith, was discovered when builders began work on a new supermarket in King's Lynn. The site, for many years derelict industrial land, had once been a church. The church, rather romantically called Saint Mary Outside the Walls, had been bombed in the war and, in the Fifties, was levelled to make way for a fish-canning factory. The factory itself fell into disrepair and now a shiny new supermarket is being built on top. But because of the site's history, the builders were obliged to call in the field archaeologists who, as was only to be expected, discovered the foundations of a medieval church. What was less expected was another discovery below what was once the high altar, of a coffin containing the remains, it was thought, of the fourteenth-century bishop.

The discovery was newsworthy for several reasons. The church was mentioned in the Domesday Book and Bishop Augustine himself features prominently in a fourteenth-century chronicle kept at Norwich Cathedral. In fact, Augustine, one of the earliest bishops, was always supposed to have been buried at the cathedral. What was he doing, then, buried under a fairly minor parish church in King's Lynn? But inscriptions on the coffin and dating of the wood pointed definitely to Bishop Augustine. The next step was carbon dating of the bones themselves, and somewhere along the line the decision was made to open the coffin in public – watched by the great and the good, including members of the Smith family.

And that's the other reason. The Smith family are still alive and well and living in Norfolk. Along the way they have been Catholic martyrs and Protestant traitors, en-nobled by Elizabeth I, and involved in a doomed attempt to hold King's Lynn for the Royalists in the Civil War. Lord Danforth Smith, the current title holder, is a race-horse trainer and unwilling local celebrity. His son, Randolph, usually to be found draped around an American actress or Russian tennis player, is more relaxed about being in the public eye and is a regular feature of the gossip columns. Previous Smiths have been rather more serious-minded and evidence of their philanthropy is everywhere in Norfolk. As well as the museum there is the Smith wing in the hospital and the Smith Art Collection at the castle. Ruth's university even has a Smith Professor of Local History, though he hasn't been seen in public for years and Ruth thinks he may well be dead.

She parks her battered car in front of the museum. The car park round the side is empty. She's early; it's only two-fifteen but still not enough time to get home and back. She might as well go into the museum and look around. Ruth loves museums, which is just as well because, as an archaeologist, she's done more than her share of looking in dusty glass cases. She remembers going to the Horniman Museum in Forest Hill as a child. It was a magical place, full of masks and stuffed birds. Come to think of it, the Horniman was probably the place where she first got interested in archaeology; they had a collection of flint tools, including some from Grimes Graves in Norfolk. She remembers the shock when she realised that these oddly shaped pieces of stone had actually been *held* by someone who had been alive thousands of years ago. The idea that you could actually go and dig up something that old – something that had been worked and honed by that mysterious creature known as Stone Age man – that idea still sends a shiver down her spine, and has sustained her through many a long and unsuccessful excavation. There is always the thought that under the next clod of earth there is the object – weathered and unrecognisable except to an expert – that is going to change human thought forever. Ruth has made a few lucky discoveries herself. But there is always the tantalising thought of the one big find, of the glass case with the inscription 'discovered by Doctor Ruth Galloway', of the articles, the book ... She pushes open the door.

The Horniman is a small museum but impressive in its way, with a clock tower at the front and glass conservatory at the back. The Smith Museum is something else. It's a low brick building, squashed between two office blocks. Overhanging gables, painted dull red, make it look as if it's wearing a hat pulled down low upon its head. Steps lead up to an arched red door with a promising sign saying 'welcome'. Ruth pushes open the door and finds herself in a small entrance lobby dominated by a stuffed bird in a case and a picture of an angry-looking man in a wig. There's a notice board adorned with a few faded flyers and a table containing some photocopied sheets labelled, somewhat optimistically, 'For School Parties', but no sign that a media event is taking place. No canapés or glasses of wine (Ruth is sure there was a mention of food), no press packs, not even a poster announcing the Grand Opening of the Bishop's Coffin. A yellowing chandelier overhead is still jangling from the opening of the door. Otherwise there is complete silence.

Ruth pushes through the swing doors and finds herself in a long room, lined on both sides with glass cases reaching up to the ceiling. There are no windows and the only light comes from the cabinets themselves, which shimmer with an eerie phosphorescence. Ruth stops and peers into one of the cases. It is labelled 'Eagle Owl' and contains a large stuffed bird which peers at her accusingly. She moves on quickly, unable to shake the conviction that the owl's eyes are following her. The next case, 'Black-backed gulls', shows a family of seagulls in the act of pecking a lamb to death. Painted blood smears the birds' beaks and the lamb looks up with an expression of resignation and cynicism. A few yards along and you are into woodland; dusty foxes gaze into brown-painted holes, squirrels are tied to tree trunks, badgers look glassily at moth-eaten rabbits, a three-legged deer is propped against a papier-mâché rock. Ruth finds herself walking faster and faster, the fur and feathers merging into one, her footsteps echoing on the tiled floor.

She crosses the room to look at the cases on the other side. Here, taxidermy gives way to Halloween. The animals on this side are skeletons, their thin bones dangling like children's mobiles against walls painted blue to resemble the sky, with white clouds and v-shaped flocks of birds. Giant otter shrew, pigmy shrew, giant golden mole, European hedgehog. They all look the same and rather sad, hanging there beside their little type-written name tags. In the biggest case is a skeleton that seems massive by comparison. Ruth is surprised to learn that, according to the label, it is only a domestic horse. The long skull and large teeth grin out of the gloom. Ruth, who rather likes horses, gives it a sympathetic smile and hurries on.

At the end of the gallery she steps from tile to carpet and, to her surprise, finds herself in a red-walled Victorian study. A stag's head looms over a painted fireplace and a man sits at a desk, frowning fiercely as he dips his quill into an inkwell.

'Excuse me . . .' begins Ruth, before realising that the man's eyes are dusty and one of his arms is missing. A rope separates her from the figure and his desk but she leans forward and reads the inscription:

Lord Percival Smith 1830–1902, adventurer and taxider-mist. Most of the exhibits in this museum were acquired by Lord Smith in the course of a fascinating life. Lord Smith's love of the natural world is shown in his magnificent collec-tion of animals and birds, most of which he shot and stuffed himself.

Funny way to show your love of the natural world, by shooting most of it, thinks Ruth. She notices a brace of guns over the head of the waxwork Lord Smith. He looks a nasty customer, alive or dead.

There are two ways out of Lord Smith's study. One says 'New World Collection' and one 'Local History.' She pauses, feeling like Alice in Wonderland. A slight sound, a kind of whispering or fluttering, makes her turn towards Local History. She feels in the mood for a soothing collection of Norfolk artefacts. She hopes there are no more waxworks or embalmed animals.

Her wish is granted. The Local History Room seems to be empty apart from a coffin on a trestle table and a body lying beside it. A breeze from an open window is riffling through the pages of a guidebook lying on the floor, making a sound like the wings of a trapped bird.

2

The body is lying on its side, legs drawn up into an almost foetal position. Ruth touches a hand, which is still warm. Is there a pulse? She can't find one but her own hands are suddenly slippery with sweat and she's not really sure what she's looking for anyway. Oh, why didn't she go on that first-aid course? She realises that she is holding her breath and forces herself to exhale, in and out, nose and mouth. It won't do anyone any good if she faints. Gently she turns the body over and has two shocks, so severe that she almost stops breathing again.

There is blood all over the face and the face is that of someone she knows.

Neil Topham, the curator, who once came to one of her lectures on the preservation of bones. Neil, polite and unassuming, who often asked her advice about exhibits. Neil, lying on the floor of his own museum, his nose and mouth covered in blood.

Hands shaking, Ruth reaches for her phone. Please God don't let her have left it in the car. No, it's here. She dials 999 and asks for an ambulance. She goes completely blank when asked for the address and can only bleat, 'The Smith Museum. Please hurry!' The voice on the other end of the phone is calm and reassuring, even slightly bored. 'A unit is on its way.' Ruth bends her head close to Neil's mouth. She can't hear or feel any breathing. But when she puts her hand inside his shirt there is a heartbeat, very faint and unsteady, but unmistakably there. Hang on in there, Neil, she tells him. Should she move the body? But all the books tell you not to. She looks desperately round the room. The bishop's coffin looms above them, dark and sinister. There is nothing else in the room apart from a glass display case in the corner and, by the window, a man's single shoe.

What can have happened to Neil? Did he have a heart attack or a stroke? But he's a young man. Young men don't just fall down and die. It is only now that Ruth realises that what happened to Neil might not be due to natural causes. She looks around the room again. The pages of the book are still fluttering to and fro. From the open window she can hear traffic, the faint shouts of children in the park. Why is the window open anyway?

With shaking hands, Ruth reaches for her phone and calls the police.

'It's the Smith museum, boss.'

'What?'

DCI Nelson is driving and his sergeant, DS Clough, is on the phone. This is a reversal of the normal order, it's usually the junior officer who drives, but Nelson hates being a passenger. At this latest news, Nelson turns to look at Clough and the car swerves across the traffic, narrowly missing a motorbike and an invalid car. Clough vows to be behind the wheel next time. His boss's driving skills, or lack of them, are legendary.

'The body. It's at the Smith Museum.'

Nelson and Clough, driving back from Felixstowe where they were following an abortive lead about a drug-smuggling ring, received a call that a dead body had been found in King's Lynn. The circumstances were suspicious and Nelson, who heads the county's Serious Crimes Squad, was on his way. It is only now, on the outskirts of the town, that Clough has managed to get the full details. He grunts, maddeningly, into his phone and Nelson swerves wildly once more.

'What? What?'

'It's the curator, boss. You know there was that big do at the museum, opening the coffin and all that? You refused to go, remember?'

'I remember,' growls Nelson.

'Well, an hour before all the bigwigs were due to arrive, one of the archaeologists gets there early and finds this curator guy, Neil Topham, lying beside the coffin, dead as a doornail.'

'Which archaeologist?' asks Nelson. But he knows the answer. He knew as soon as Clough mentioned the Smith Museum.

Clough relays the question over the phone.

'It was Ruth, boss. Ruth Galloway.'

The car swerves across the road.

* * *

When Nelson arrives at the museum, Rocky Taylor is standing by the front door, a circumstance that does nothing to ease Nelson's troubled mind. He regards Rocky, a local lad, as a typical slow-moving country bumpkin. Nelson, who was born in Blackpool, still thinks of himself as a Northerner, which, in his mind, is synonymous with sharp wits and a proper sense of humour. On entering the lobby, he is slightly relieved to find Tom Henty in attendance. Tom, though born and bred in Norfolk, is Nelson's idea of the perfect police sergeant – steady, tough, unflappable. He's going to need all those qualities today. Tom is standing beside a glass case containing a particularly hideous stuffed bird. Next to him, on a hard chair, looking pale but in control, is Ruth Galloway.

'Ruth,' Nelson nods at her.

'Hallo Nelson.'

Clough, following in Nelson's wake, is rather more forthcoming. 'Ruth! Long time no see. How's that baby of yours?'

'Fine. She'll be one tomorrow.'

'One! Can't believe it. Seems like only yesterday that she was born.'

'Less of the chatting, Sergeant,' says Nelson, not looking at Ruth. 'This is a crime investigation, not a coffee morning.' He turns to Henty. 'What happened?'

'Got a call at two-twenty.' Henty flips open his notebook. 'Came through to the duty desk. Dr Galloway was at the museum and found the curator, Neil Topham, lying on the floor beside the coffin. The one that was due to be opened at three. Dr Galloway called the emergency services – police and ambulance. Taylor and I got here the same time as the ambulance. Paramedics took him to hospital but he was DOA.'

'Damn.'

That was bad news for Neil Topham admittedly, but also for the investigation. The body will be covered with the prints of the well-meaning paramedics. And the only evidence of the crime scene will be the one witness. Ruth Galloway.

'Have next of kin been informed?'

'DS Johnson's at the hospital now.'

That's good. Judy Johnson's the best at that kind of thing. Get bad news from Clough and you might never recover.

Nelson looks at his watch. It's now three-thirty. 'Did you manage to stop the vultures descending?'

Henty coughs deprecatingly. 'I rang Superintendent Whitcliffe and informed the local press.'

'Whitcliffe isn't coming is he?'

'No. He said he'd let you deal.'

I bet he did, thinks Nelson savagely.

'Rocky turned away the rest of the public,' says Henty. 'Your friend was there. The warlock.'

Nelson grunts, recognising the description without difficulty. 'Cathbad? Of course he was there. Opening a coffin would be just his idea of fun.'

'He said he wanted to talk to you,' says Henty impassively. 'Something about skulls and the unquiet dead.'

Nelson grunts again. 'Well it'll have to wait. Can you show me the room where the body was found? Clough,

wait here with Dr Galloway.' And he stalks away without
a backward glance.

There is something strangely calm about the Local History
Room. It's a long, narrow space, slightly too high for its
width, as if it was once part of a larger room. The floor,
like the rest of the museum, is covered in black and white
tiles and the walls are painted in cheerful primary colours.
The window is open and the breeze blows the dusty
curtains inwards. The coffin, with its straining sides,
stands four-square in the centre of the room. There is a
single glass case in a corner containing what looks like
a stuffed grass snake. The only other objects on the floor
are a guidebook and a single shoe, a brown suede slip-
on, about a foot away from the coffin. Nelson stares at
it dispassionately. Typical arty shoes. Real men – real
Northern men – always wear lace-ups.

'Think that's his? Topham's?'

Henty shrugs. 'I suppose so.'

'Did you see him earlier? You delivered this thing didn't
you? You and Rocky.'

'Yes. I saw him. Only a few hours ago.'

'How did he seem?'

'I don't know. A bit excited. Wound up. I suppose he
was looking forward to the big event.'

Henty does good deadpan; Nelson approves. The man
could be a Northerner.

'No palpitations? Signs that he was going to drop down
dead?'

'No. He was youngish. Not overweight. Looked in reasonable health. A bit overwrought, as I say. Screamed at Rocky when he knocked something over.'

'We all scream at Rocky. That doesn't mean anything.' Nelson looks around the room. 'You haven't touched anything in here.' It's a statement more than a question.

'No, sir. Scene-of-the-crime boys are on their way.'

Quite right. That was the way modern policing worked. Don't touch anything until the SOCO team get there with their space-age suits and brushes and little plastic boxes. In the old days, when Nelson was a young PC in Blackpool, they'd be in there right away, moving the body, getting their fingerprints over everything. Now Nelson rotates slowly on the spot, taking in the crime scene at a distance. If it *is* a crime scene.

There are a few streaks on the floor which might be blood and the tiles, though obviously recently swept, are still grubby in places. That's good. The forensic boys love a bit of dirt, perfect for catching prints, DNA, all the stuff they like. The curtains flap more wildly. The wind is getting up.

Nelson turns to Henty. 'Was the window open when you got here?'

'Yes.'

Strange to have an open window in October. Nelson walks over to it and looks out. They are on the ground floor and it would be fairly easy to get in that way. Outside is the car park, a few dustbins and a charity recycling box. No handy soil for footprints but someone in the adjoining offices may have seen something. He'll have to send Rocky house-to-house.

Nelson walks slowly round the room. He realises that the patterns on the walls are in fact a series of pictures. Norfolk Through The Ages. One scene in particular catches his eye: a circle of wooden posts on a beach, a crudely drawn figure in a white robe in the centre of the circle, arms stretched out like a scarecrow, an improbably yellow sun shining overhead. Nelson goes closer. 'Bronze Age wooden henge on Saltmarsh Beach,' he reads, 'discovered in 1997 by Professor Erik Anderssen of the University of Oslo.' And by Ruth Galloway, he thinks. He thinks also of the Saltmarsh, the bleak expanse of wind-blown grass, the treacherous stretches of quicksand, the tide rushing in across the mudflats, turning land into sea – a fatal trap for the unwary. Nothing could be further from the cheery blue and yellow beach scene on the wall. He looks at the next wall. 'Roman Villa at Swaffham, believed to be part of a garrison town.' A white-pillared house stands smugly in landscaped grounds, like something from an upmarket housing estate. Nelson frowns at it. He doesn't like the Romans any better than he likes the Bronze Age idiots. Between the Roman Villa and the henge is a cartoon which could, if charitably interpreted, be said to represent a girl lying on her side. 'Iron Age girl, discovered in 2007 by Dr Ruth Galloway of the University of North Norfolk.'

'Boss?'

Nelson turns round, grateful that Tom Henty can't see his thoughts.

'Do you want to speak to Dr Galloway? Only she was saying something about having to collect her little girl from the childminder's.'

Nelson sighs. 'OK. When the SOCO boys come, get them to check over by the window. I think there may have been forced entry.'

'Do you think it's murder then, boss?'

'I don't know. Could have been natural causes, I suppose, but I don't like the open window. Looks as if there may have been a break-in. Is Chris Stephenson on his way to the hospital?'

Chris Stephenson is the police pathologist. Not high on Nelson's list of favourite people (admittedly, that's not a long list).

'Yes. Apparently he was at some Halloween party with his kids.'

'Well, maybe he'll fly there on his broomstick.'

Nelson doesn't like Halloween. Old people frightened by feral teens in fright masks, eggs thrown at cars, bricks through windows. He thinks that Michelle may have taken their daughters trick-or-treating when they were little but it seemed a gentler affair in those days. The girls always refused to dress as anything as unaesthetic as witches anyway. He remembers a couple of Disney fairies dancing off to the neighbours to collect handfuls of Haribos. Admittedly, Rebecca did go through a vampire stage, but that was later.

'Right,' he says. 'Is there an office or something where I can talk to Dr Galloway?'

'Curator's office is just down the corridor.'

'Grand. Send her down to me will you?'

He finds the office without difficulty. It's at the end of a corridor that also doubles as an art gallery, another succession of gloomy oil paintings. Here there are trestle tables laid out with wine boxes and plastic glasses, the only signs so far that the museum was expecting visitors that day. Nelson takes a crisp from a bowl as he passes. He's meant to be on a diet but murder always makes him hungry. Halfway down the corridor there's a door marked 'Fire Exit.' Nelson tries the handle. Locked. A breach of health and safety rules. Or maybe someone wanted to block off possible escape routes?

Inside the curator's office Nelson finds himself in a confused space of cardboard boxes and exhibits from the museum, maybe removed for repair or because they were in some way surplus to requirements. He pushes past a stuffed beaver and a wall-eyed Viking in a one-horned helmet. There's a pile of DIY tools on the floor. Perhaps Topham meant to mend the exhibits himself.

The desk is covered with paper, which irritates Nelson whose desk at King's Lynn Police Station is famously clear apart from his ever-present To Do List. Nelson loves lists and feels that a few lists would have done Neil Topham the power of good. Might even have stopped him being killed. 1. Come to work. 2. Tidy office 3. Avoid being murdered by a knife-wielding maniac. But there is no knife and he doesn't even know for sure that Neil Topham was murdered. At some point he'll have to search the office properly, but first, Ruth Galloway.

The door is pushed open. 'You sent for me?' Ruth's voice is heavy with irony.

'I just thought we should talk somewhere private.'

Ruth's sarcastic expression is replaced by something a little more ... what? Wary? Vulnerable?

'So.' Nelson clears a space on the desktop, pushing aside old editions of *Museums Today*, and gestures at Ruth to sit down. 'You arrived at the museum when?'

'Are you taking notes?' The sarcastic note has returned.

Nelson produces a notebook with a flourish. He nods encouragingly.

'I arrived at approximately two-sixteen p.m.—'

'Bit early wasn't it? I thought the bun fight started at three.'

'I'd been to the supermarket. Didn't think it was worth driving home and back.' She looks at Nelson. 'It's Kate's birthday tomorrow. I was shopping for her party.'

There is a long silence. Nelson flinches as if her words cause him actual, bodily pain. Then, as if continuing a conversation started a long time ago, they both speak at once.

'I'm sorry . . .'

'I didn't . . .'

They both stop. Ruth's face is flushed, Nelson's very pale. She looks away. The window is high in the wall, too small to see out of if you're sitting down, but she gazes at it anyway.

'I didn't mean to upset you. I know you don't want to talk about her.'

'It's not that.' Nelson looks down at the untidy desk, starts to move objects randomly. A fossil paperweight here, a pile of unopened bills there. 'It's just . . .' He stops. 'I promised.'

'I know. You promised Michelle you wouldn't see her.' Ruth's voice is flat. 'Or me.'

'It was the only way I could save my . . . make it up to her.'

'I understand. I said so at the time, didn't I?'

'You've been great. It's just me.' He shifts the paper-weight again and gives a sigh that is almost a groan. 'I've messed things up for everyone.'

'Oh, spare us the Catholic guilt Nelson.' Ruth gets out her phone and checks the time. A new phone, Nelson notices. Rather a smart one. 'Let's get on with it. I thought you were meant to be conducting an investigation here.'

'Fine.' Nelson squares his shoulders. 'You arrived at two-sixteen. Was anyone else here?'

'No. I thought it was odd. After all, the event was in less than an hour's time. Anyway, the place was deserted so I thought I'd just have a look round. I went through the Natural History Gallery . . .'

'The one with all the stuffed animals?'

'That's right.'

'Gives me the creeps.'

'Me too. Then I went into the Local History Room and there he was, lying by the coffin.'

'Did you recognise him?'

'Not at first but when I turned the body over—' She stops.

'Are you OK? Do you want a glass of water?'

Ruth smiles faintly. 'Is this your softly softly inter-viewing technique? No. I'm OK. I'd only met Neil once or twice before but I recognised him.'

'Where was he lying?'

'Next to the coffin. He was on his side, legs drawn up, one arm over his head.'

'Was there any blood?'

'Yes. On his face.'

'As if he'd been battered around the head?'

'No. Around his nose. Almost as if he'd had a nose bleed.' She stops.

'Did you touch him?'

'Yes,' Ruth's voice is sharp. 'Of course I touched him. I wanted to see if he was alive.'

'And was he?'

'I wasn't sure,' Ruth admits. 'His skin was warm but I couldn't find a pulse at first. I called an ambulance, then I thought I felt a faint heartbeat. I don't know anything about first aid.'

'When did you call the police?'

'About a minute later. It suddenly occurred to me that someone might have done this to him.'

'You thought he might have been murdered?'

'I didn't know what to think. He looked as if he might have had a fit. Maybe he was epileptic or something.'

'We'll find out if so. Chris Stephenson's on his way to the hospital.'

Ruth grimaces. A dislike of Stephenson is something she and Nelson have in common.

'Was the window open?' asks Nelson.

'What?'

'The window in the room where you found the body. Was it open?

'I think so, yes. There was a book on the floor and the breeze was turning the pages.'

'I'll get SOCO to look at the book. Might be prints on it, I suppose.'

'Do *you* think he may have been murdered then?'

Nelson is about to answer when there's a peremptory knock and the door opens to admit a man – tall, bronzed, grey-haired with a decided air of command. He has a large, hawk-like nose which seems to enter the room a few seconds before the rest of him. He also looks vaguely familiar. Rocky Taylor is hovering in the background.

'I said I wasn't to be disturbed,' snaps Nelson.

'Danforth Smith.' The tall man holds out his hand. Nelson ignores him and looks at Rocky.

'Lord Smith.' Henty appears and makes an apologetic introduction. 'The owner of the museum.'

'I came at once,' Danforth Smith is saying in confident upper-class tones that set Nelson's teeth on edge. 'Dreadful thing to have happened. Poor Neil. Is it true that he's dead?'

Nelson's holds up a hand. 'How did you know about Mr Topham?'

'Gerald told me.'

That figures. Gerald Whitcliffe, Nelson's boss and a friend to the great and good.

'I was all set to come to the opening when I got the phone call from Gerald. I've been trying to reach Neil's parents. They'll be devastated.'

'Sergeant,' Nelson addresses Tom Henty over Smith's head. 'I'm conducting an interview here.'

'It's OK, Nelson.' Ruth stands up. 'I've got to go anyway and we've finished, haven't we?'

She looks at him, her chin lifted.

'Yes,' says Nelson. 'We've finished.'

* * *

Lord Danforth Smith sits in Ruth's vacated chair and stretches out his legs as if he owns the place. Which he does. Rocky scurries off to make coffee. Bloody serf. Come the revolution, he'll be first against the wall. (The aristocrats will have scarpered long ago.)

'DCI Nelson,' Nelson introduces himself.

'I know who you are,' Smith says affably. 'Gerald speaks very highly of you.'

'Does he? Well, Lord Smith, you probably know as much as we do. Dr Galloway arrived at the museum early to find Mr Topham lying beside your ancestor's coffin. She called an ambulance but he was dead on arrival at the hospital.'

'How terrible. Does anyone know how he died? I mean, he was a young man.'

'How young?'

'Thirties I think. I'd have to check. Thirty sounds young to me these days.' Lord Smith smiles, showing long, equine teeth. He is a racehorse trainer, Nelson remembers.

'How long had Mr Topham worked for you?'

'About five years. Absolutely super chap. Very enthusiastic.'

'No health problems?'

'Not that I know of.'

'Was he in trouble of any kind? Anything worrying him?'

For the first time, Lord Smith looks slightly uneasy. He crosses and recrosses his legs. Handmade shoes, Nelson bets. Lace-ups.

'Last time I spoke to him it was about the opening of

the coffin. He seemed fine, very excited about having the event here. He hoped that Bishop Augustine could stay in the museum permanently.'

'Must have been a strain, organising an event like that?'

'Maybe, but that was Neil's job. He loved it. He loved getting people to visit the museum. We've got a fine collection here and it doesn't get the recognition it deserves. Look here, Inspector, what's all this about? Is there something odd about Neil's death?'

'I'm not sure yet.' Nelson looks at him blandly. 'But you'll be the first to know if so.' He realises where he has seen that nose before. It's in half the bloody oil paintings outside.

After Lord Smith has left, bowed out by Rocky and Tom Henty, Nelson does what he's been waiting to do: opens the locked drawer in Neil Topham's desk. The key had been hidden, rather inadequately he can't help thinking, under the flint paperweight.

The drawer proves worth inspection. Inside, Nelson finds a plastic bag full of white powder and a pile of handwritten letters. No envelopes, but they are all on the same sort of paper, cream notepaper, expensive-looking. Love letters? Well, love is always a good motive for murder. Nelson smoothes out the first sheet and reads the bold, blue handwriting:

You have ignored our requests.
Now you will suffer the consequences.

3

Ruth drives straight to the childminder's house to collect Kate. Sandra looks after Kate while she is at work, but this is a Saturday and Ruth feels it is an imposition. Sandra doesn't seem to mind though, and Kate, up to her elbows in flour making cakes, seems to be having a whale of a time. As usual, Sandra has several other children there, all organised in benign labour – making cakes, sticking things on paper, playing a giant (wipe clean) snakes and ladders in the sitting room. Sandra's own kids are grown up so these must also be the offspring of mothers too disorganised to arrange weekend childcare. Ruth can't be the only one, surely? At least she is paying Sandra, which means it's a clean commercial transaction, unlike those murky arrangements with friends. Could you do me a favour? Are you sure you don't mind? I'll do the same for you one day. Much better like this, cash in hand.

Ruth likes Sandra but never knows what to say to her, so she thanks her, picks up Kate – floury hands on her best jacket – and backs out of the small terraced house. Sandra waves her goodbye, a child on each hip.

'She hasn't slept, kept going all afternoon, so you might be lucky tonight,' she says.

There was a time when Ruth wouldn't have understood this sentence. She is wiser now. Kate hasn't slept. This means that if Ruth keeps her awake all the way home, she may fall asleep at six and not wake until the morning. Kate and Ruth still haven't really got the sleeping thing sorted. Get her into a routine, the books say, but the only bedtime routine that suits her daughter is Ruth staying with her for hours, reading stories, singing lullabies, or just lying there holding her hand. If Ruth tiptoes out of the room, Kate starts to wail. Let her cry, say the books, but Ruth can't bear to. Maybe it would be better if there was another parent, someone to pour her a glass of wine and tell her to be strong, but on her own Ruth weakens. Before she has got downstairs, she's back in attendance, singing, story-telling, hand-holding. She usually falls asleep too, lying beside Kate's cot, and wakes up stiff and dry-mouthed at midnight. When morning comes, horri-fyingly early, one of them is bright-eyed and raring to go and it isn't Ruth.

'Mum,' says Kate now. 'Mum mum mum mum.'

This is a new development, one which never fails to bring a lump to Ruth's throat. She likes the way that Kate says 'Mum' and not 'Mummy', as if she's a tiny teenager. Ruth's more comfortable with mum anyway. Mummy sounds twee and home counties. She's sure that Shula and David Archer call their mother 'Mummy'.

Slightly more disturbingly, Kate has also started saying 'Dada.' As there's no male person currently standing in this relation to her, she employs a scatter-gun approach and has so far bestowed the title on Ruth's cat, Flint, her grandfather, Cathbad, and the postman. Ruth's father and Cathbad were delighted; Flint and the postman underwhelmed.

As she drives through the King's Lynn streets, past the quay and the customs house and the market square, Ruth keeps up a merry flow of prattle designed to keep her daughter awake. 'Look Kate, look at that dog! He's spotty isn't he? Just like the hundred-and-one Dalmatians. Mum will read you that one day. It's brilliant. Much better than the film. Look, children dressed as witches! And some more of them! And here are some children dressed as mass-murderers. How cute!' As afternoon turns to evening, more and more of these mini-devils swarm onto the streets. When did trick-and-treating become so ubiquitous? She's never going to let Kate do it. But then, there are no neighbours where they live, only the sea and the miles of whispering marshland. Perhaps she should move. Ruth winds down the windows, hoping that the cold will keep Kate awake. She ejects Bruce Springsteen and puts in a tape of children's songs. 'My Bonnie lies over the ocean, my Bonnie lies over the sea.' All in vain. Kate's head droops.

Ruth's not too disappointed. She knows she'll pay for it later but right now she could do with the quiet. Maybe Kate will stay asleep when they get home and Ruth can carry her up to her cot. Mum needs to think, Ruth tells Kate silently. She's a bit churned up because she saw your dad today. Dad. Kate has never called Nelson 'Dada' but then she hasn't seen him for six months. In the first few months of Kate's life, Nelson was a frequent visitor, torn with guilt over Michelle but also fascinated by this new, unexpected daughter. Kate was born after Ruth and Nelson spent one night together, a few hours stolen out of a horrendous sequence of events which had begun with a murdered child. Ruth had always known that Nelson would never leave his wife and his other daughters, and she had prided herself on asking him for nothing. But Nelson hadn't been able to leave the situation alone, had wanted to give Ruth money, had wanted to be part of Kate's life. He had even insisted that Ruth have the baby christened and that he and Michelle should be godparents. But at the christening, Michelle had found out.

Ruth still doesn't know how it happened, but two days after the short ceremony at a Catholic church, Nelson had turned up on her doorstop, so ashen-faced that for a second she had barely recognised him. Michelle knew that he was Kate's father. 'She asked me a straight question and I couldn't very well lie, could I?' Ruth had her own opinion on that but she had wisely kept silent. Nelson had admitted everything and he and Michelle had 'had it out'. They had argued furiously ('It was terrible, Ruth, we argued for two days. We never argue.' 'Really?') and the upshot was that Nelson had agreed not to see Ruth or Kate again. Ever. 'It was the only way I could save our marriage. I'm sorry.' What if they met in the course of work, Ruth had asked, stony-faced. 'She accepts that that might happen, of course.' Nelson had wanted to make a 'financial provision', to give her money every month, but Ruth had refused. She hadn't realised how far Nelson would go to save his marriage. Or how much it would hurt.

Seeing Nelson at the museum had been worse, far worse, than seeing poor Neil Topham's body curled up beside the bishop's coffin. Her feelings for Nelson are so complicated that she has long since stopped trying to make sense of them. As soon as she sees him she always feels, in quick succession: irritation (he's the bossiest person she knows), respect (he's very good at his job), pleasure (he makes her laugh), and undeniable attraction. Does she love him? She has stopped asking herself this question too. She knows that she never wants to live with a man again. Ten years ago, when Peter moved out, she remembers the way the house itself seemed to sigh with relief. It was just Ruth and the cats and the wild skyline, alone at last. And now it's just Ruth and Kate and Flint. But it had been nice having Nelson around. He may be a male chauvinist pig but he's quite useful in a crisis.

Bring back, bring back, oh bring back my Bonnie to me . . .

She has reached the Saltmarsh. It is dark now but she can hear the sea sighing in the distance. The road is raised up over the flat marshland, and at times like this it feels as if you are arriving at the end of the world. She may have left the plastic ghouls and miniature witches behind but this is the real thing. The dark, the unknown. Ruth has known real terror on the Saltmarsh but still she loves it. Her cottage is one of three but one is empty and the other is a holiday home, seldom occupied. It's a lonely place but, on the whole, Ruth enjoys the solitude. So, when she parks outside her house and the security light (installed two years ago by Nelson) illuminates the Sold sign on the house next door, she feels a familiar irritation, almost anger. The house has been bought for rental, she knows, and any day now she'll have some trendy couple leaning over the fence and inviting her round for sushi, or some bearded loner who wants to show her his dried seaweed collection. Or some—. Stop, she tells herself, unlocking the door and carrying Kate inside. It may well be a new soul mate, or someone with children the right age to play with Kate, but the truth is that Ruth doesn't really want any new friends. She has enough trouble with the ones she's got.

Nelson drives to the hospital in a similarly uncomfortable state of mind. Seeing Ruth again had been as bad as he had imagined it would be. And when she mentioned Katie! Nelson's feelings for Ruth are so tied up with guilt and fear that he finds them impossible to untangle. His feelings for Katie, on the other hand, are crystal clear. He loves her, the baby he has only held three times in his life, and he wants to be her father. But that's impossible.

The events at the christening six months ago are still so painful that Nelson finds his thoughts veering away whenever he tries to approach the recollection. Now he forces himself to remember. Michelle had been fine at first. She had been keen to be a godmother; in fact she had always taken a special interest in Ruth and Kate,

something which, when he thought about it, had had
the power to make him feel almost ill with guilt and fore-
boding. But like an idiot, he had ignored his misgivings.
He had insisted on a Catholic christening because he'd
been brought up a Catholic, and Cathbad's naming day
ceremony held a few months earlier had made him acutely
uncomfortable. Worse, he felt that they were ill-wishing
Kate in some way, invoking those faceless, bloodthirsty
Gods that Cathbad admires so much. He'd wanted some
protection from the angels and saints of his own childhood. So he had persuaded Ruth to have Kate baptised
and had asked Father Hennessey, a Catholic priest whom
he had met on a previous case, to perform the service.
Ruth had agreed, partly because she too had been
impressed by Patrick Hennessey and, he suspects, partly
because Ruth herself had come close to death just a few
weeks earlier.

And, at first, it had been a happy occasion. A beautiful
May day, he remembers, with blossom on the trees and
the promise of summer in the air. He had held Kate (the
third time) and Michelle, who loves babies, had been in
her element. Cathbad and Shona, the other godparents,
had been no madder than they could help. Afterwards
they had driven to a country pub with Ruth and Kate in
the back of the car. Michelle had chatted happily to Ruth
on the journey but as Ruth got out of the car, Michelle
had detained Nelson with an imperious hand. Despite
trying not to, he can see her face now, an expression so
glacial with anger that he can only describe it as terrifying.

'She's yours, isn't she?'

'What?'

'Kate. She's yours. I was looking at her just now and she's got this little whorl of hair that goes a different way from the rest. You've got one just like it. So has Rebecca.'

At first he denied it outright. They had stood there, in the car park of The Phoenix, hissing at each other as the happy families walked past them, heading for a pub lunch in the sun.

'You must be mad,' he had said. 'What are you talking about, a whorl of hair?'

Michelle had looked at him disdainfully. 'Don't bother lying about it. Everything fits. I wondered why you were always so concerned about Ruth. I thought you might be becoming a nicer person in your old age. How wrong can you be?'

He tried for bemusement. 'What are you on about, love?'

'Don't call me love. You slept with Ruth, she's had your baby, and now you're trying to deny it. I never knew you were such a coward, Harry.'

And he is a coward. He knows that now. They had been forced to go into the pub, to drink Kate's health and laugh at Cathbad's jokes. Michelle, brittle and beautiful with self-righteous fury, had even held the baby in her arms, thoughtfully stroking the telltale swirl of dark hair. When they got home Michelle had given him an ultimatum. He must never see Ruth or Kate again. 'But I work with her,' he had protested. 'You know what I mean. You can speak to her as a colleague but

never, never as anything more than that.' And he had
agreed.

He had known all along that he could never break up
his family, turn Laura and Rebecca into resentful
strangers and Michelle into that age-old stock character
'the ex-wife.' Although his daughters are both at university now, they still need him. They need both their
parents, they need a home. And Michelle. He has loved
her for almost all his adult life. She's still one of the
most beautiful women he's ever seen and she's the
mother of his beloved daughters. How could he ever leave
her? Once he fantasised that he could have both women,
all three children, but that's not the way the world works.
But in honouring his wedding vows Nelson has betrayed
Ruth. He can hear himself now, blustering, gabbling away,
denying that there was ever anything between them. A
phrase from the Good Friday gospel comes back to him.
Before the cock crows, you will have denied me three
times.

Nelson sighs as he turns into the grounds of the
hospital. 'Car Park full. Current waiting time: 30 minutes.'
He has sinned and the wages of sin are death. Death has
come uncomfortably close in the last few years. He can't
afford to make the Gods angrier than they already are.
And, in the meantime, he has a dead body and Ruth
Galloway is the only witness.

The whole case bothers him. Neil Topham could have
died from natural causes but the idea of the body lying
beside the other, long-dead, corpse disturbs him. And those
letters. Once before Nelson had had to deal with a case

involving anonymous letters and there were enough echoes in the missives found in Topham's desk to make the hairs on the back of his neck rise.

> *You have ignored our requests.*
> *Now you will suffer the consequences.*
> *You have violated our dead.*
> *Now the dead will be revenged on you.*
> *We will come for you.*
> *We will come for you in the Dreaming.*

Nelson screeches to a halt in a bay reserved for emergency vehicles. Detective Sergeant Judy Johnson comes out to meet him. She's one of Nelson's best officers: bright, hard-working, excellent at the touchy-feely stuff. She got married earlier in the year and Nelson lives in dread of her announcing that she's off on maternity leave. 'That's the trouble with promoting women,' he grumbled to his boss. Whitcliffe had been shocked. 'Harry! You just can't say things like that these days.' The list of things that Nelson can't say seems to be getting longer by the minute. Still, he's sure that Whitcliffe knows what he means. All that trouble training up an officer only to have her quit the moment she starts getting really useful. Or she'll try and juggle work and babies and be constantly tired and stressed. Judy hasn't said anything about starting a family though; come to think of it, she's been rather quiet these last few weeks.

'Hi boss.'

They are standing in the entrance to A and E. A steady

stream of injured revellers, some still in Halloween masks, trail past them. The walking wounded. And it's not six o'clock yet.

'Dead on arrival?' Nelson greets Judy.

She nods. 'He's in the morgue. I've contacted his parents. They're on their way.'

'Chris Stephenson had a look?'

'Yes. He says he'll do a post-mortem tomorrow.'

'Say anything else useful?'

'Signs of drug use.'

Nelson thinks of the white powder found in the desk drawer. Was it for Topham's private use only? What was going on at the Smith Museum?

'Cause of death?' he asks, stepping aside to let a reeling man dressed as a mummy go past.

'Not sure. Could have been heart attack.'

'I'd better have a look.'

Judy follows Nelson across the car park, towards a discreet sign saying 'Hospital Morgue'. On their way they pass a couple of nurses wearing witches' hats and a disturbingly realistic vampire, swigging Bull's Blood from the bottle.

4

It seems impossible that six children can make this much noise. Ruth's little house seems to be swelling with sound, its sides straining under the pressure of chocolate fingers, party games and an exuberant rendering of 'Happy Birthday Dear Katie'. This last reminds Ruth uncomfortably of Nelson, who persists in calling her Katie. Why can't people just accept that Ruth knows her own daughter's name, even if it does scan better with an 'ie' on the end?

Kate's little friends include two toddlers, both clients of Sandra's, who ignore each other and run round bursting balloons, and two older children belonging to a colleague of Ruth's. The older kids, who are called Daisy and Ben, try to organise the babies but end up playing pass-the-parcel solemnly by themselves. Ben wins a rag doll and hands it silently to his mother.

Shona, radiant in a pink velvet tunic, sits on the floor with Kate so that people who don't know her say 'she'll make a lovely mother.' Ruth smiles noncommittally. She has known Shona a long time. They first met on a dig, twelve years ago. It was on this dig that Erik had his finest hour, the discovery of the Bronze Age henge. Cathbad too had been centre stage, organising protests against the removal of the henge to a museum. Shona had sympathised with the protesters, as had Ruth and Erik too, up to a point. But the henge had been removed, and though there is no trace of it now on the shifting sands of the Saltmarsh the repercussions of that summer are still being felt in many people's lives. Ruth had once felt betrayed by Shona, beautiful Shona who could have any man she wanted, but her need for a friend had been too strong and they managed to repair their relationship. Now Shona is living with Ruth's boss, Phil, and expecting his baby. She is blissfully happy and so Ruth, who wonders just how her glamorous friend will cope with broken nights, mother-and-toddler groups and endless reruns of In The Night Garden, keeps her doubts to herself. Shona does seem good with Kate and maybe she'll take to motherhood with perfect ease. If so, Ruth must remember to pick up some tips.

As an entertainer, though, Shona is quite outclassed by Cathbad, who arrives late and promptly leads the children in a wild game of follow-my-leader: over the sofa, up and down the stairs, rampaging through Ruth's tiny, overgrown garden.

'Does he have children of his own?' asks one of the toddlers' mothers, picking her offspring out of a bramble bush.

'One daughter. She must be almost grown up now.'

'He seems very . . . energetic.'

'He is.'

'How do you know him?'

'He works at the university.' Ruth doesn't feel up to going into her whole history with Cathbad. How she first met him on the henge dig, how he reappeared when a child disappeared on the Saltmarsh. How he keeps appearing whenever her life is in danger. How he has appointed himself as unofficial guardian angel, not just to Ruth and Kate, but also to a markedly ungrateful DCI Harry Nelson.

'He's Kate's godfather,' she offers.

'Oh.' The mother looks relieved, as if Cathbad's presence has at last been satisfactorily explained. Ruth doesn't think it's worth mentioning that Cathbad is also a druid. Thank God he's not wearing his cloak.

Cathbad proceeds to eat most of the party food and to initiate a game of throwing quavers in the air. Ruth looks at her watch. Five o'clock. Surely they'll all be going home soon? She decides to open the wine.

'Not for me,' says Cathbad, who is performing conjuring tricks with scotch eggs. 'I'm driving.'

'You're high on E numbers anyway.'

'Just having fun.'

'It was nice of you to come.'

Cathbad grins. He has a rather piratical face, dark-skinned, with greying hair in a ponytail. 'All part of my godfatherly duties. As you know, I'm always on the side of chaos. Tell me, Ruth ...' He lowers his voice. 'What really happened at the museum yesterday?'

Ruth is instantly on her guard. As an expert on forensic archaeology she has been involved in three police investigations. Each time, Cathbad managed to get involved as well, once to devastating effect. She finds it suspicious that he already knows about the death at the museum.

'How do you know about that?' she asks, rather sharply.

'I came for the opening of the coffin and was turned away by PC Plod. I heard that the curator was found dead.'

'Yes.' Ruth doesn't see any point in denying it as the story will be in the papers tomorrow. 'There's not necessarily anything suspicious about it though. Poor guy may have had a heart attack.'

Cathbad looks at her. 'Is that really what you think?'

A typical Cathbad response. Trying to get her to say more than she wants to.

'I don't think anything,' she says, starting to collect squashed sandwiches. There is definitely more food on the table and on the floor than in the kids, though Daisy is slowly working her way through the chocolate fingers. 'Why are you so interested anyway?' she asks.

Cathbad throws a cocktail sausage into the air and catches it in his mouth. It's quite a neat trick. Daisy, the only child still sitting at the table, watches him with awe.

'Have you heard of the Elginists?' he asks, when he has finished with the sausage.

'No,' says Ruth. 'Should I have?'

'I don't know,' says Cathbad maddeningly. 'Should you?'

Ruth is about to tell him not to be so bloody enigmatic when Kate wanders up, holding a balloon and a scotch egg. She hands both to Cathbad before climbing purposefully onto his knee.

'Dada,' she says.

* * *

It is seven o'clock before everyone goes home. Daisy was sick on the stairs and Kate is spark out on the sofa, still holding a piece of birthday cake. Ruth covers her with a blanket and carries on tidying up. She is aware of two specific concerns fighting their way to the surface of her ever-present amorphous mass of worries (Who will look after Kate if she falls ill or dies? When will she ever have time to write an article or a paper and will Phil fire her if she doesn't? Why can't she lose weight? Who is Kerry Katona and what's happening to the world?). The first is a nagging feeling that Nelson should have rung. She knows what he said about no contact but she just can't believe that he would ignore his own daughter's birthday. On Kate's 'naming day' he and Michelle had turned up with an embarrassingly large present. But that was before Michelle had found out. Before Ruth was officially the scarlet woman of North Norfolk. She feels sad for Kate. Everyone should have a present from both parents on their birthday. Even her parents had given presents, though after they found God these did take the form of Children's Bible Stories or gruesome books about missionaries in China. But even Bible stories are better than nothing. What will she say to Kate when she is old enough to notice this lack? Perhaps she'll have to pretend that Cathbad is her father.

Cathbad had left without expanding on the Elginists. Elgin composed music didn't he? No, that was Elgar. Elgin was the guy with the marbles. What could the Elgin Marbles have to do with the Smith Museum in King's Lynn? As far as she could see the place was full of stuffed cats.

And that brings her to her biggest current worry. Where the hell is Flint? He had taken flight the moment six children descended on him yelling 'Kitty Kitty!' Ruth didn't blame him. She assumed that Flint would lurk in the garden for a bit and be back for his tea. Flint normally eats at six o'clock, the time Ruth usually gets back from work, but though Big Ben was chiming from the radio Flint's ginger face did not appear at the cat flap. Ruth went into the garden, shaking his biscuit box. 'Flint! Supper!' She noticed dimly that a van was parked outside the cottage next door. So the dreaded trendy couple are moving in at last, but at the time Ruth could only think about Flint. Maybe he was chasing birds on the marshes and too busy to think about cat biscuits. But now it is pitch black and still no sign of Ruth's precious boy.

She knows that she is slightly neurotic about Flint. Once she had another cat, a beautiful little black and white shorthair called Sparky. Sparky had been quieter than Flint and less demanding, but a character none the less, cheerful and independent. Ruth had loved her and, one night, had opened her door to find Sparky on the doorstep with her throat cut. Just thinking about it now makes Ruth feel like crying. Sparky's death had been part of a whole nightmarish series of events, culminating in murder. Ruth knows that the killing of a human is more serious. She may love her cats but she has a sense of proportion. At the university they are always on the alert against attacks by animal rights groups and, whilst Ruth feels squeamish about the use of animals in experiments, she can see that it might occasionally be necessary. She doesn't place the rights of animals above those of humans but she does, undoubtedly, prefer her cats to many humans. And now, with Flint not responding to her calls, she feels sick and panicky. He's a cat, she tells herself. They do what they want. But she can't help imagining Flint's mangled body, his lovely marmalade fur clotted with blood . . .

Stop, she tells herself, scrubbing the stairs for the tenth time. He's probably having a lovely time chasing voles through the long grass. But Flint is a creature of habit and he is always in by this time, stretched out on the rug, purring like a tumble dryer on spin. She has never met a cat who purrs so loudly. Oh, where is he?

The trouble is, because of Kate, she can't go out on the marsh and look for him. She walks to the end of the garden and back, listening for the telltale movement in the wind-blown bushes that means Flint is nearby. Nothing. Silence, apart from the sea roaring in the distance and the far-off cry of an owl. The owl. Hecate's symbol. Ruth has a rather close relationship with the goddess of witchcraft so she prays to her as well as to the other, more macho, God; neither of whom she believes in.

She goes back into the house. Maybe she should carry Kate up to bed but she is sleeping so peacefully it is tempting to leave her where she is for the moment. How can she sleep when Flint is missing, presumed mangled? The room still smells faintly of sick, she'd better clean the stairs again.

The knock on the door makes Ruth stand stock-still,

floorcloth in hand. Visitors are rare on the Saltmarsh, and at this hour they rarely bring good news. She's not scared, she tells people, living in such an isolated place, but she is *wary*. 'Who is it?' she calls.

'I've got a cat,' shouts an unfamiliar voice. 'I wondered if it was yours.'

Ruth has the door open in a second. Even a mass murderer would be welcome if he had found Flint.

A squat dark-haired man stands in the doorway, holding Flint in his arms. When the cat sees Ruth he meows accusingly.

'Flint!' Joyfully, she reaches out for him. He feels extremely heavy and squeaks when she squeezes him.

'I see you know each other,' says the man, sounding amused.

'Oh yes. Thank you! How did you ... Where did you ... ?'

'He'd managed to get himself shut in my outhouse. I was moving in and may have left the door open. I'm sorry.' The man holds out his hand, smiling broadly. 'I'm your new next-door neighbour, Bob Woonunga.'

'Oh,' Ruth puts Flint down and reaches out to shake his hand. 'Pleased to meet you.' He doesn't look like half of a trendy couple, she tells herself.

'By the way,' says Bob, 'there's a parcel out here for you.'

He hands her a box inexpertly wrapped in pink paper. 'To Katie,' Ruth reads. 'From Dad.'

5

Nelson drives slowly through narrow wooded lanes. He drives slowly because the countryside always makes him feel nervous, because it has been raining and there are gullies of water running in the ditches and because, every few yards, there are signs warning him to be careful of racehorses. Nelson takes the frequency of the signs to mean that he is nearing Lord Smith's racing stables. 'Hope you don't mind coming to see me down on the farm, so to speak,' Smith had said on the phone. 'It's just that it's hard to take time off from the yard.' 'I'll come early,' Nelson had promised. 'Great,' replied Smith, 'I get up at five. The first lot pulls out at six.' Nelson had no idea what this meant but he knew when he was beaten. He agrees to arrive at seven.

As he takes the turning for 'Slaughter Hill Racing Stables' he sees a line of horses coming towards him, jogging gently through the mist. Nelson stops the car as they go past, the horses wearing blankets and catching at their bits, heads flying up, hindquarters swinging out as if they can't bear this tedious pace for a single second more.

Nelson has come to speak to Lord Smith about the death of his curator. The autopsy on Neil Topham had proved inconclusive (though Chris Stephenson had tried his best not to use this word). Topham had died from acute pulmonary haemorrhage which could, according to the pathologist, be attributed to a number of causes including tuberculosis, lung abscess or Factor X deficiency. 'What's Factor X when it's at home?' Nelson had barked. It sounded like one of those dreadful TV programmes his daughters watch. 'It's a coagulation factor that allows the blood to clot; people with Factor X deficiency are prone to pulmonary haemorrhage.' 'But you said it could be caused by all sorts of things?' 'Yes. Pulmonary haemorrhage can be brought on by infection, or drug use, or even by shock.' 'So we're no nearer to finding out what killed the poor bastard?' 'No,' Stephenson had admitted.

The body has been released to Topham's parents for burial but Nelson is still reluctant to close the case. There's the little matter of the drugs, for one thing. The powder found in Topham's desk drawer had turned out to be one hundred per cent pure cocaine. The curator's body had shown clear evidence of drug use. Nothing odd in that, maybe. As far as Nelson can make out, most arty types are on drugs. But were the drugs for Topham's sole use (there was a hell of a lot there, according to the drugs squad, thousands of pounds worth) and what caused Neil Topham, a man apparently in good health at half past one, to be found dead by two-twenty? And there are the letters too. Someone evidently had it in for Neil Topham and the Smith Museum and Nelson wants to know why.

There are security gates across the track but they open at Nelson's approach. He parks beside a modern bungalow with a sign saying 'Visitors Please Report Here'. Nelson rings the bell but there is no reply. There are cars in the car park, among them a showy blue Ferrari, but no one seems to be about. Opposite is a high wall with an archway and a clock tower. After waiting impatiently for a few minutes, Nelson marches through the archway, wishing he'd thought to wear boots. Place will be swimming in mud after all that rain.

He is wrong. The archway leads into a huge quadrangle, lined on three sides with stables. In the middle is a square of grass as smooth and green as a bowling pitch. There is not a speck of mud to be seen. The stalls have a kind of v-shaped rail in the top half, and through this horses' heads are poking, each one looking as impatient as Nelson himself. He walks up to the first head and the horse rolls an angry eye at him, nostrils flaring.

'Better not go too close,' says a voice behind him. 'He's a bit of a tinker, that one.'

Nelson turns and sees a woman wearing jodhpurs and a reflective jacket. At her approach the horse neighs, though whether in welcome or anger he can't tell.

'Can I help you?' she says, eyebrows raised. She is tall, with black hair hanging loose over her shoulders. Nelson supposes she is quite-good looking but she's not his type. She has dark eyes, straight black brows that almost meet in the middle and a decided nose. She also looks rather familiar.

'DCI Nelson from the Norfolk Police,' says Nelson. 'I'm here to see Danforth Smith.' He's buggered if he's going to add the 'Lord.'

'Oh, you want Dad,' says the woman. 'You'd better come to the office.'

Surprisingly, given the extreme order of the yard, the office is a mess. There are racing papers everywhere, half-drunk cups of coffee, even a slightly chewed doughnut. A large ginger cat squats by the computer, eyeing the doughnut beadily. The cat – and the doughnut – remind Nelson of Ruth. Racing silks, clashing pink and purple, hang on the door.

'Sorry about the state of this place,' says the woman, 'but I've got to get the declarations done by ten.'

'Declarations?'

'Saying which horses are running where.'

It's a foreign language, thinks Nelson. He is experiencing the unusual sensation of being in an entirely alien habitat. A horse and rider pass by the door. To Nelson's untrained eye, the animal looks magnificent, its plumy tail swishing against silken hindquarters. He is struck by how big the horse is close up. The rider's stirrups are on a level with the window. Other horses are coming out of their stables now, breath steaming in the cold air. More men (and women, he thinks) in yellow reflective jackets are putting on saddles and swinging themselves up on the narrow backs. Soon the yard is full of sidling, prancing horses parading slowly around the square of grass.

Though he has never told a living soul, Nelson loves horses. He still remembers his father's horror when, as a child, he had asked for riding lessons. He soon realised that he had made a terrible mistake; ponies were for girls, football was for boys. He had quickly switched his request to football training and had the pleasure of seeing his father's face when he scored his first goal for Bispham Juniors. Archie Nelson had attended all his son's matches, yelling himself hoarse on the touchline, though he was a quiet man in all other ways. His sisters had both done ballet, he remembers, but this had not counted in the house the way Harry's football had counted. He's sure his father never went to a single dance performance, although his sisters were both meant to be quite good.

So Nelson had suppressed his fascination with horses, had limited it to yearly bets on the Grand National. He even enjoys watching the racing on TV, the horses swirling into the paddock, cantering up to the starting post with the wind in their tails. It seems incredible that the jockeys can stay on, perched up on the necks of these twitchy muscle-bound monsters. Nelson has never been on a horse and it's too late now.

'The second lot's just going out,' says the woman, who has been checking something on the computer.

'Where are they going?' asks Nelson, wondering if this is a stupid question.

'To the gallops.'

'For exercise?'

She turns and gives him a slight smile. It doesn't suit her; her features are designed for tragedy. 'Six furlongs, uphill. It's exercise all right.'

The word 'uphill' reminds him of something.

'Funny name this place has got. Slaughter Hill.'

'There was a battle here ages ago,' the woman says vaguely. Then, with evident relief, 'Here's Dad now.'

Danforth Smith appears in the doorway. He too is wearing jodhpurs and boots. Uniform of the upper classes, thinks Nelson. But it looks kind of impressive all the same.

'Hope you haven't been waiting long,' says Smith genially. 'Caroline been looking after you?'

'She has,' says Nelson. He is surprised to see Caroline blushing.

'Let's talk in the house,' says Smith. 'We'll be more comfortable.'

'Sorry about the mess,' says Caroline, blushing again. Her demeanour has changed completely with the arrival of her father. 'Are you declaring Tommy Tuppence for Newmarket?'

'No,' says Smith. 'He's still not right. I'll turn him out later on today. This way, DCI Nelson.'

Smith leads the way across the grass to the far side of the yard. The horses are heading out through the archway now, hooves clattering on the tarmac.

'How many horses have you got here?' asks Nelson.

'Eighty,' says Smith with some pride. 'Both flat and jump. The flat season's nearly over but the jump season's just beginning. We've got an all-weather track so we can ride out all year round.'

'Do the same horses run in flat races and jump races?' asks Nelson.

'Good God no.' Smith stops by a box at the far end of

the yard. 'Completely different game. Look at this fellow now. Classic jump horse. Stands every bit of seventeen hands. Got real bone on him.'

Again, Nelson has no idea what this means but there, in the wood-smelling gloom, is the biggest horse he has ever seen, jet black except for a white stripe running down his face.

'The Necromancer,' says Smith, in awed tones. 'Just come from Dubai. He's a real prospect for next year's National.'

'I'll remember,' says Nelson.

The black horse looks steadily at them for a moment and lowers his head to his food.

As they pass through another, smaller, yard, Nelson is surprised to see two rather different animals eating from a haynet tied up inside a barn.

'Are those . . . donkeys?'

Smith laughs. 'Some horses don't like the company of other horses. The Necromancer for one. But they're herd animals. They don't like to be alone. So we brought in these little fellows to keep them company. They're from a local horse rescue place. We call them Cannon and Ball because they're such jokers.'

Nelson doesn't see that this follows at all. He pats one of the donkeys, marvelling at how soft its fur is. He sees that both animals have cross-shaped markings on their backs. His mother once told him that all donkeys carry this mark because it was a donkey that carried Christ into Jerusalem. These two don't look as if they are too bothered by religious significance. They carry on tearing at their hay, large ears twitching.

'Jolly little fellows,' says Smith with casual affection. Cannon (or Ball) looks at him out of large long-lashed eyes. Their feet are tiny, like goat's hooves.

Leaving the jolly donkeys behind, they pass another barn stacked with hay and cross a concrete carport to a large, modern-looking house. Nelson is disappointed. He'd expected a Lord to live in a mansion at least.

'Is this the country seat?' he asks.

'Afraid not,' says Smith. 'Slaughter Hill House was pulled down. You can see the ruins in the grounds.'

Again, Nelson is struck by the strange, rather sinister name. He asks Smith about it.

'There was a battle here in the Civil War. King's Lynn was Royalist, you know, and the Earl of Manchester attacked the place for the Parliamentarians. There was a great battle hereabouts. Hundreds died.'

Nelson bets he knows which side Lord Smith would have been on. He's ambivalent himself – he can't see any particular harm in the Royal Family (he was quite shocked when Ruth once referred to them as 'parasites') but he has always admired Cromwell's warts-and-all approach. And he likes the sound of the Earl of Manchester. He imagines him looking like Sir Alex Ferguson.

'It's the hill that gets me,' he says now. 'There are no hills in bloody Norfolk.'

'There's a slight rise in the park,' says Smith, 'that's why I put the gallops there. It's good for the horses to go uphill. Builds stamina. But I believe that the name derives from the great mound of bodies after the battle.'

Charming, thinks Nelson. Name a house after a great

pile of festering bodies. Aloud he says, 'Why was the house pulled down?'

'It was falling to pieces,' says Smith sadly. 'Too far gone to save. It was demolished in the Sixties. Great shame. It was the house I grew up in, lots of memories.' He stares up at the modern house, frowning slightly, then visibly pulls himself together. 'But this is better in many ways, far more convenient. And it's near the horses. I can come over if there's a problem in the night. My daughter Caroline lives in the cottage by the gate.'

'Caroline works for you, does she?'

'Yes. She's my yard manager. Good girl. Does all my paperwork and still rides out three times a day. She's never caused me a day's worry.' There is a slight emphasis on the 'she'.

They enter through a back door into a gleaming red and white kitchen.

'Coffee?'asks Smith.

'Please.' Nelson had not expected Lord Smith to be making him coffee. Surely there's an elderly retainer around somewhere? He asks.

'No,' says Smith. 'There's a housekeeper but she's not here today. My wife's out at work. Most of the time it's just me and Randolph.'

'Randolph?'

'My son. Would you like biscuits? I'm diabetic so I've got some ghastly sugar-free rusks. But there are some Hobnobs somewhere.'

Nelson thinks he would like a Hobnob very much indeed. He is just wondering about the mysterious son (maybe he's locked in a turret room somewhere) when the door opens and a handsome, dark-haired man bursts into the room.

'Morning all.'

Smith does not turn round but plunges the cafetière with unnecessary violence.

'What time do you call this?' he says.

'I don't know,' says the man pleasantly. 'What time do you call it?'

'You've been out all night. Your mother was worried sick.'

'I doubt that,' says the man who must, surely, be the errant Randolph. 'Ma never worries about anything. Ah, coffee. Superb. I could murder a cup.' He turns and seems to register Nelson for the first time.

'Hallo there,' he says. 'I'm Randolph Smith.'

'DCI Nelson.'

'DCI Nelson's come to talk to me about Neil's death,' says Danforth, speaking loudly and clearly as if to someone deaf or deficient in understanding. It's almost as if he wants to convey a message. Or a warning. Nelson watches Randolph with interest. For a second he looks wary – almost scared – then the cheerful unconcern is back in place.

'Oh, the mysterious death at the museum. Does the detective suspect foul play?'

'It's not a laughing matter' says Danforth Smith reprovingly.

'No.' Randolph rearranges his handsome features. 'Desperately sad. Poor Neil.'

'Yes indeed,' says Smith, putting cafetière and dark green cups on a tray. 'I've written to his parents of course. And we should all attend the funeral.'

'Will it be here or in Wales?'

'I've no idea,' says Smith. 'We'll take our coffee into the study, Detective Inspector.'

Nelson follows Lord Smith out of the room, wondering how Randolph Smith knows that Neil Topham's family comes from Wales.

Smith ushers Nelson into a luxurious study with sofa, drinks cabinet and vast mahogany desk. The walls are lined with shelves containing leatherbound volumes and plastic files. In the occasional clear space, there are photos of horses, some standing in fields, some sweaty and magnificent after winning a race. A glass cabinet is crammed full of trophies.

'Do you have children, Detective Chief Inspector?' asks Smith, seating himself behind the desk.

'Two daughters,' says Nelson, sitting in the proffered visitor's chair, which swivels rather alarmingly. He hates saying this; it feels as if he is denying Katie. At least he sent her a birthday present, he thinks. He couldn't bear to let the day go completely unnoticed.

'Daughters are easier. My two girls have never given me a day's trouble. Caroline you saw. She's a real hard worker. Tamsin's a lawyer, lives in London, husband, two children. But Randolph! He hasn't done a day's work since leaving university. Caroline's travelled all over, seen the world. All Randolph seems to see is the inside of night

clubs. And he drinks with the most dreadful people . . .'
He stops himself with an effort. 'Still, you don't want to
hear about my domestic problems.'

'It must be hard work, running an operation like this.'

'Bloody hard work. Up at five every day. The horses
have holidays but we don't.'

'Do you have much time left for the museum?'

Smith's face becomes serious. 'Not as much time as I'd
like. I left all the day-to-day running to Neil. Poor chap.'
He looks up and meets Nelson's eyes. 'Have you discovered anything about how he died?'

'Earliest indications suggest that death was the result
of pulmonary haemorrhage,' says Nelson cautiously. Is it
his imagination or does Danforth Smith relax slightly?

'How ghastly. Did he have weak lungs?'

'We won't know until we've looked at his medical
records but it's quite possible. But I wanted to talk to you
about another matter.'

'Yes?' Smith leans forward across the acres of polished
wood. His tone is one of polite interest but Nelson notices
that one hand is clenched tightly around a fountain pen.
As Nelson watches, Smith seems consciously to relax his
grip, letting the pen roll across the desk.

'Yes,' says Nelson. 'Were you aware of any letters sent
to Neil Topham?'

'Letters?'

'Threatening letters.'

Nelson places a file on the desk. He takes out some
loose papers and pushes them towards Danforth Smith,
who puts on a pair of half-moon glasses and peers at the

hand-written pages. Nelson watches him intently. At first
Smith seems to show only polite interest then something
makes him look harder. It's almost a classic double take.
What has Lord Smith seen in the letters that surprises
him so much? Nelson continues to watch as, once again,
Smith seems deliberately to calm himself. When he speaks,
his voice is completely steady.

'Where did you get these?'

'From Neil Topham's desk. Have you seen them
before?'

There are three letters in total. The first is dated August
2009:

> To whom it may concern,
>   You have something that belongs to us, something that
> belongs to the spirit ancestors. If you do not return it,
> you are violating the harmony of the spirit world.
> Remember that the spirits are strong and can exact
> revenge. I advise you to think carefully about your
> actions. Every event leaves a record on the land and, if
> you continue to disrespect our dead, your life may well
> be in danger.
>   In the brotherhood of the spirit.

The second letter is dated September 2009:

> You have chosen to disregard our first warning. In your
> arrogance you think you can ignore the wrong that you
> have done to us but the spirits are everywhere and they
> see all and know all. You cannot escape. The spirits cry

out for vengeance. If you persist in defying us, the wrath
of the Great Spirit will destroy you. Consider carefully.

The third letter is dated October and reads simply:

You have ignored our requests. Now you will suffer the
consequences. You have violated our dead. Now the dead
will be revenged on you. We will come for you. We will
come for you in the Dreaming.

Nelson looks at Smith, who has taken off his glasses
and is rubbing his nose.

'Lord Smith, have you any idea who sent these?'

Smith says nothing. Outside a horse neighs and a
woman laughs. The silver cups glint in the autumn sun.

'We have some heads,' says Lord Smith at last. 'At the
museum.'

'Heads?'

'Aborigine skulls. They were originally acquired by my
great-grandfather. We used to have them on display but
now they're kept locked up. About a year ago I got a letter
from a group calling themselves the Elginists. They
demanded the return of the skulls. Said they should go
back to Australia and be buried in their ancestral ground
... said they needed to enter Dreamtime, or some such
rubbish. I gave them short shrift. Those heads belonged
to my great-grandfather. They're very rare. One's been
turned into a water carrier. I couldn't just turn them over
to some bunch of nutters. I mean, these artefacts are valuable, they need special care.'

'Have you still got the letter?'

'I don't know. I'll look.' Smith gets up and starts to search in a steel filing cabinet. What is it filed under, wonders Nelson. N for Nutter? I for Ignore?

'Here it is.' Smith puts a single sheet of paper in front of Nelson.

This letter looks very different from the missives found in Neil Topham's desk. It's typewritten for one thing and is on actual headed notepaper, with a logo that seems to represent the moon above a meandering river.

Dear Lord Smith,

We are writing on behalf of the Elginists, a group dedicated to the repatriation of sacred artefacts. It has come to our attention that your museum currently holds four Indigenous Australian skulls which have been forcibly removed from their ancestral ground. As you may know, it is an important tenet of Indigenous Australian belief that the remains of the ancestors should be returned to Mother Earth so that they may enter the Dreaming and so complete the cycle of nature. We respectfully request that you return these skulls, which were unlawfully removed and which, therefore, can only bring bad fortune to you and your family. Be warned that the Great Snake will have its revenge.

Please contact us at the above address to arrange repatriation.

There is no signature just 'The Elginist Council.'

Nelson looks at Smith. 'Did you reply?'

'No.' Smith looks haughty. 'I wouldn't dignify it with

a response. If you ignore these sorts of people, they go away. I've learnt that over the years.'

'And did they go away?'

'I assumed so. They didn't approach me again.'

'Did you know that Neil Topham had received these letters?'

'No.' Smith looks genuinely shocked but there's something else there too, thinks Nelson. Anger? Fear? 'I'm surprised Neil didn't tell me,' he says now. 'We spoke every week. I felt that we had a good working relationship. I trusted him.'

'When you last spoke to him Neil didn't seem disturbed? Worried?'

'No. We talked about Bishop Augustine. He was really excited about having the bishop's relics at the museum.'

Nelson looks back at the letter. On the face of it, there's nothing too alarming in it, except maybe the mention of 'bad fortune' to the Smith family. But Nelson's eye is drawn to two things: the logo, which he now perceives to be a snake slithering under the moon, and the words, *the Great Snake will have its revenge.*

And he thinks of the room with the coffin and the open window and the single glass case containing the stuffed body of a snake.

6

Ruth drives to work on Monday feeling that several hurdles have been overcome. Kate's birthday party (she knows she shouldn't think of this as a hurdle, but still) went off OK and the new neighbour didn't turn out to be a trendy sushi-lover or a weird seaweed collector. True, he had looked a little weird at first with his hair in a sort of sumo-wrestler knot and his feet, despite the weather, in leather flip-flops. And the name! She'd had to ask him to repeat it.

'Bob Woonunga.' He had grinned, showing very white teeth in a dark brown face.

'Oh. That's . . . unusual.'

'It's an Indigenous Australian name,' he had explained. They were sitting in Ruth's kitchen by this time, drinking tea. Kate was still asleep on the sofa.

'Safe in dreamland,' Bob had said. 'Don't wake her.'

Indigenous Australian? Did that mean Aborigine? Were you allowed to say Aborigine anymore? Ruth had settled for: 'You're a long way from home.'

'I'm a bit of a wanderer,' Bob smiled. He had an Aussie

accent which, Ruth realised, was one of the things that made her trust him. Why? Because of *Neighbours* and other warm-hearted Antipodean soap operas? Ruth doesn't like to admit it but it's probably true. As a student she had been addicted to *Neighbours*. And now she has a real-life Australian for a neighbour.

She had wanted to ask more about Mr Woonunga's wanderings but he had volunteered little except that he had a temporary post at the University of East Anglia, teaching creative writing. Or, as he put it, 'I've got a gig at the uni.' He has rented the house next door for a year.

'Are you a writer then?' asked Ruth.

'Poet mostly, but I've written a few novels.'

Ruth was impressed. Like many academics, her ultimate goal is to turn her thesis into a book but so far she hasn't progressed far beyond the title, 'Bones, Decomposition and Death in Prehistoric Britain'. To think that someone can be so blasé about their success that they can shrug it away like that. 'I've written a few novels.' And he must be a successful writer if he's teaching on the UEA course, even if she hasn't heard of him.

'What made you choose this place?' she had asked. 'It's quite a way from Norwich.'

'A friend recommended it,' said Bob, stroking Flint, who seemed to have become surgically attached to his new neighbour. 'And I like the place. It has good magic.'

Good magic. Ruth, negotiating the turn into the University of North Norfolk (definitely the poor relation to the prestigious University of East Anglia), wonders why she hadn't recoiled as she usually does at any mention of religion or the supernatural. Was it partly because she agreed with Bob Woonunga? Cathbad would say that the Saltmarsh is sacred to the Gods. Erik used to call it a symbolic landscape. Nelson usually refers to it as a dump. For Ruth it is home, but she sometimes wonders why someone born and brought up in South London should be so drawn to such a desolate place. Does *she* feel that there is magic in the shifting sands and secret pools? No. But, although she has experienced both fear and danger on the Saltmarsh, she knows that she wouldn't live anywhere else. It's not entirely rational, she's willing to admit that.

Ruth's office is in the Natural Sciences Block which is separated from the main campus by a covered walkway. It's fairly pleasant in summer, with views over the ornamental lake, but on this grey November morning everything looks forlorn and unloved. The paint is peeling in the lobby and someone has scrawled 'Abandon Hope All Ye Who Enter Here' above the main doors. Ruth climbs the two flights of stairs to her office, noticing that the fluorescent lights are flickering again. She'll have a headache by lunchtime. She opens her door with a key card and sits down at her desk.

Ruth's office is tiny, only just big enough for a desk and a chair. One wall is full of books, the other has a window overlooking the grounds. It's too hot in summer and too cold in winter but Ruth loves it. It's a place where she can be Doctor Ruth Galloway, expert in forensic archaeology, not Kate's mum, running late as usual, or Ms Galloway, single mother. 'You're very brave,' someone said recently, 'to bring her up on your own.' What choice did I have ? Ruth wanted to say. Expose her on the hillside? Leave her to be adopted by a friendly wolf pack? But she did have a choice, she recognises, right at the beginning. A choice she supports. It was just that when it came to it she realised she wanted a baby very badly indeed. And, if she never sees him again, she will always be grateful to Nelson for this at least.

Nelson's birthday present was a large stuffed monkey. Ruth had looked at it for a long time, trying to find some hidden meaning in the blond acrylic fur and beady eyes. Why a monkey? Why a present at all? Hadn't Michelle forbidden all contact? And when did Nelson deliver it? When the children were singing 'Happy Birthday Dear Katie'? When Cathbad was rampaging round the garden? She doesn't like the idea that someone can just drive up to her house, leave an offering on her doorstep, and disappear. Though it has happened before.

Ruth sighs and starts opening her post. November is a busy time, there are assessments to be made, essays to mark. They are more than halfway through the autumn term. She needs to read through her lecture notes for the morning but first she needs a coffee. Maybe a doughnut too. The canteen does a tolerable espresso but the trick will be getting there without running into Phil. She'll risk it. He's probably still at home, sleeping off last week's conference.

'Ruth!'

'Hi Phil.'

Caught just outside her office, coffee money in hand.

'Going for a coffee?'

'Er . . .'

'Great idea. I'll go with you. Though I'm off coffee at the moment. Keeping Shona company.'

When, last year, Phil had left his wife of fifteen years to move in with Shona, few had felt confident that the relationship would survive. Even Shona seemed shocked at the transformation of her married lover into full-on live-in partner. Ruth had thought that Shona might lose interest in Phil once she had prised him from his wife (it had happened before) but then Shona had become obsessed with having a baby. Maybe it was because Ruth had just had Kate; maybe Shona just felt that the biological clock, though on silent for many years, was not to be denied. But for whatever reason, she had wanted a baby and Phil had obliged. Now Shona's pregnancy is all that he can talk about. He seems to feel that Ruth is interested in every twinge of heartburn, every swollen ankle. Was he like this when his first children were born? Ruth wonders. She didn't know him then but she bets not. Phil is embracing older fatherhood as he does every new fad, with tail-wagging enthusiasm. It's quite sweet, she supposes, though she draws the line at discussing piles.

Phil, though, has something else on his mind. He buys a Smoothie and a banana ('Shona's got a real craving for them') and steers Ruth to a discreet table near the window.

'Terrible thing at the museum on Saturday.'

'Yes,' says Ruth. She bets Phil was gutted to miss the excitement.

'That poor curator. Do police know how he died?'

'I've no idea,' says Ruth. 'They don't confide in me.'

Phil looks at her curiously. Ruth knows that he has always been intrigued by her relationship with Nelson. She keeps her face blank and takes a sip of coffee. It is thick and bitter and perfect.

'Anyway,' says Phil, obviously deciding that there is nothing more to be gained in that direction. He pauses impressively. 'I had a call last night from Lord Smith.'

'Oh yes?' The name means nothing to Ruth. She looks longingly at her doughnut, the grease just starting to ooze through the paper bag.

'The owner of the Smith Museum.'

'Oh. Danforth Smith. What did he want?'

'It's a delicate matter.'

Phil looks positively delighted. He loves any intrigue. Ruth raises her eyebrows. She is desperate for a bit of doughnut but doesn't want to look greedy in front of Phil – especially as Shona, even pregnant, is thinner than she is.

'You know the museum has a large collection of New World artefacts?'

Ruth dimly remembers a room labelled New World. But she had plumped for Natural History and the stuffed animals. 'Yes,' she says warily.

'Well, they contain a number of skeletal remains.' He lowers his voice. '*Human* bones.'

'Human bones?'

'Apparently Lord Smith's great-grandfather brought home a number of skulls and other bones from Australia. They're thought to be the relics of Aboriginal Australians.'

Ruth's head is like a switchboard, lights flashing, bells ringing.

'And now a pressure group is demanding the return of these artefacts,' says Phil.

'This pressure group, is it called the Elginists by any chance?'

'How did you—?'

'Just a lucky guess.' Cathbad's interest in the museum is now explained. She also wonders about Bob Woonunga and the mysterious 'friend' who recommended the Saltmarsh as a place to live. Isn't it a bit of a coincidence that an Indigenous Australian should suddenly move in next door?

'Well, the heads are fairly obvious and Lord Smith is adamant that they're not going anywhere. But he needs someone to look at the other bones, to check if they really are human. And he asked for you.'

'Why?' asks Ruth.

'Well, you're our bones expert. I presume he asked around.'

I bet he did, thinks Ruth. And I wonder who he asked.

Back in her office, she makes an internal call to Cathbad. He works in the chemistry department as a lab assistant, though he originally trained as an archaeologist.

'So, tell me about the Elginists.'

Cathbad laughs, not at all abashed. 'I knew you'd come round to the Elginists.'

'Apparently Lord Smith wants me to look at some Aboriginal relics.'

'Indigenous Australian,' Cathbad corrects her. 'And they're not relics, they are remains of the ancestors, the Old Ones. They need to go back to their own country, so that they can enter the spirit world and be one with their mother, the Earth.'

Ruth marvels anew at how Cathbad comes out with the stuff, just as if he is reciting a chemical formula. She is used to him going on about Mother Earth, though the Indigenous Australian link is new.

'How come you're involved in all this? I thought you were a druid.'

'All the great religions are one,' says Cathbad impressively, but Ruth thinks it is a typically religious phrase because it sounds good and means absolutely nothing.

There is a scratchy, electronic pause. 'I got involved with the Elginists when we were protesting about the henge,' Cathbad says at last. 'They offered their support. They agreed that the henge should stay where it was.'

Ruth remembers the protests about the henge, Cathbad standing within the wooden circle, staff upraised, defying the tide itself. There had been rumours that the entire archaeology team had been cursed, that anyone who touched the timbers would be dead in a year. Well, Ruth is still here and even Erik survived for a good many years after the dig. Ruth wonders what sort of help the Elginists offered.

'Cathbad,' says Ruth. 'Do you know Bob Woonunga?'

Cathbad laughs again. 'Bob's an expert on repatriation. He's a poet too. He's written lots of beautiful things about the Dreaming. I met him at a conference.'

'And you recommended that he move in next door to me?'

'I thought it would suit him. He's a good bloke, Ruth. You'll like him.'

'I met him last night.'

'There you are then.'

'Why do I feel that there's something you're not telling me?'

'Relax, Ruthie. Look, we're having another meeting next week. Why don't you come along? There'll be lots of archaeologists there. It's all above board, I promise you. Your friend from Sussex is coming. Max Whatshisname.'

'Max Grey.'

'That's the one. It'll be a laugh. We're going to end with a real Aboriginal smoke ceremony.'

'Indigenous Australian,' says Ruth but her heart's not in it. She is thinking about Max.

7

Nelson drives back to the police station thinking about snakes, racehorses and the sheer arrogance of the British upper classes. Lord Smith had been polite, charming almost, but there's no doubt that he thinks that he has a God-given right to do what he likes with his horses, his museum, his great-grandfather's grisly trophies. *Those heads belonged to my great-grandfather.* It's a short step from saying 'those slaves belonged to my great-grandfather.' Nelson can just see Smith as a plantation owner, slaves toiling in the fields, no-good son lolling about on the porch drinking Bourbon – or whatever they used to drink in *Gone With The Wind* (Nelson's mother's favourite film).

Could there be a link between the letters and Neil Topham's death? Nelson thinks about the open window, the snake in the case, the words 'now the dead will be revenged on you.' But Nelson is not going to fall into the trap of assuming that the letter-writer is a killer. Like every detective in Britain, he remembers the Yorkshire Ripper and the infamous 'I'm Jack' tapes. The police had wasted valuable time assuming that the voice on the tape was the voice of the Ripper when, in the end, it had just been some nutcase wanting his moment of glory. Nelson has been there too. Years ago he started to receive letters about the disappearance of a little girl. Those letters had haunted his dreams for years. Were they from the killer? Did they contain cryptic clues which, if only he could crack the code, would lead him to Lucy Downey? It had been the letters which had formed the first real bond with Ruth. She had interpreted them, explaining arcane mythological and archaeological terms. Her expertise had almost cost her her life.

But Chris Stephenson thinks that Topham's death was from natural causes. The coroner will probably find the same way. Neil Topham died from a sudden pulmonary haemorrhage which could have been brought on by his drug-taking. The letters, the snake, the strange tableau with the coffin – it could all be irrelevant. But Nelson knows, knows from the depth of his twenty-odd years with the force, that something is wrong. He saw it in Lord Smith's face when he looked at the letters, the sudden shock of anger (or was it fear?) crossing the haughty features. He saw it in Neil Topham's office, amongst the broken exhibits and unread paperwork. He saw it in the room with the coffin, the pages of the abandoned guide-book fluttering in the breeze.

The horses had been impressive. Before he left, Smith had taken him to watch them on the gallops. That had been some sight, seeing the horses coming up the hill, three abreast on the black all-weather track, steaming in hazy autumn sunshine. As they passed they had made a noise that was something between panting and snorting, heads straining against tight reins, manes and tails streaming out.

'They're beautiful,' he hadn't been able to stop himself saying.

Smith had looked at him with real pleasure. 'They're my pride and joy,' he had said.

There was no doubt that Smith loved his horses but he was still an arrogant bastard. And there is something about the whole set up – the stables and the museum – that smells funny to Nelson. But is it enough? For the past three months Nelson and his team have been working flat out trying to crack a drug-smuggling ring. The county has suddenly been flooded with Class A drugs and no one really knows where they are coming from. Nelson has been liaising with a shadowy body called the Tactical Crimes Unit, but so far no one has been able to identify the tactics involved. Smuggling usually involves the ports, but though Nelson has been mounting round-the-clock surveillance nothing has turned up. And still the drugs keep surfacing. He can't really afford to take officers off the case to investigate – what? Some crackpot letters? A feeling that things aren't quite what they seem?

The first person he sees at the station is Judy Johnson. She looks exhausted. He knows that she was at the docks last night.

'Any luck?' he asks.

'No.' She yawns. 'And I had to sit in a car with Clough all night.'

'Did he eat all the time?'

'Even when he was asleep.'

Clough's capacity for food is legendary. He's a good cop but Nelson wouldn't like to spend the night in a car with him.

'Go home after the meeting,' he says. 'Get some sleep.'

'Thanks boss.'

Nelson keeps the briefing short. Judy Johnson gives an account of last night's abortive stakeout. They discuss possible leads. Clough gives it as his opinion that the drugs are coming from Eastern Europe. Nelson shifts uncomfortably in his seat. Over the last few years, a great number of refugees from Eastern Europe have come to settle in King's Lynn. It's customary for the press, and some police officers, to blame every crime on the new arrivals. Nelson knows it's his job to stamp on such talk. Didn't he recently attend a briefing on 'Policing in a Multicultural Society'? Actually, he had fallen asleep after ten minutes but he still knows that Clough's comment isn't helpful.

'Have you got any evidence for that, Cloughie?' he growls.

'Well, Russians ...' says Clough unrepentantly. 'The Russian mafia. They're up to their necks in drugs. Like the Chinese triads.'

There's a big Chinese community in King's Lynn too.

'Like I say,' says Nelson. 'No evidence.'

'Not many boats in the port from Russia,' says Judy.

Clough glares at her. 'They use mules, don't they? Some

poor sucker forced to swallow the goods. Quick shit and bingo. Kinder Egg.'

'Kinder Egg?' repeats Judy faintly.

'Yeah, that's what they call it. Surprise every time.'

'I'll see what Jimmy has to say.'

Nelson has an informer who only speaks to Nelson and then only under conditions of elaborate secrecy. He trusts this man as far as he would trust any untrustworthy bastard.

'OK,' he says now. 'We'll give it another night at the port. Fuller, you can do a stint with Tom Henty.' Tanya Fuller, an extremely keen DC, looks pleased. It'll do her good to have some responsibility and Henty will keep an eye on her. Nelson turns to the Smith Museum, giving a brief description of events on Saturday. He tries to keep it as flat as possible but he can tell that the team are intrigued.

'Were there clear signs of a break-in?' asks Tanya.

'Nothing definite. I'm sending some PCs house-to house and I'll wait to see what the SOCOs come back with. Johnson, can you liaise with them?'

Tanya looks disappointed, Judy stifles a yawn.

'So it may just be natural causes,' says Clough, biting into a Mars bar.

'Stephenson thinks so. Cause of death was pulmonary haemorrhage. Bleeding on the lungs,' he explains for Clough's benefit.

'What could cause that?'

'Lots of things including infection or drug-taking.'

'Did he take drugs, then? This curator bloke?'

'His body showed signs of persistent drugs use. And I found a hundred grams of cocaine in his office.'

Clough whistles. 'That's a lot of Charlie.'

'Do you think it was natural causes, boss?' asks Judy.

Nelson pauses. 'Most likely. There are a couple of odd things though.' He tells the team about the letters. 'Fuller, can you do some digging on the Elginists? Find out if they've ever been involved in anything dodgy. Clough, you and I might pay Lord Smith another visit.'

'Great,' says Clough, to general laughter. 'Might get a tip for the National.'

'The Necromancer,' says Nelson. 'He's got a lot of bone apparently.'

As Ruth nears her house, she is aware of a strange humming noise on the air. Is it a bird, a low-flying plane, the coastguard's helicopter? Perhaps it's a bittern, whose low, booming call she sometimes hears at night. Thinking of birds reminds her of David, her previous next-door neighbour, who was the warden of the marshes. David knew every stick and stone of the Saltmarsh, he could recognise the call of any one of the hundreds of birds that use these wetlands as a pit-stop on their journey south, he could find his way across the treacherous quicksand in the dark and had once saved Ruth's life. But David has gone, and if there's a new warden, she hasn't met them yet. As Ruth gets closer she sees that the sound is coming from Bob Woonunga, who is sitting on the grass in front of his house playing something which, from memories of Rolf Harris, she recognises as a didgeridoo.

She parks outside her cottage and gets Kate out of her car seat. Kate is now walking. She started at ten months, which is early according to the books. And while Ruth was proud of her daughter for reaching this milestone ahead of time (walking at ten months = first class honours degree from Cambridge), she can't help thinking that it was easier when she could carry her everywhere. Now Kate struggles to be put down and totters purposefully over to Bob and his didgeridoo. Ruth follows, more reluctantly. Flint, lurking by Ruth's front door waiting for his dinner, jumps over the fence and is the first to reach their new neighbour, rubbing himself lovingly around his legs.

'Want,' says Kate, pointing at the didgeridoo. This is one of her new words.

Bob puts down the long wooden pipe and says, 'Hallo little neighbour. You were asleep when I met your mum.' He reaches out and strokes Flint, who arches his back appreciatively. Ruth is shocked at the cat's infidelity.

'Mum,' says Kate, putting a hand on the painted wood of the didgeridoo. 'Mum, mum, mum.'

'Careful Kate,' says Ruth.

'Oh, don't worry.' Bob's smile seems impossibly wide. 'It's good to touch things. That's how we learn, right?'

Ruth agrees that it is. Touch is an important sense for an archaeologist. She remembers how Erik could tell just by holding a stone tool how it had been made, and what it had been used for. He used to shut his eyes, she remembers, while running his thumb along the sharp edges of a flint. She supposes that one day she'll stop thinking about Erik.

'Is it hard to play?' she asks, indicating the didgeridoo.

'Have a go.' He grins his endless grin again.

Ruth sits down on the grass and puffs and puffs but all she achieves is a sort of feeble farting noise. Kate laughs delightedly.

Bob blows again, an undulating, reverberating sound that seems oddly right out here in the wind and sky.

'I'm not an expert on the didge,' he says, putting the instrument on the ground, 'but it's a way of keeping in touch with home.'

'Where is home?' asks Ruth, settling herself more comfortably. It's a mild evening and it's curiously pleasant to be sitting out here on the grass as if it's summer. The moon is up but it's still light over the sea, the waves breaking in bands of silver and grey. A pair of geese fly overhead, calling mournfully.

'Our home is in Dreamtime,' says Bob. Then, laughing, he relents. 'I'm one of the Noonuccal people from Minjerribah, the islands in the bay. North Stradbroke Island to you.'

This doesn't mean very much to Ruth, whose only contact with Australia is a friend who emigrated there and now sends her irritating Christmas cards featuring Santa in swimming trunks. The islands in the bay have an exotic, foreign sound that seems to belong more to the Caribbean than to the land of surf and barbecues and good neighbours becoming good friends.

'I think you know a friend of mine,' she says. 'Cathbad.'

'Cathbad. Yes. He's a brother.'

'A brother?'

'In spirit. We belong to a band of brothers. A group of like-minded people.'

'The Elginists?'

Bob doesn't seem surprised. 'That's right. We're committed to the repatriation of our ancestors.'

'Like the skulls at the Smith Museum?'

A shadow crosses Bob's face, or maybe it's just the evening light. The sky seems to have grown much darker in the last few minutes. Kate climbs onto Ruth's lap and starts pulling her hair experimentally. Flint has wandered away.

'Right. But they're not just skulls. They're our ancestors. They need to be returned to their Spirit Land so they can enter the Dreaming.'

This is more or less what Cathbad had said but it sounds so much more impressive coming from Bob, out here under the darkening sky. Ruth shivers and holds Kate tighter.

'Look out there,' says Bob. He points over the Saltmarsh. You can't see the sea any more but you can hear it, a rushing, urgent sound in the twilight. 'This is sacred land. My people believe that the world was created in the Dreamtime when the spirit ancestors roamed the Earth. This place, it was made by the Great Snake. You can see its shape as it meandered over the land, creating all these little streams and rivers. That's why I feel at home here. The Snake's my tribal emblem. We need to take the Old Ones back so they can be at one with the Dreaming. For the Aborigines there's no life and death, no yesterday and today, it's all one. We need our ancestors with us so they can be part of the oneness. We can't leave them to rot in some whitefella's museum.' He grins as he says the last bit, perhaps parodying himself, but Ruth doesn't smile. She is thinking of Cathbad, all those years ago, demanding that the henge stay here, on the Saltmarsh, rather than be taken to a museum. 'It belongs here,' he had said, 'between the earth and the sky.' No wonder he and Bob are friends.

'Won't the museum return the . . . your ancestors?' she asks, tentatively, thinking that she knows the answer.

'No.' Bob's face darkens further. 'I tell you Ruth, Lord Danforth Smith is a seriously bad man.'

Nelson sits at his desk, wondering whether it's time to go home. It's dark outside and there's no real need to sit here, going over Chris Stephenson's report and wondering what's happening down at the docks. If there's anything to report he'll soon hear from Tanya and Tom Henty; he might as well wait in the comfort of his own sitting room. But still he sits in his office, drinking cold coffee and reading about pulmonary haemorrhage. The truth is that he doesn't want to go home.

When Nelson had agreed not to see Ruth any more, he and Michelle had fallen into each other's arms and into bed. It was the most emotional experience of his life. He had felt full of tenderness for Michelle, full of gratitude and remorse. At that moment, he would have promised her anything. But the euphoria hadn't lasted. Michelle had not seemed able to stop talking about Ruth. 'What was she like in bed? Was she better than me? What

was it like sleeping with someone so fat?' 'Don't,' Nelson
had begged. 'Can't we just forget it?' But that, of course,
was impossible. Now, six months later, Michelle fluctu-
ates between tearful intensity ('Promise you'll never leave
me') and seeming indifference. Last night she had gone
out with some of the girls at work and not returned
until midnight. He had rung her several times but her
phone was switched off. When she'd finally got in, he'd
been sitting up waiting for her. In fact, he'd been
wondering whether to call up a squad car. 'I didn't think
you'd be interested,' she'd said when he asked where
she'd been. She had flounced off upstairs as if he'd been
in the wrong, but later, in bed, had sobbed in his arms
and asked if he thought she was too old to have another
baby. Wondering which wife will be waiting for him at
home – the frosty businesswoman or the reproachful
angel – he decides to stay on and do some more work.
He'll find out some more about these Elginist people for
a start.

Nelson is bad at technology but can just about manage
to use Google. Soon the screen is full of pictures of marble
horses, grinning skulls, totemic objects. There's the logo
again, the crescent moon with the snake beneath it. The
Elginists, he reads, are dedicated to the return of cultural
artefacts to their countries of origin. There is a bit about
the Elgin Marbles and a whole site dedicated to someone
called the Amesbury Archer, a Bronze Age skeleton found
near Stonehenge whose return is demanded by a group
of druids. Nelson immediately thinks of Cathbad. What
had Tom Henty said? That Cathbad had wanted to talk

to him about 'skulls and the unquiet dead'. Could Cathbad be mixed up with these people? It seems only too likely. Nelson, who enjoys what can only be described as a friendship with Cathbad, decides to speak to him as soon as possible.

But most of the hits come up with the words 'Aboriginal remains'. The Elginists have been active around the country, demanding the return of Aboriginal relics held in private collections. In some cases, it seems they have been successful, and the internet provides pictures of smiling Aboriginal chiefs in animal-skin cloaks embracing embarrassed-looking museum officials. But there are many reports of collectors refusing to hand over their ill-gotten spoils, of threatening behaviour, bitter recriminations. Nelson can't see that the police have been involved but he'll check the files. Could this group, who seem both organised and determined, be involved in Neil Topham's death?

'Boss?' Judy Johnson is standing in the doorway.

'I thought you'd gone home,' says Nelson. 'You look knackered.' He realises that this is hardly tactful but Judy *does* look exhausted, grey-faced and almost shell-shocked.

'I'm going in a minute,' she says, 'but I got the report from SOCO on the Smith Museum. There were some fingerprints found at the scene so I thought I'd run them through our database, see if there were any matches.'

'And were there?'

'Just one.'

She puts a print-out on Nelson's desk. It informs him that fingerprints found at the scene match the prints of one Michael Malone.

Michael Malone. Alias Cathbad.

8

The Newmarket pub is on a crossroads leading to King's Lynn via one fork, Downham Market via the other. Rumour has it that there was once a terrible stagecoach accident at the junction, and even today Danforth Smith's horses sidle and spook if they pass this way. Stories of spectral carriages and ghostly horses are almost certainly unsubstantiated but, nevertheless, there is something unsettling about the location of the pub, backed by woodland, dense and inhospitable, and the only other building in sight is a deserted garage, with rusty Esso signs that creak in the wind. Despite these drawbacks, the pub is the watering hole of choice for the staff of Slaughter Hill Racing Stables and tonight, Karaoke night, it is full to bursting. Caroline Smith and her friend Trace have just left the microphone to tumultuous applause following a spirited rendering of *I Will Survive*. They give way to four stable lads who share a love of Queen's oeuvre and an almost total lack of musical talent.

'What will it be this time,' wonders Trace, as they fight their way to the bar, '*Bohemian Rhapsody* or *We Will Rock You?*'

'I've got an awful feeling about *Radio Gaga*,' says Caroline, pushing her damp hair back from her face. 'We haven't heard that for a while.'

But the quartet surprise them with *We Are The Champions*. Caroline and Trace escape with their beers to a relatively quiet corner of the pub.

'We had a policeman round our place today,' says Caroline. 'Called Nelson. Do you know him?'

Although Trace, in her leather trousers and artfully ripped top, hardly looks like the sort of person who would be on cordial terms with the police, she is going out with Dave Clough and so is regarded as an expert on King's Lynn's finest.

'Yeah, I know him. He's Dave's boss. Dave thinks a lot of him but he's always seemed a bit of a Neanderthal to me. What did he want?'

'I don't know. He wanted to see Dad. I thought it might be about that thing at the museum.'

'To do with the bishop's coffin?' Trace is part of the field archaeology team who first discovered Bishop Augustine.

'Yes. You know the curator dropped down dead?'

'I'd heard. Why are the police investigating? Do they think he was bumped off?'

'I don't know. I thought you might know.'

Trace shakes her head. 'I try not to let Dave talk too much shop. If I wanted to know about police stuff, I'd watch *CSI Miami*. Much more interesting.'

Caroline laughs. 'This Nelson guy seemed to be talking to Dad for an awfully long time, that's all.'

'Why don't you ask your dad about it?' asks Trace, though she thinks she knows the answer.

Caroline's face darkens. 'I can't talk to him about anything at the moment.'

'So you didn't discuss the pay rise?'

'No.' Caroline stares into her lager in order to avoid Trace's expression of amused exasperation. 'I told you, it's so hard to talk to him. He's busy in the yard all day and he goes to bed straight after supper. He was in bed before I came out.'

'Then make an appointment with him. You're not just his daughter, you're an employee, a valuable employee. You practically run that yard.'

'Well, Len does a lot with the horses, especially the ones from abroad.'

Trace dismisses Len Harris with an airy sweep of the hand that almost knocks her glass to the floor. 'But you do all the paperwork and you ride out and you look after all the press and publicity. You designed the website and you organised the open day.'

'Len hated the open day. Said it upset the horses.'

'Forget Len. He's a miserable bastard. It was a great success. You should get more recognition for the things you do.'

'I know. It's just . . . things are difficult at the moment. Dad's always arguing with Randolph and Randolph just lazes around winding Dad up. He doesn't even ride any more, just sits around watching daytime TV and drinking vodka at lunchtime. '

'What about your mum?'

'She's never home. She's always at work or out with her friends. And she's not interested in the yard anyway. She says it's cruel to make horses race because they never jump over fences when they're out in the fields, just when someone's on their back hitting them.'

'She's got a point,' Trace glances at her watch. She sympathises with her friend but she doesn't want to listen to Caroline banging on about horses all night. There are limits after all. And she'd like to do another song.

'Oh no,' says Caroline earnestly. 'Horses love to race. It's in their blood.'

'Maybe it's not in yours. You've travelled, you've got loads of other experience. Why don't you get out, get a job miles away? Forget about your mum and dad and Randolph.'

Caroline's face takes on a closed, stubborn look.

'I can't. There are things I need to do.'

Trace is about to ask what things when a stable-girl called Georgina comes over to ask them to form a three-some to sing *Material Girl*. Trace jumps up at once; she's always thought that she has a lot in common with Madonna.

Danforth Smith is, in fact, finding it hard to sleep. Usually he collapses into bed at ten, worn out by a hard physical day. His wife, Romilly, sleeps in another room and, anyhow, she's out 'seeing friends'. It occurred to Danforth recently that he no longer knows any of his wife's friends. He looked on her Facebook page recently and didn't recognise half of the names on it. 'Business acquaintances,'

she had said airily but, if so, they are business acquaintances who send very unbusinesslike messages ('love you
babe') and include pictures of themselves sunbathing
topless in the Maldives. Romilly has her own life, her own
job (as an interior designer), her own friends, her own
bank account. She leaves the house at nine, driving her
white Fiat 500, and is back at six, just when Danforth is
organising the evening feeds. Then she is often out again,
'networking' at various arty parties. Danforth usually eats
with the lads; Romilly, when she's home, eats with
Randolph in front of the TV. She gets on much better
with Randolph than he does. 'He's resting,' she says, whenever he raises the subject of their only son. 'Resting? He's
not a bloody actor.' 'He might be,' Romilly had countered.
'He's thinking of doing a course.' Danforth had stomped
off to the stables, disgusted. In his opinion, going on a
course is only another word for being unemployed.

So Romilly is now out somewhere discussing French
films or Italian wine (Danforth's idea of these events is
based on magazines his nanny used to read in the Fifties)
and Danforth tosses and turns in the ancient double that
once belonged to his parents. He gets up, goes to the loo,
drinks some water, tries to recite bloodlines in his head.
The house is silent; he can hear the occasional stamp and
whinny from the stables, but these are soothing sounds
usually guaranteed to make him feel that all is well with
the world. Why does he feel tonight that there's something very wrong with the world? Is it poor Neil's death?
He feels sorry for the curator certainly. Neil always seemed
a nice guy, a bit nervous maybe but fundamentally decent

and very bright, committed to turning the Smith Museum into something more modern and 'interactive' (whatever that might mean). But now Neil is dead, found lying beside the coffin of Danforth's illustrious ancestor. Is it this gruesome scenario which is preying on his mind? The coffin and the snake. *The Great Snake will have its revenge.* Nonsense, of course. Neil died from natural causes. Absolute tragedy and all that but life must go on. He'll offer the parents some money to fund some research or something in Neil's name. Make sure his memory lives on. He shifts uncomfortably under the duvet. Why can't he get to sleep?

And he's worried about Caroline. Danforth might say to Nelson that Caroline has never caused him a day's worry but the nights are another matter. Whenever he can't sleep, Caroline's face appears in front of him, reproachful and slightly angry. Why should she be angry with him? He's always done his best, though the kids haven't been easy at times. Tamsin was always the clever one, straight As, degree in law, now a successful career. Tamsin was always organised, the sort of girl who drew up a revision timetable in four different-coloured felt-tips. Randolph was another matter, brilliantly clever when he tried, infuriatingly stupid when he didn't. But even he managed to get a degree, though what he's going to do with it is another matter. Randolph isn't helped by being so good-looking. All his life teachers, friends and, later, girlfriends, have fallen over themselves to make excuses for him.

Caroline doesn't have that problem. She and Tamsin are actually very alike – striking without being beautiful

– but where Tamsin's dark hair is usually pulled back into a neat chignon, Caroline's is often loose and slightly unkempt. And while Tamsin always looks smart, Caroline slops around in jodhpurs or weird hippy dresses. And Caroline is so intense, always getting into a state about something or another. Animal rights, racehorses shipped off to die in Belgium, abandoned greyhounds, the age-old wrongs of every godforsaken tribe in the world. Her schooldays were one long drama of tears and tantrums, professions of love and hate. Caroline hadn't gone to university, she'd travelled the world instead and come back with a whole new list of things to care about. That's all fine, but why does she look at him as if he's the one responsible for the world's ills? He didn't wipe out the bloody American Indians, for God's sake. And why hasn't Caroline got a boyfriend? Always hanging out with that shaven-haired girl from the university. Maybe she's . . . But Danforth's imagination doesn't stretch that far.

He sighs and goes downstairs to make some cocoa. He'll put a swig of brandy in it too.

Randolph is in a bar, a very different drinking establishment from Caroline's. The lighting is subdued, the ambiance expensive. Two burly bouncers at the door stop passing riff-raff getting further than the gold ropes. Randolph drinks a glass of champagne without noticing, as if it's medicine. The first glass is free, to soften the fact that the rest of the drinks cost the equivalent of a two-bedroomed house (with garage). Randolph doesn't really notice the prices either. There's plenty in the bank, and if there isn't, what are overdrafts for? He's thinking about Clary, his current girlfriend. She's developed an awful habit of ringing him up on a Monday night. Monday nights are meant to be sacrosanct. And she's been making ominous noises about meeting his parents. Sunday lunch at home with Mummy and Daddy, Dad bellyaching about the cost of hay, Caroline brooding on the world's wrongs, horse shit all over the place. It's just not going to happen.

'Drinking alone?' The question comes from a young man in his twenties, vaguely Russian-looking, with a shaven head and definite biceps.

'Not now,' says Randolph.

Romilly Smith downs her beer in one gulp. She'd like another but she has to drive home and, besides, she needs her head to deal with this lot.

'Violence has to be justifiable,' she says. 'I'm not against it. I just think we need to choose our moment. And we have to make a case for it.'

Her audience, two men and a woman, all in their twenties and dressed in various items of camouflage, look at her resentfully. Romilly, in her white trousers and grey cashmere jumper, could not look more out of place in the dingy pub with her dingy companions, but there is an air of authority about her, an indefinable sense of superiority that makes the woman address her almost respectfully as she says, 'Who do we have to make the case to?'

'To whom,' corrects Romilly kindly. 'To the public, of course. And to the press. Something like this can't be hushed up and we wouldn't want it to be. We need the publicity.'

'What does it matter what the press think?' says one of the men. 'Bunch of Tory tossers.'

Romilly sighs. The group are really distressingly stupid sometimes. Not that she's got any time for Tories. She was in the Socialist Workers' Party before this lot were even *born*.

'It matters because they control public opinion,' she says. 'We have to be clever. We have to play the game. We have to spin things our way.'

'Nothing matters,' says the woman mutinously. 'Nothing matters except the cause.'

She sounds like Caroline in one of her sulky moods, thinks Romilly, except that Caroline would never have the guts for Direct Action. This group, for all their faults, don't lack guts.

'Of course dear,' she says soothingly. 'Nothing matters except the cause.'

Danforth makes cocoa in the empty kitchen. The time on the stainless steel range says 00.15. Fifteen minutes past midnight. Though the kitchen is deserted, it isn't quite silent. Various machines whirr and hum. The dishwasher is still ploughing through its umpteenth cycle. Ecologically unsound, says Caroline. She does all her washing up by hand. Well, she's welcome to it. Danforth rinses a cup, mindlessly rubbing a mark from one of the shiny red units. He's never been keen on them himself but Romilly insisted. He'd prefer an Aga like his parents had, mismatched cupboards, an old oak table. But their kitchen lies in ruins in the grounds of the park, weeds growing through the sandstone tiles where he used to lie on a summer's day, watching the ants march under the scullery door.

The milk starts to boil and Danforth removes it from the heat. A horse neighs outside, another answers. Danforth pauses, dripping milk onto the floor. It is rare for the horses to neigh at night. A neigh is often a warning, a signal to the rest of the herd. Perhaps he should check the CCTV cameras in Caroline's cottage? No, it would be impossible for an intruder to get past the electric gates. Danforth pours the cocoa, blinking in the glare. Then he stops again. There shouldn't be any glare, just the discreet spotlights above the range (Romilly is excellent at lighting). But the room is bathed in an unnatural white glow.

The security lights are on.

Danforth goes to the window. He can see through the arch and into the yard, see the horses heads silhouetted in the sudden brightness. Maybe a fox has got in. Only yesterday one of the lads had had some story about seeing a big cat 'the size of a cheetah' prowling on the edge of the wood. There are always stories about big cats, lions escaped from the nearby zoo, panthers living wild in suburban gardens. But a loose animal could disturb the horses. They need their sleep too.

Barbours and boots are kept by the kitchen door. Danforth shrugs on a coat and treads into his gumboots. He walks quickly across the carport where his Range Rover is parked in solitary splendour. Romilly's Fiat and

Randolph's Porsche are both missing. Romilly is probably watching a dreary film with subtitles and doubtless Randolph is out with some highly unsuitable girl, two-timing that nice Clary. Danforth walks quickly around the house. The stable cat, Lester, appears from the darkness and rubs himself round his legs. Was it Lester who sparked the rumour about the big cat?

The yard is still lit up. Some horses are peering sleepily out of their stalls but most are hidden. The clock over the archway says twelve twenty-five. The grass is grey in the moonlight, the stable doors ghostly white. Lester runs happily along the plastic-coated hay bales, his tail in the air. There is nothing and nobody to be seen.

Danforth Smith stomps back to the house. Maybe now he'll be able to sleep. He'll definitely have a brandy, perhaps a double. He stops by the back door to take off his boots. It is some minutes before he notices the dead snake on the doorstep.

9

Morning at Slaughter Hill, and the horses are thundering over the gallops. Caroline is clinging to the saddle of a grey gelding and hoping that he'll stop when she asks him to; she had too much to drink last night and the horse knows it, even if her father doesn't. Danforth Smith, also feeling slightly fragile after his broken night, is in the office sorting out the declarations. He has told no one about the snake. Lester the cat found the body on the manure pile and has taken it behind the barn to investigate. Head Lad Len Harris is getting the next lot of horses ready, giving a leg up to a young jockey and thinking sourly about the immigration laws. Romilly Smith is in the bathroom, getting ready for a hard day designing curtains. Randolph is still asleep.

Len Harris looks in through the office door.

'That new boy – Ali Baba or whatever his name is – thinks a lot of himself, doesn't he?'

Danforth sighs. He's not exactly politically correct himself but Len's casual racism depresses him.

'His name's Mikelis,' he says. 'He's from Latvia and he's an excellent jockey.'

'If you say so,' grunts Len. He's been at Slaughter Hill for twenty years and Danforth couldn't run the place without him. Doesn't stop him wishing that he could sometimes.

'I've got to be at the museum this morning,' he says. 'Can you manage here?'

'Course I can, governor.' Sometimes Len gives a good impersonation of a faithful old retainer. He almost tugs his forelock. It doesn't fool Danforth for a minute, but he needs Len. Caroline is a good manager but she's too soft with the horses, and with the owners. Randolph . . . but Danforth doesn't even finish this sentence in his own head.

'I'm meeting some archaeologist woman,' he says, turning back to his paperwork. 'Hope she's not the squeamish type.'

Ruth is not the squeamish type but she does hope, as she parks in front of the museum, that all traces of Neil Topham's final agony have been cleared away. She has had roughly four hours' sleep and doesn't think she could cope with bloodstains or police tape. But as she approaches the entrance, the building has the smug, shuttered look of a place that has been empty for years. A sign on the door says 'Closed Until Further Notice'.

It doesn't seem possible that anyone could be inside, but almost as soon as Ruth has pressed the bell the door is opened. Almost as if someone was lying in wait for her.

'Dr Galloway? Danforth Smith. Do come in.'

Ruth recognises Danforth Smith from Saturday but she can see that he has no recollection of ever having met her before. He's polite though, almost gracious, as he ushers her through the dusty entrance hall. The museum, although it has only been closed for two days, already looks distinctly unloved. A pile of post has been pushed to one side of the door and cobwebs are starting to shroud the face of the Great Auk.

'So good of you to come,' says Danforth. 'I'm sure you're a very busy lady.'

Ruth smiles. She doesn't deny that she is busy or mention that she doesn't like the word 'lady'. There's no point; Smith, like Nelson, is probably beyond re-education. Besides she's keen to see the infamous collection.

Danforth leads the way through the National History Room, their footsteps echoing on the black and white tiles. Ruth tries not to imagine the glass eyes following them.

'When's the museum opening again?' she asks.

'Lord knows.' Danforth Smith stops to examine a particularly mangy badger who stares grimly back. 'I've got to find a new curator and people might not be so keen to work here after what happened to poor Neil.'

'Have you found out how he died? I found his body,' she explains hastily, in case she is sounding ghoulish.

Danforth looks at her with new interest. 'I'm sorry ... I didn't realise. No, they haven't said for certain. DCI Nelson mentioned something about a pulmonary haemorrhage.'

'Nelson?'

'Yes. The detective chappie. Rather a rough diamond but bright enough, I think.'

'I know Nelson.'

'I suppose you do, in the course of your work.'

'Yes.'

'Well,' Danforth turns back to the badger. 'I got the impression that Nelson thought that Neil died from natural causes. It's just that . . .'

Ruth waits. Knowing when not to speak is one skill that she shares with Nelson.

'Doctor Galloway, have you heard of the Elginists?'

'Someone mentioned them to me the other day.'

'Really?' Danforth looks up and Ruth thinks that he looks tired, almost haggard. She hasn't much liked Lord Smith up until now but suddenly she feels almost sorry for him.

'About a year ago I had a letter from a group called the Elginists demanding the return of the . . . the artefacts I'm about to show you. It turns out that they also wrote to Neil. Terrible letters, threatening him, saying that his life was in danger.'

Ruth's head reels. She looks at the stuffed animals, envying them their painted idyll. Could Cathbad and his friends have written threatening letters to Neil Topham? It's not impossible, and this realisation stirs memories that Ruth would rather have left undisturbed. Could Cathbad be involved in the curator's death? And what about Bob Woonunga, her charming didgeridoo-playing neighbour? What's his role in all this?

'Does Nelson,' her voice sounds high-pitched and odd,

'does Nelson think that the letters had anything to do with Neil's death?'

'I don't think so,' says Danforth, 'but it's a strange coincidence, don't you think?'

'Very strange.'

'The whole thing's odd. Neil dropping dead like that beside the bishop's coffin. I don't believe in jinxes,' he laughs, 'but still, it's odd.'

'What's happened to the coffin?' asks Ruth. 'It's not still here, is it?'

Danforth Smith seems genuinely surprised. 'I thought you knew. It's at the university. Your university. Apparently it needs to be kept in a controlled environment. Phil Trent was talking about opening it next week. Just a low-key affair this time. He said you'd be there.'

Thanks a lot Phil, thinks Ruth. He hadn't mentioned the coffin when he'd spoken to her in the canteen, too busy going on about bananas and Natural Childbirth.

'Where are these bones you wanted me to look at?' she says.

'This way.'

They pass through the Victorian study where Lord Percival Smith is frozen in the act of writing, wax hand holding wax quill. Danforth Smith leads the way into the long gallery where the portraits of long-dead Smiths look down their noses at them. The door to the Local History Room is firmly shut. Smith sees Ruth looking at it.

'The police have finished with the room now. There's nothing to see.' But he doesn't open the door.

At the far end of the gallery is the curator's office, and at the opposite end a little door that Ruth hadn't noticed before. Smith opens it now. 'The storerooms are down here.'

The staircase leads down into a brick-lined cellar. Ruth has never liked underground spaces and now, after the events of two years ago, finds them almost unbearable. As she descends the stairs, the air seems to get thicker and hotter. Heating pipes snake overhead making a low humming noise. She takes a deep breath and tries to feel professional. This is a museum, not a dungeon. At the foot of the stairs, Danforth Smith stops to fumble for a key. Ruth only just avoids crashing into his tweed back.

'Ah, here it is.'

In front of them is a plasterboard wall with two doors. Danforth is unlocking the left-hand door and reaching for a light switch. Rather reluctantly, Ruth follows him.

A flickering fluorescent light illuminates a narrow room with brick walls and cement floor. The walls are curved, a half-circle bisected by the plasterboard wall. The straight side of the room is lined with metal shelves and the shelves are stacked with cardboard boxes. Each box is scrawled with a single word. Bones.

The room is full of bones.

Ruth is an expert on bones; her students even once presented her with a life-size cardboard cutout of Bones from *Star Trek*. She has excavated mass graves, dug up prehistoric bodies, but she has never seen anything like this. Boxes of bones just piled up together in a cellar. No names, no dates, just 'bones'. Are they all human? she wonders. There must be fifty, maybe sixty, boxes here.

She suddenly realises that Danforth is speaking to her and, incredibly, there is pride in his voice.

'My great-grandfather was a real character. Travelled to Australia in the 1800s, the pioneer days. He was after gold. Did you know that gold was discovered in Australia in the 1850s? My great-grandpa started a gold mine in New South Wales. Had a few clashes with the old Abos over the land, but he must have been a fierce old codger because he stuck to it and made a mint. Came back to England in about 1870 but he was never the same again, apparently. My pa remembered him as quite dotty. Anyhow, he brought his collection back with him, God knows how. There's some wonderful stuff. We've got some of it in the museum downstairs: snakeskins, dingo traps, branding irons, convict-made bricks.'

Great-grandpa must be Lord Percival Smith, adventurer and taxidermist, thinks Ruth. Clearly his collecting extended beyond slaughtering and stuffing local wildlife. She was right when she thought he looked an ugly customer.

'Where do the bones come from?' asks Ruth. She is starting to feel seriously uncomfortable. There isn't much room to stand in the space between the boxes and Danforth Smith seems to be looming over her. He has to duck his head under the curved ceiling. She can see the sweat on his forehead. It's very hot and there's a faint smell of gas in the air.

'They're Aboriginal bones. And the skulls too. I think the old man had the idea that the Abos were put together differently from us, that they were linked to cave men or some such. So he started collecting bones. There must be hundreds here.'

Ruth shakes her head. As an expert in prehistory she detests the term 'cave men', but that almost fades into the background compared with the mind-boggling idea of a man who collected human bones for fun and a great-grandson who seems almost proud of the fact.

'Where did he get the bones?' she asks faintly.

'From all over. Some of them come from one of the islands. Those are the ones that these Elginist nutters are on about. My great-granddad had a share in a salt mine on one of the islands.'

The word 'island' rings a faint bell. Does salt come from mines, wonders Ruth irrelevantly. It sounds like something from *Alice in Wonderland*, one of Cathbad's favourite books. She remembers how, the first time she visited the museum, she had felt like Alice, plunged into an underground world, faced with arbitrary but somehow sinister choices. The little door or the big one. Eat me. Drink me. Aloud, she asks, 'But where did they come from? I mean, did he just dig them up or . . .' Or what, she thinks.

'Oh I think so,' says Danforth airily. 'The Aboriginals just dumped their dead bodies in the ground, no coffin or anything.' He sounds disapproving.

'So he *dug up the bodies*?' Ruth can't believe her ears.

Danforth registers her tone and becomes more defensive. 'He paid good money for them, I'm told. The Abos probably spent it on drink from what I've heard.'

'And now the Elginists want the bones back?'

Danforth's face darkens further. 'They don't know what they want. Burial of their ancestors and all that tosh. I mean, these . . .' He gestures towards the cardboard boxes stacked on the shelves. 'These aren't their ancestors. They're just *bones*.'

Ruth doesn't know where to start. 'But they're human bones, human remains. They deserve a decent burial.' She tries to think of an example that will mean something to Smith. 'Look at Bishop Augustine. He's your ancestor. You wouldn't want his bones kept in a cardboard box. You'd want them treated with dignity and respect.'

'But that's different. He was a bishop.'

'Well some of these people might be bishops or the equivalent. Holy men and women.' Ruth pauses, aware that she's hazy about Indigenous Australian religion. She thinks of Bob Woonunga. *My people believe that the world was created in the Dreamtime when the spirit ancestors roamed the Earth.* She doesn't think that there is any point telling this to Danforth Smith.

'So,' she says briskly. 'What do you want from me?'

Danforth, too, seems relieved to have left the spirit world behind. 'I want you to tell me if these bones really are human. I mean, they could be bloody dingo for all I know. The skulls are staying here, they're important objects – especially the water carrier. But if the bones *are* human, I suppose these Elginist people can have them. They're not doing much good here, after all.'

'All right,' says Ruth. 'I'll take a look at the bones.'

'Righty ho.' Danforth rubs his head, which he has just knocked against the doorpost. 'Oh I almost forgot.' In the corner of the room is a kind of wire cage. Danforth Smith takes out another key to unlock this. Inside is a metal box, rather like a large camera case. 'Here are the skulls,' he says. 'Beautiful aren't they?'

Ruth, left alone with the bones, takes off her jacket, wipes her hands on her legs and takes a water bottle from her bag. 'Why do young people carry these bottles everywhere?' her mother always asks. 'I don't feel the need to gulp down water all the time.' Maybe not Mum, thinks Ruth, but even you might feel like a drink in these circumstances. She drinks slowly, trying to concentrate. The heat is making her sleepy. Last night hadn't been a good one. Kate, worn out after the excitement of the didgeridoo, went to sleep at half-past seven. But as Ruth was tiptoeing downstairs at eight she woke up again. And again at ten, at midnight, at half-past three. Today Ruth feels as if she is sleepwalking or seeing everything through thick glass. She puts the bottle back in her rucksack. She'd better get on with it. She has a lecture at twelve. Come to think of it, the heat can't be doing the bones much good either. Like Bishop Augustine's coffin, they should really be kept at an ambient temperature. She takes down a box from the nearest shelf. She peers into the nearest box. Bones are piled high inside, yellow-white, some of them with numbers and dates printed on them. At first glance, they are almost definitely human.

She had planned to lay the bones out anatomically but

soon gives up. Danforth Smith's great-grandfather (such a character) must simply have scooped up everything buried in the soil of the island salt mine. There are adult bones, children's bones, animal bones, all mixed together in a ghastly colonial stew. There are also a few interesting stone tools, which Ruth puts aside to study later.

What would Cathbad make of this? she wonders. Cathbad and his Elginist friends who want the bones reunited with Mother Earth. She decides to call him. She wants to hear his voice, to reassure herself that Cathbad, her friend, who has been so kind to her, could never have anything to do with letters that threatened to take a man's life. A man who subsequently died. Besides, she tells herself, she wants to ask him about the 'repatriation' conference. It's work, she tells herself, nothing to do with Max. So much has happened since she last saw Max, not least the birth of Kate, that she no longer knows how she feels about him anyway. She conjures him up: tall, curly-haired, slightly watchful. She met Max when he was excavating the Roman Villa near Swaffham but their relationship soon became overshadowed by other events, including murder. Cathbad was involved in that case too. He really does seem to have discovered the art of omnipresence.

Except today. Cathbad isn't answering his phone. This is unusual because, although he claims that using mobile phones causes brain cancer, he's usually pretty quick to answer a text or voicemail. Where can he be?

Ruth puts aside the bones and opens the box containing the skulls. There are three of them, more or less intact.

Beautiful, Danforth had said, and, in a way, Ruth can see what he means. A human skull is a gift to an archae-ologist, telling so much, free from the trappings of flesh. But it's also a person, as Ruth always tells her students, and three people, three real people who were born and died thousands of miles away, have ended up with their heads locked in the basement of a Norfolk museum. Why? How?

The fourth object in the box makes Ruth catch her breath. It's the top half of a skull, the iliac crest, scooped out to resemble a bowl. This must be the famous water carrier. What sort of person would want to drink out of someone else's head? She turns the object round in her hands, wondering about its owner. Without carbon-14 dating it's almost impossible for her to tell how old it is, or even if it belonged to a man or a woman. The complete skulls are easier, the sloping brow-ridge and the pronounced nuchal crest at the back tell her that they are all male. One has scars which may be indicative of syphilis. But it is the last skull that makes her sit back on her heels, as shocked as if she had suddenly come face-to-face with Smith Senior and his grave-robbing friends.

The skull has cut marks all over it. Clean cut marks unhealed, which shows that they were made at the point of death or soon after. The position of the cut marks indi-cate that the head has had the skin cut from it. It has been scalped.

10

Cathbad's silence is easily explained. He is helping the police with their enquiries. Or rather, he is entertaining Nelson and Judy in his caravan on the beach at Blakeney. Cathbad seems determined to keep the occasion social, offering them tea and brownies, enquiring after Michelle and the girls. Nelson answers brusquely. He's annoyed with Cathbad for putting him in this position. Why the hell did his fingerprints have to be found at the scene? Does the man get everywhere?

He doesn't think that Cathbad killed Neil Topham but he's mixed up in it somehow. He was at the museum that day and, as for the Elginists, they have Cathbad's name written all over them. Cathbad loves nothing more than a fight with authority and this one would be right up his street.

'I expect you know why we're here,' is Nelson's opening gambit.

'I'm sure you'll tell me,' replies Cathbad genially.

Progress through the caravan is difficult. Objects hang from the ceiling and there is furniture everywhere, mostly draped in material so that it is hard to know whether it's a chair or a table that you've just fallen over. Nelson gets tangled up in a dreamcatcher made of seashells and swats at it wildly. It breaks.

'Sorry,' he says, not sounding it.

'It doesn't matter,' says Cathbad. 'I can make another.'

'Do you sell them to gullible tourists?' asks Nelson, landing with relief onto a bench seat.

'No, I give them to special people in my life,' says Cathbad. He looks at Judy, who looks away.

Nelson, who is the not-so-proud owner of two of Cathbad's dreamcatchers, gets straight down to business.

'We found your prints at the museum. Are you going to tell us what's going on?'

Cathbad settles himself in a tall wizard's chair. He smiles. Nelson glowers at him. He distrusts Cathbad's smile.

'I was in the museum on Saturday,' he says. 'You know that. I came for the opening of Bishop Augustine's coffin.'

'But how come your prints were found in the Local History Room, which was closed to the public?'

Cathbad sighs. He turns to Judy. 'Have you ever been to the Smith Museum?' he asks her. 'Fascinating collection.'

Judy is fiddling with her phone. She looks tired again today, thinks Nelson, and she hardly spoke on the drive from the station. Christ, he hopes she isn't pregnant.

Judy meets Cathbad's eyes. 'I went once when I was at school. I thought it was boring.'

Cathbad seems delighted by this answer. He laughs.

'Then you should look below the surface. There are horrors underneath.'

Nelson has had enough of this. 'Give me a straight answer,' he growls, 'or we'll conduct this interview at the station. Were you or were you not in the Local History Room that day?'

'Yes, Detective Chief Inspector,' says Cathbad, with deceptive meekness. 'I was. I arrived at about two o'clock. There was no one to be seen, though all the drinks and goodies were laid out in the long gallery. I went into the Local History Room to pay my respects to Bishop Augustine.'

'Why?'

'He was an interesting character. People thought he was a saint. Apparently he could bilocate, be in two places at once.'

Nelson can see exactly why this would appeal to Cathbad. 'When you went into the room,' he asks, 'did you see the curator?'

'No. There wasn't a soul about.'

'Did you know Neil Topham? Did you ever meet him at one of your weirdy gatherings?'

'I met him once or twice at events organised by the museum,' says Cathbad with dignity. 'I wouldn't say we were friends.'

'But you didn't see him that day?'

'No.'

'Was there anything unusual in the room when you went in?'

Cathbad raises his eyebrows. 'Apart from it having a dirty great coffin in the middle? No.'

'Nothing on the floor? No exhibits out of place?'

'No. I don't think so.' Cathbad is definitely curious now.

'Was the window open?'

'I'm not sure . . . No, I remember thinking how hot it was in there.'

'Hot?'

Cathbad looks innocent. 'Yes, hot. Close.'

'What else did you do?'

'Went up to the coffin. Said a prayer to the good spirits. Then I had a quick look round the room. There's a picture of the henge, you know.'

'Have you seen this before?' Nelson holds out a copy of the museum guidebook. It's not the book found in the room with the dead body (that's still with forensics) but it's folded back on the same page.

'It's from the museum, isn't it?'

'Take a look at this page. Does it mean anything to you?'

'The Smith Family,' Cathbad reads aloud in a polite, interested voice, 'have lived in Norfolk since the middle ages. The first recorded Smith was Augustine, Bishop of Norwich from 1340 to 1362. Bishop Augustine was much loved for his charitable work and when he died hundreds visited his body as it lay in state. There is a statue to him at the cathedral. In the sixteenth century Thomas Smith aided Henry VIII in the Dissolution of the Monasteries and in 1538 was rewarded by the gift of Slinden Abbey, which had previously been a monastery. Thomas reverted to Catholicism during the reign of Mary Tudor but reverted again to become a loyal protestant under

Elizabeth I. He was knighted in 1560. In the Civil War, Slinden was the scene of a particularly bloody battle and was renamed Slaughter Hill. Lord Edmund Smith fought on the Royalist side and was killed in the battle. Other prominent Smiths have included Hubert Smith, an actor who performed with Beerbohm Tree, and Sir Gilbert Smith, a Conservative MP in the Eden government. The present Lord Smith is a successful racehorse owner and trainer.'

The words 'died', 'Slaughter' and 'killed' have been underlined.

'A fascinating family,' says Cathbad.

'Have you seen this guidebook, with these words underlined, before?'

Cathbad looks up from examining an engraving of Slinden Abbey. 'No. Why?'

'It was found in the room with Neil Topham's body.'

'It wasn't there when I went into the room.'

Nelson glares at Cathbad, who looks back at him with wide, innocent eyes. The dreamcatchers sparkle overhead.

'What did you do next?' asks Nelson. 'When you left the Local History Room.'

'Had a look round the other rooms and then went to meet some friends for a spot of lunch.'

'You can give their names and addresses to Detective Sergeant Johnson later.'

'I'll be glad to.'

Cathbad smiles at Judy, who looks down at her phone again. Nelson says, 'Cathbad, are you a member of the Elginists?'

Cathbad doesn't miss a beat. 'Yes I am.'

Nelson counts to ten and gives up on five.

'You didn't think it was worth mentioning this?'

'You didn't ask.'

'Did you write the letter to Lord Smith demanding the return of the Aborigine relics?'

'I was one of the people who drafted it, yes.'

'Can you give me the names of the others?'

'I suppose so. We've got nothing to hide. The group's quite open and above board. We've even got a website.'

But that, as even Nelson knows, proves nothing. These days every nutcase has got a website. Nelson leans forward, trying to force Cathbad to take him seriously. But Cathbad is still looking at Judy with that infuriating smile on his face.

'Cathbad, did you, or anyone in the group, write letters to Neil Topham?'

Cathbad is still smiling. 'To Neil? No. Not that I know of. Why?'

'Because threatening letters were sent to him. *Handwritten* letters.' Nelson glares at Cathbad, remembering other handwritten letters, death threats written in flowery poetic language but no less sinister for all that. Cathbad drops his eyes first.

''I don't know anything about any letters to Neil Topham,' he says, 'I helped draft the letter to Lord Smith, that's all.'

'You helped draft the letter that threatened Smith with the vengeance of the Great Snake?'

Cathbad frowns. 'I think we put it better than that. More poetically.'

'Stop taking the piss,' says Nelson. 'These are serious accusations.'

Cathbad opens his eyes wide. 'What exactly are you accusing me of?'

That's the problem; Nelson doesn't know. But he does know that something went on in the museum that day. Henty and Taylor delivered the coffin at half-past one. If he is to be believed, Cathbad visited the museum at two but didn't see Neil Topham. Ruth arrived at two-sixteen, by which time Topham was already dead.

'We'll be in touch,' he says, standing up. 'Don't leave the country.'

Rocky and Clough are not having much luck with their door-to-door enquiries. Most of the buildings around the Smith Museum are offices and so are closed on Saturday. The people in the garage opposite didn't see anything, nor did the owner of the corner shop. They are just about to give up when the shopkeeper suggests they talk to 'old Stanley'.

'Who's old Stanley when he's at home?' asks Clough, who is stocking up on chocolate.

'He's the caretaker of the flats behind the museum. He's always in the grounds, sweeping up leaves, doing odd jobs. Old Stanley sees everything.'

'Then we'll see him,' says Clough grandly. 'Come on Rocky.'

Stanley lives on the ground floor of the mansion flats directly behind the museum. His flat is crammed with pictures of his children and grandchildren but his main interest seems to be keeping the grounds clear of dog mess.

'They used not to allow dogs in the flats,' he explains. 'But the residents complained and now their bloody dogs crap everywhere.'

'Don't they use pooper scoopers or whatever they're called?' asks Clough. He'd like a dog but Trace is asthmatic, or so she says.

'Don't talk to me about pooper scoopers,' Stanley's face darkens. 'Little plastic bags full of crap everywhere. There's no respect.'

'Right,' says Clough. 'Look, Mr ... er, Stanley. We're investigating an incident which happened at the museum on Saturday. We wondered if you were in the grounds on Saturday between about midday and two-thirty.'

'Might have been,' says Stanley cautiously.

'Did you see anything suspicious? Anyone entering or leaving the museum.'

'There was that one man.'

Clough sits up straighter and even Rocky looks interested.

'What man?'

'He was in the car park. Must have been after two o'clock because I always have my radio with me and *Any Questions* had just finished. Then it's *Any Answers*, all these busybodies ringing in. Haven't they got anything better to do?'

'The man,' prompts Clough. 'What was he doing?'

'Just walking through the car park. I watched him. He went up to the recycling box and put a shoe in. One shoe! What's the good of that to some poor bastard?'

'What did he look like?'

'I only saw his back. Tall. Wearing a dark suit and a hat. I thought he looked like a businessman. People don't wear suits so much these days. There are no standards.'

Clough, wearing jeans, ignores this. 'What did he do next?'

'Just walked off. I think he turned right, towards the town. A few minutes later there was all the excitement. Ambulance, police cars, the lot.'

'Why didn't you come forward with this earlier?'

Stanley shrugs. 'Didn't think it was my business. I'm not a nosy parker.'

Clough drives back to the station elated at having found a possible clue but full of contempt for Stanley and the public in general.

'Didn't think it was his business. Old nutter. Too busy going on about dog shit.'

'I'd like a dog,' says Rocky. 'A Labrador. Labradors are clever.'

'Cleverer than you, certainly,' says Clough.

Nelson and Judy are also driving back to the station.

'Bloody Cathbad.' Nelson is still steaming. 'Every bloody thing that happens in this county, he's involved some-where. I'm beginning to think he can bi-whatsit like that Augustine fellow. Be in two places at once. Remember when he turned up in the snow that time? At Ruth's place.'

'Yes,' says Judy.

Nelson turns to look at her, causing the car to swerve

sharply. 'Are you OK, Johnson? You seem to have taken a vow of silence today.'

It is very rare for Nelson to ask his staff how they are. Judy realises that he is trying to be kind. 'I'm fine,' she says. To distract herself, and him, she looks down at the list of names given to her by Cathbad.

'Jesus, boss. You should see the people Cathbad says he was having lunch with on Saturday. Akema Beaver, Derel Assinewai, Bob Woonunga. Are these people for real?'

'All Cathbad's mates have weird names. What are their addresses?'

'All local— Bloody hell!'

'What?' The car swerves again.

'Bob Woonunga's address. No 1, New Road. He lives next door to Ruth.'

Back at the university, Ruth goes to the canteen for a restorative cup of coffee. The first person she sees is Irish Ted. Ted is a member of the Field Archaeology Team and Ruth has come across him many times before. He's almost a friend, although Ruth doesn't feel she knows him very well. He once told her that his name wasn't even really Ted.

Now, though, he greets her enthusiastically. 'Ruth! Long time no see. Come to join me?'

Though it's only eleven o'clock, Ted is tucking into a huge slice of pizza, washed down by a can of lager.

'I can't stay long. I've got a lecture at twelve.'

'Why bother? Most of the students can't speak English anyhow.'

It's true that these days most of Ruth's students come from overseas. She teaches postgraduates and the university needs the money. But in fact their English is usually perfect.

'They speak better English than me,' she says. 'How are you, Ted?'

'Fine. Can't complain.' He grins, showing two gold teeth. 'I hear you're involved with the cursed coffin.'

'What? Oh, Bishop Augustine. Did you find him then?'

Most of the Field Team's work is on building sites. Contractors are obliged to call in the archaeologists if they are working on a historic site. However, there is pressure on the team not to find anything so valuable that building work is delayed. Big business tends to outrank historical research.

'Yeah,' says Ted. 'It was on the new Asda site. We knew there'd been a church there once, one of the early ones. But we didn't expect to find chummy there, all sealed up in his coffin. Gave us quite a turn.'

'Did you know who it was?'

'Well, there's a pretty big clue on the coffin itself.' The word 'Augustin' and a bishop's staff are carved into the coffin. 'And we'd heard the legend.'

'What legend?' asks Ruth, despite herself.

'Old Augustine put a curse on anyone who opened his coffin. It's all in the records up at the cathedral. If anyone despoiled his body, a great serpent was going to come and devour them.'

'A great serpent?' A memory stirs in Ruth's brain.

'Yes. Satan himself, presumably. Augustine was known

for being able to cast out devils. His statue in the cathedral shows him with his foot on a snake. Maybe the devil was about to have his revenge.'

He grins and swallows the rest of his pizza in one easy bite.

11

The setting for the second opening of the coffin is very different from the first. Instead of canapés and wine boxes, a sterile room in the university's science block. Instead of the press and assorted dignitaries, a small group of people in disposable coveralls: Phil, Ruth, Chris Stephenson, Lord Smith and – to Ruth's surprise and discomfort – Nelson. She is also surprised that Cathbad hasn't managed to con his way in; he works in the science department after all. But Cathbad is still not answering his phone. Ted was invited to represent the Field Team who had discovered the coffin, but he had declined. He was scared of the curse, he said.

But despite the bland surroundings there is a definite frisson in the room. The coffin itself, balanced on two trestle tables, looks neither sterile nor scientific. In fact it looks almost sinister, a brooding dark shape amidst the white. Next to the coffin is a table covered with a white sheet, intended for the Bishop's skeleton. It is this more than anything that reminds Ruth that there is a person inside the wooden box, a direct ancestor of the tall grey-haired man currently chatting to Nelson about horse-racing. Who knew that Nelson was interested in horses? Ruth and Nelson have not yet exchanged one word.

The door opens and a technician comes in, carrying a hammer and a chisel. These instruments, placed beside the trestles, look far too B&Q-ish to suit the occasion but Ruth knows that the coffin lid may be hard to shift, there are a lot of nails in it.

'Shall we start?' Phil asks Ruth rather nervously. The technician gets out a camera – he is going to video the whole thing. Ruth prays she won't end up on YouTube.

'What's the coffin made of?' asks Lord Smith.

'Oak,' says Ruth. 'It's good-quality wood. Some coffins from this time are made from lots of small pieces of wood nailed together but these are good, large pieces. Look how the top forms a ridge. That's quite unusual too. The shape as well, tapering to a point. We're just starting to see this in medieval coffins. Previously they were basic rectangles.'

'You know your stuff,' says Smith approvingly. Ruth, who has spent several days reading up on medieval burial practices, tries not to look pleased.

'Is there another coffin inside?' asks Chris Stephenson.

'No. We've scanned it and all that's inside is a body wrapped in some kind of cloth or shroud. Some bodies from this time were buried in lead inner coffins but it's rare. There was a body excavated from the site of a monastery in St Bees in Cumbria buried in a box within a box within a box, like a Russian doll. But, like I say, it's rare. Besides, lead was expensive.'

'But he was a bishop,' protests Smith, perhaps stung by the suggestion that his ancestor couldn't afford the best.

'Maybe he gave all his money to the poor,' says Ruth. It's unlikely, given what she knows of medieval bishops, but it effectively silences Danforth Smith.

Phil, rather gingerly (he's not known for his DIY skills), starts to prise up the nails, which come out easily. Too easily, thinks Ruth, though she keeps this thought to herself. The nails, thick and black, made from badly rusted iron, are laid aside for further examination. The atmosphere becomes tenser, people move closer to the coffin. Then, just when Phil removes the last nail, Ruth's phone rings.

She curses inwardly. She'd meant to turn her phone off. She almost does so now, but a glance at it tells her that the caller is Cathbad. Backing away from the main group, she hisses, 'Cathbad? I can't talk now.'

Cathbad sounds amused. 'Is it the great unveiling?'

'Yes. Why aren't you here?'

'I wasn't invited.'

That's never stopped you before, thinks Ruth.

'Can we talk later?' she asks.

'Sure. I'll come round to your house at about six.'

This isn't quite what Ruth had in mind but she hasn't got time to argue. She sees, to her annoyance, that the lid has been lifted and Nelson and Lord Smith are peering into the open coffin. The technician is videoing frantically.

'I've got to go,' she says. 'Bye.'

'Over to you, Ruth,' Phil says graciously, though he is probably cross with her about the phone call. Getting closer, she sees that the skeleton is wrapped in something that looks like silk, though it has a strange waxy sheen to it. Next to the head is the crook of a bishop's crosier, beautifully preserved.

'Bishops were often buried with their crosiers,' Phil is saying. 'An interesting survival of the superstition that you take your goods with you into the next life. This one might even have been specially made for funerary use. The crook looks as if it's made of jet.' The tip of the staff does indeed have a dull black gleam to it.

Ruth pulls on her gloves and leans into the coffin. The silk is well preserved due, no doubt, to the thin coating of wax. 'Beeswax,' she says, 'a natural preservative.' Gently she unwraps the silken shroud. Behind her, there is a sharp intake of breath as the bishop's skeleton is revealed.

It is a perfect skeleton, laid out on its back, arms crossed across the chest. There is a ring on one of the fingers and below the feet something that looks like a shoe. But, looking closer, Ruth realises something else.

Bishop Augustine is a woman.

'So the old boy was really an old girl. How priceless!' Cathbad leans back in his chair and laughs uproariously. Kate, who is watching him closely, laughs too. 'Are you sure?'

'Of course I'm sure,' says Ruth with some asperity. 'Female pelvic bones are quite different from male. The female pelvis is shallower and broader, the pubic ramus is longer. It was a woman's skeleton all right.'

'Do you think the bodies were switched, or was Bishop Augustine a woman all along?'

'I don't know. There was meant to be a pope who was a woman, wasn't there?'

'Pope Joan,' Cathbad nods, taking a swig of wine. 'She was only found out because she gave birth in the middle of a public procession.'

'Well, that would tend to give it away,' says Ruth, filling up their glasses. She hadn't really wanted Cathbad to come over (entertaining is too much of a pain these days) but now he's here it's surprisingly pleasant. Cathbad had spent the first ten minutes playing wildly with Kate and now she looks satisfyingly sleepy, though she is keeping her eyes fixed on him in case he does anything fun. He also brought wine, which is always welcome. Ruth offers to make some pasta. She's not much of cook but she's hungry and Cathbad is hardly a demanding guest. He's a vegetarian (of course) so all she has to do is shove some pesto on top. Kate loves pesto too. Then, with any luck, she'll go to sleep.

'What did Lord Smith say?' asks Cathbad, pulling a funny face at Kate behind his wine glass. 'Was he shocked that his famous ancestor turned out to be a cross-dresser?'

'He was flabbergasted,' says Ruth. 'He kept asking if I was sure. Phil was delighted. It makes more of a story for the press.'

Cathbad pulls another face, not entirely for Kate's

benefit. 'Typical. He's a publicity junkie, that man. Poor Shona. I don't know how she puts up with him.'

Cathbad's affection for Shona and antipathy towards Phil go back a long way but Ruth isn't about to let him get away with this. 'She puts up with him because he does everything she tells him. She's not exactly down-trodden.'

'I know. She's a warrior maiden at heart. But what about the bishop? How are you going to solve the mystery?'

'I'm going to go to the cathedral, look at the archives. And there's a local historian who's meant to be an expert on Bishop Augustine.'

Cathbad nods. 'Janet Meadows. Yes, I know her, she'd be the perfect person to ask. I bet the bishop *was* a woman though, otherwise why would she be buried with the bishop's staff?'

'The crosier? Yes. And she had the bishop's ring on her finger. There was a single shoe in the coffin too. I don't know what that was meant to signify.'

'That she was a left-footer?' suggests Cathbad, grinning.

'They were all Catholics then,' says Ruth dismissively. 'I'd better go and get the pasta on.'

But just as Ruth has wrestled Kate into her high chair and put the pasta on the table, there is a knock at the door.

'I'll go,' says Cathbad, jumping up.

He seems very keen to greet the visitor and Ruth isn't altogether surprised to see Bob Woonunga's smile coming through the front door.

'I hope I'm not intruding, but I heard Cathbad's voice.'

'I'm not surprised,' says Ruth, 'the noise he and Kate were making.'

'I've brought some fireworks.' Bob holds up a small, brightly coloured box. 'That's traditional here, right? I thought Kate might enjoy them.' It is firework night. Ruth's drive home was punctuated by explosions and random flashes of red and green light. She is rather frightened of fireworks and intends to keep Kate as far away from bonfires as possible. Still, it's a nice thought.

'Thank you,' she says. 'That's very kind. Would you like to stay for some supper?'

'If you've got enough.' Bob sits at the table and waves at Kate, who screws up her face and blows an impressive raspberry.

'Kate!' Ruth doesn't know where to look.

'She's playing the didge,' says Bob. 'She remembers. That's one bright kid you've got here.'

'She's very clever,' says Cathbad, pouring more wine (Ruth has produced a second bottle). 'She's an old soul.'

'You said that about my cat once.'

'Flint? Well, he's an old soul too.'

'Yeah,' agrees Bob. 'He's a wise one, all right.'

At last, reflects Ruth, collecting garlic bread from the kitchen, Cathbad's found someone who speaks his language. The last person who had seemed entirely on Cathbad's wavelength was Erik. Come to think of it, there's something about Bob that reminds her of Erik in his gentler moments.

'How did you two meet?' she asks, sitting down beside Kate.

'At a conference to discuss cultural repatriation,' says Bob. 'Cathbad was interested in some bones found near Stonehenge, I was just beginning to find out how many of our ancestors were in private hands. That's when we decided to form the Elginists.'

'I saw Lord Smith's collection the other day,' says Ruth, thinking that 'collection' is entirely the wrong word. What is the right one? Ossuary? Mausoleum?

Bob seems instantly to become more alert. He flicks a glance at Cathbad. He has dark eyes with very long eyelashes which give the impression of great innocence. Ruth isn't sure though. She thinks Bob, like Flint, is a wise one.

'Did you see the skulls?' asks Cathbad. 'Is it true that one's been turned into a water carrier?'

'Yes,' says Ruth. 'It's a horrible thing.'

Bob leans forward. 'Were you able to tell how these people died? I know you're an expert.'

Ruth is aware of the flattery but it has its effect all the same. 'I couldn't tell the cause of death. The skulls were all male. One showed signs of disease, probably syphilis. One . . .' She stops. Should she tell Bob about her other, even more gruesome, discovery? She doesn't owe Smith or his ancestors any discretion after all, and it might help the case for repatriation.

'Yes?' says Bob.

Ruth sighs. 'There were cut marks on one of the skulls. It looked to me as if the head had been skinned shortly after death. Scalped.'

Bob and Cathbad look at each other. Bob makes an odd

gesture, holding his hand, palm outwards, against his
forehead. He looks genuinely shaken. For the first time
since she's met him, the smile has disappeared altogether.

'Scalped,' says Cathbad. 'Why would anyone do that?'

'It was a trophy,' growls Bob. His face has darkened,
his brows drawn together. He looks quite frightening.
'This wasn't a fellow human to him, it was a hunting
trophy. Like a stag's head on a wall.'

Ruth thinks of the fake Victorian study at the museum,
the waxwork figure at the desk, the stag's head on the
wall. She wonders if Danforth Smith's ancestral mansion
is full of such objects. She feels compelled to say, 'Well,
this wasn't Smith himself. It was his great-grandfather.
It was a long time ago. Attitudes then—'

'Were exactly the same as now,' Bob bursts out. 'To a
man like Danforth Smith black people aren't human. He
venerates his own ancestors but ours are nothing to him.
We're animals. Less than animals. I hear he worships his
horses. We're less important to him than his horses.'

'I did try to reason with him' says Ruth, feeling rather
ashamed at having provoked such an outburst. 'I said
that your ancestors were as valuable as his. Bishop
Augustine, for example, you know, the medieval bishop
whose coffin we were due to open that day.' She looks at
Cathbad, warning him not to say anything more.

Cathbad smiles and contents himself with muttering
something about 'mother church'. He seems far less
shocked than Bob by the scalping revelation. Ruth,
watching him, can't imagine that Cathbad would be so
incensed about the museum keeping the skulls that he

would write and threaten Neil Topham's life. But someone did.

'It's to do with ownership,' says Ruth. 'Smith thinks the bones are his because they were taken by his great-grandfather. It's a really fixed mindset.'

'Typical British upper classes,' says Cathbad, still smiling. 'You should point the bone at him, Bob.'

'Point the bone?' says Ruth. 'What does that mean?'

'It's an Aborigine curse,' says Bob, shooting a glance at Cathbad. 'It brings about certain death.'

'You don't believe that though?'

Bob shrugs. 'Plenty of people do. You know, there are tourists who take rocks from Australian national parks. Weeks, months, later they send the rocks back saying that they've had nothing but bad luck since they took them. When the rocks are back on native soil, the curse is lifted. Think how much worse it is to take the very bones of our ancestors and keep them on the other side of the world. That's a lot of bad juju.'

'Well, perhaps Danforth Smith will change his mind,' says Ruth. 'He can't display the relics after all. What's to be gained from keeping them shut up in a storeroom?'

'You'd be surprised, Ruth,' says Bob. 'You must come to the meeting at the weekend. We'll tell you stories about whole tribes being wiped out. About Victorian adventurers who hunted the Aborigine like animals. Fine gentlemen like Lord Danforth Smith.'

'It's incredible,' says Ruth. 'I had no idea.'

'I once knew a whitefella who kept an Aborigine skull on his mantelpiece. Boasted about it. Used to put a Santa hat on it at Christmas. Funny old Abo head to amuse the children.'

'What happened to him?' asks Cathbad.

'He's dead now,' says Bob. 'The ancestors are powerful.'

Ruth feels a real shiver running down her spine. For a moment she is sorry that she ever saw the cellar room at the Smith Museum, with its boxes of bones. Did she handle them with enough reverence? Will ancestors be after her next? She is glad that penne with pesto contains no bones. She is about to say something – anything – to break the mood, when Kate causes a distraction by falling asleep with her head in her pasta.

When Kate has been put to bed, Bob and Cathbad go into the garden to light the fireworks. Ruth watches from the window. Her excuse is that she wants to hear if Kate wakes up, but really she wants to keep away from the frightening little packages with their warnings of death and disfigurement. One large rocket even has a skull and crossbones on it. Surely this should warn any sensible person to steer clear? Besides, it's freezing out there.

Cathbad and Bob are having a great time though. Bob seems to have got over his moment of darkness. Ruth remembers how completely his face seemed to change when he talked about curses and 'bad juju'. Ruth has known Cathbad long enough to understand that some people do believe in curses, in ill-wishing, in bad karma, but nevertheless the concept still disturbs her. Can there really be these malignant forces out there just waiting to strike or, worse, waiting to be directed? And can Bob, her smiling next-door neighbour, really direct death itself by pointing a bone? Ruth, who has spent years resisting her parents' beliefs, is a resolute rationalist but, still, there is something troubling about a man who believes he can visit bad luck upon another human being. Or does he believe it? Maybe it's all an elaborate joke. She watches Bob laughing as he hammers in a stake for the Catherine wheels. Who was Catherine and why did she have a wheel? Ruth has a feeling that the answer is sure to be nasty. She decides against asking Cathbad.

But surely Bob is harmless. He's just a passionate man, a poet, someone who believes in honouring the past and respecting the dead – just like Cathbad. And like Erik. Ruth wishes she could stop thinking about Erik, especially on the Saltmarsh late at night, times when, as Erik would have said, the restless spirits walk the earth looking for the light. She wishes she could just remember Erik as a brilliant archaeologist and her beloved mentor. But darker memories insist on emerging. A stormy night, lightning illuminating the sky like fireworks, a hidden room, a terrible secret. Ruth pushes these images aside with an effort. She must only think about the good things. With Bob too. He's a good neighbour, a kind creative person who plays the didgeridoo and likes children. And Flint, whose judgment Ruth trusts, adores him. Flint is currently asleep on the spare-room bed. He hates firework night.

Cathbad bends to light a fuse. Nothing happens. He goes back to try again. Ruth opens the back door.

'You shouldn't return to a lighted firework.' She learnt that from *Blue Peter*.

'It's OK, Ruth.' Cathbad brandishes his taper. 'Fire always obeys me.'

Famous last words, thinks Ruth. But she shuts the door again. The wind is getting up, making the whole lighting business more hazardous than ever. Maybe they'll give up soon. She wonders if they'd notice if she sneaked off to watch *Newsnight*.

But suddenly there is a slight hiss and a little gold tree springs up in front of her. The tree spins, shedding gold and silver leaves. Bob laughs aloud and Cathbad performs a rudimentary, capering dance. Ruth smiles, despite herself. This sort of firework seems harmless enough, rather beautiful, in fact. A few more like that and she can put the kettle on.

In fact, there are many many more. How can Bob's little box hold so much? Fountains, stars, spinning wheels, shrieking rockets – Ruth watches them all from the back door. What is it, this desire to fill the night with noise and light? It goes back hundreds of years before poor old Guy Fawkes. Probably another attempt to stave off the horrors of the night and of winter, like cockerels crowing at dawn. And like the cockerel, there seems to be a certain element of macho posturing involved. Bob and Cathbad are determined not to come back indoors before every last touch paper has been lit. Ruth doesn't know a single woman who really likes fireworks.

But, finally, they do come back in, smelling of gunpowder and the sea.

'How about that?' says Cathbad triumphantly.

'Amazing,' says Ruth. 'Would you like a cup of tea?'

'I'd like something stronger.'

'I might have some brandy left over from last Christmas.'

'Perfect.'

So they sit in front of the fire and drink brandy and talk about bonfires, paganism and Aboriginal smoke ceremonies. Ruth feels her eyelids drooping but she enjoys sitting there, listening to the ebb and flow of conversation. If only she didn't keep thinking that Kate would wake up any minute. Surreptitiously, she looks at her watch. Eleven-thirty. Even at the most optimistic assessment Kate will be awake in six hours. Ruth stifles a yawn, feeling her jaw lengthening.

'We should go,' says Bob. 'Ruth has to be up in the morning.'

'Oh, Ruth's a night owl,' says Cathbad, pouring more brandy.

'I used to be,' says Ruth. 'Now I'm a lark. A reluctant one, I grant you.'

'Come on Cathbad.' Bob stands up, turns to Ruth. 'Thank you for a lovely evening.'

'Thank you for the fireworks.'

Bob grins. 'Well, the sun god needs his sacrifice. Isn't that right, Cathbad?'

'Undoubtedly.'

'Can I give you a lift?' It hadn't occurred to Ruth that Cathbad didn't bring his car. He rarely drives. He has a car but it is the oldest vehicle that Ruth has ever seen. Erik used to speculate that it dated from the Bronze Age.

'No, I'm fine. I like walking at night.'

'I'll give you a lift as far as Snettisham.'

'OK.'

Ruth watches them go. The Saltmarsh is dark and silent, the Gods of night still reigning. As Bob's tail lights disappear into the blackness, Ruth goes back inside and bolts her door.

12

The Necromancer is cantering along the all-weather track. He is going uphill, neck arched against the bit, powerful quarters pushing him onwards in a series of huge, bounding leaps. When he takes the turn at the top of the hill, his great round hooves strike sparks from the churned earth. He rises in the air, eyes red, mane and tail ablaze. He flies over the house. The Milky Way is his race track, the stars his hurdles. The asteroid belt writhes and twists beneath his feet. It is a snake that falls, hissing, to earth. It is a snake that is bigger than the sky, bigger than the earth. It is a snake that is small enough to whisper in his ear: 'You are going to die.'

Danforth Smith wakes with a sudden lurch of the heart. He can hear his breathing reverberating around the empty room. His duvet is drenched with sweat. He reaches out for his water but touches a dead hand. He is lying beside the bishop's corpse, the ghastly skeletal face turned to his. He tries to scream but his voice has been stolen. With horror, he watches as a snake emerges from the skeleton's rib cage. The creature, green as death, weaves itself in

and out of the protruding bones. Smith knows that it
has come for him, but with equal certainty he knows
that he will not be able to move, not even to stretch out
a hand as the dryly slithering body presses itself against
his.

Will it come for him, the black coach with its six horses,
the headless coachman? He hears Niamh's voice, her sweet
Irish voice, clear as a bell. 'When it stops at your door,
there's no escape. Your time has come.' The sky is alight
with gold and silver stars, the black horse gallops across
the heavens. Romilly appears briefly, hand-in-hand with
a shadowy figure that he doesn't recognise. Then
Randolph, laughing and laughing. Then Tamsin, but her
face is turned away. Then Caroline. She's trying to tell
him something but he can't hear. Now Lester the cat
appears, swollen to the size of a lion. Lester opens his
mouth and a man's voice says, 'The great snake will have
its revenge'.

The snake has reached his face. He can see its yellow
eyes. In the background, Randolph laughs harder than
ever. He wants to say that he's sorry but he knows it's
too late. *The great snake will have its revenge.* He prays that
it won't hurt, that he'll be able to see his horses galloping
one last time.

The yellow eyes are level with his. The black horse waits
for him outside.

13

Nelson is not normally much of a one for breakfast. He likes to leave early and grab a bacon butty on the way to work. Sometimes he even accompanies Clough for a traditional McDonald's breakfast. What he doesn't do is sit at his breakfast bar consuming the Full English and trying to make conversation with his wife. But today, 6 November, is his birthday and Michelle announced that she was going to 'cook him a proper breakfast for once'. The trouble is that it's only seven-thirty and neither of them feels much like eating. All Michelle has on her plate is a single piece of toast.

'Have some of this bacon, love.'

Michelle shudders. 'I couldn't.'

'It's too much for me. You know I'm trying to lose weight.'

Michelle's face falls. 'I thought you'd like a proper breakfast. You always used to when we lived in Blackpool.'

Nelson and Michelle are both from Blackpool. They lived there when they were first married and Nelson has noticed that, in the last few months, Michelle has increasingly been harking back to those days. It's as if she wants to remember a time before Norfolk, before the children grew up, before Ruth.

'I was young then. I didn't have to watch my weight.'

'You should come to the gym with me. You said you were going to.'

In the euphoria of reconciliation, Nelson and Michelle had agreed to do more things together. Nelson would go to the gym, Michelle would watch football matches, they would go out for meals, book mini breaks. So far Nelson has been to the gym once, they have had two unsatisfactory meals out and Michelle has leafed through a brochure full of details of spas and golf links but coy about prices. Nelson did try to get tickets when Blackpool played Norwich but neither of them had been too disappointed when he was unsuccessful. Michelle hates watching Blackpool; orange isn't her colour.

'I haven't got time,' he says now, gulping his tea. 'Work's a nightmare. We're getting nowhere on the drugs case.'

'I thought we'd have more time together now the girls have left,' says Michelle. Both daughters are now at university. Laura reading marine biology at Plymouth, Rebecca doing media studies at Brighton. Nelson is rather in awe of higher education (he and Michelle both left school at sixteen) but he wishes his daughters would study subjects he understood. Still, Brighton's a grand place. Perhaps they could have a mini break there.

'We'll go out for a meal tonight,' he says, kissing Michelle on the cheek. 'I'll try to get off early.'

She smiles, rather forlornly. 'Happy birthday Harry.'

Nelson leaves the house feeling depressed. He's not wild about his birthday at the best of times and forty-three sounds worryingly old. His dad died at fifty. Bloody hell. Only seven more years. And Michelle had seemed so sad, so unlike the confident woman he had married. How can he make things better, short of obliterating the last two years? It's ironical that now he thinks about Ruth more than ever. In the past, he was able to forget her when he was with Michelle but now she is there all the time, the invisible presence. The elephant in the room. He smiles thinly to himself. She'd love that description, he's sure. He notes with irritation that there are two spent rocket cases in his garden. Why can't people go to organised bonfire parties rather than trying to set themselves alight in their own gardens? It just makes more work for the emergency services. He opens the garage and starts up the Mercedes. He'll make sure that he's home early, take Michelle somewhere nice for dinner. But, before he has even left the cul-de-sac, he gets a message on his phone: *Danforth Smith found dead.*

Ruth has no one to cook her breakfast and right now she's glad. Kate woke up twice in the night and then, inexplicably, slept in until eight. Ruth has got used to Kate being her alarm clock and so no longer sets the other kind. She rose in a panic, flinging on clothes and ignoring Kate (and Flint's) demands to be fed. She usually drops her daughter off at Sandra's at eight, and even then it's a rush to be at the university for nine. She gets in early these days because she does so much more of her work there – home no longer being a place where she can read for hours and forget the rest of the world. And today she has a lecture at ten. Bloody hell. No time for make-up, she'll just have to scare her students with her naked face. Maybe they'll think she's wearing a Halloween mask.

Ruth slops cat food down for Flint, stuffs porridge into a resistant Kate and is just heading out to the car when her phone rings. The landline. She hesitates. Should she leave it? Surely if it was important they'd ring her mobile, but it might be her parents who regard mobile phones as the work of the devil (they are experts on the Prince of Darkness). Ruth goes back inside, still carrying Kate. Flint, delighted by this turn of events, climbs onto the table, purring loudly.

'Doctor Galloway?' Not her parents then.

'Yes.'

'This is Janet Meadows. I'm a local historian. Cathbad said that you wanted to talk to me.'

Not for the first time Ruth marvels at the efficiency of Cathbad's information service. He left her house last night at nearly midnight yet has already had time to network. She looks at her watch. Nearly nine. Ruth hates being late, she can feel her facial muscles knotting into a tension headache.

'That would be great. It's just that I'm in a bit of a–'

'What about today? Midday. At the cathedral refectory.'

'I don't think I can . . .' Ruth tries to conjure up her timetable. She doesn't think she has any lectures between eleven and three.

'Cathbad said it was important.'

Why is Cathbad so keen for Ruth to meet this woman? It's not important in any real sense but still ... Ruth would like to talk to someone about Bishop Augustine before the press gets hold of the story. And lunch in the cathedral cafe sounds tempting. Weird but tempting.

'OK,' she says. 'I'll see you there.'

Nelson is surprised to find that it's business as usual at the yard. He meets a string of horses coming through the gates and another set are being saddled up in the quadrangle.

'Horses can't wait, I'm afraid,' says a leathery individual who identifies himself as Len Harris, Head Lad. 'They need to be exercised. We've got runners today and the owners expect to see their horses run. So life goes on.' He grimaces as if he realises how inappropriate this sounds. 'Though we're all devastated about the governor.'

Nelson can't see any evidence of devastation in the faces of any of the riders but he has begun to realise that jockeys and stable lads don't give much away. There is something watchful, almost withdrawn, about them. Perhaps it's the strain of keeping their weight under ten stone. The only creature who seems at all upset is Lester the cat, who is meowing piteously in the office. When Nelson walks through the yard towards the house, Lester follows him.

This time, Nelson knocks at the front door, which is opened immediately by Randolph. He *does* look upset, Nelson acknowledges, his eyes are red and he seems almost unhinged, running his hands through his hair and talking at random. 'Detective ... ah ... good of you to come ... we're all ... ah ... well ... you can imagine ... yes.'

Nelson follows Randolph, still gibbering, into a large, light sitting room. There, looking rather lonely on a vast leather sofa, are two women. One he recognises as Caroline, the other is a slim woman with short, grey hair. The wife, presumably.

'I'm sorry for your loss,' he begins formally. 'Do you feel up to talking to me?' He wishes Judy Johnson were here; he has asked her to join him as soon as possible.

'Of course,' says the woman, who introduces herself as Romilly Smith, Danforth's wife. 'It's just been the most terrible shock. I've only just got back from the hospital.'

'Was your husband taken ill in the night?'

'It was so sudden,' says Romilly. She's about sixty, Nelson reckons, but still powerfully attractive .The sort of woman confident enough not to dye her hair. She's distressed now, holding her handkerchief tightly in one hand, but still very much in control. 'He seemed fine yesterday,' she says. 'He was full of the opening of the coffin, finding out that the skeleton was female. He was really intrigued.'

Randolph, who is pouring himself a whisky, lets out a sudden laugh.

'Isn't it a bit early?' his mother indicates the drink.

'I've had a shock, Ma.'

'We've all had a shock,' snaps Caroline. She, too, looks very shaken. Her dark hair is pulled up in a bun which makes her look older but rather beautiful.

'So Lord Smith didn't seem unwell yesterday evening?' says Nelson, sitting in a squashy armchair which seems about to digest him.

'No. He was his usual self,' says Romilly. 'We had supper together and he told me all about the bishop's coffin and how impressed he was with your colleague Dr Galloway, and he said goodnight about ten. He goes to bed early because he gets up so early. I stayed up to watch the news and *Newsnight*, then I went to bed. I was woken up at about eleven-thirty by Dan calling out ...' She stops.

'He called out?' Nelson prompts.

Romilly Smith takes a deep breath, holding her handkerchief to her eyes. Caroline pats her arm rather ineffectually.

'I heard him shout something. I went to his room and he seemed to be having the most dreadful nightmare. He was pouring with sweat and his eyes were open, but he didn't seem to be able to see.'

'Did he say anything? Anything that you could understand?'

'He was ranting on about a coach and horses. Afterwards I realised what that meant. Dan had an Irish nanny when he was little. Niamh she was called. She sounds like a real ghoul but he was devoted to her. She told him about this black coach that's meant to come for people when they're dying. It's pulled by six black horses and the coachman's headless.'

'It's called the Coach-a-Bower,' says Caroline. 'The black

coachman knocks three times on your door and when you open it he throws a bucket of blood in your face.'

'I thought it was a banshee in the coach,' says Randolph, still standing by the drinks trolley. 'You heard her voice and you knew your time was up.'

'So you know this story too?' asks Nelson.

'Dad used to tell it to us' says Caroline. 'At bedtime.' Charming, thinks Nelson. Nothing like a banshee and a bucket of blood to make children sleep well. He's glad that he was just a working-class dad who stuck to Winnie-the-Pooh.

'So your husband was talking about this coach,' says Nelson. 'Was he delirious?'

'I think so. He kept saying that the coach was coming for him and he kept talking about a snake.'

'A snake?'

'He said a snake was there on the bed with him. He said he could see its eyes. They're burning, he kept saying.'

'What did you do?'

'I felt his forehead. He was boiling hot so I called the doctor. I tried to sponge Dan down, to get him to have some water, but he was beside himself, yelling and . . . and crying.'

'What time was this?'

'About midnight.'

'Was anyone else in the house?'

'I was out,' says Randolph, sounding rather sheepish. 'I arrived back at the same time as the doctor. I couldn't believe the state Dad was in.'

'You should have called me,' sobs Caroline.

'I'm sorry.' Her mother touches her hand. 'But we just didn't know how serious it was. Everything happened so quickly.'

'What did the doctor say?'

'He said that we should get Danforth to hospital. He was dehydrated and needed liquids intravenously. He called for an ambulance. They were very quick but Dan died on the way to hospital.'

Just like Neil Topham, thinks Nelson. Another man in apparently good health one minute, dead the next. And he doesn't like the mention of the snake. He doesn't like it at all. A line from one of the letters comes back to him. *We will come for you. We will come for you in the Dreaming.*

'Did they offer a cause of death?' he asks. 'I'm sorry if this is hard for you.'

'Heart attack, the paramedics said, but someone at the hospital said it might have been a lung infection.'

There'll have to be an autopsy, thinks Nelson. Of course, Danforth Smith *could* have died of natural causes – heart attacks can happen to anyone – but two suspicious deaths in six days, both connected to the museum?

'Did Lord Smith have any heart problems?' he asks.

'No.' Romilly seems exhausted by her account. She leans back against the sofa cushions and shuts her eyes. 'He always seemed as strong as a horse.' She laughs sadly. 'Of course, the horses were his life. Maybe he worked too hard. I don't know.'

'He was diabetic wasn't he?' asks Nelson.

Romilly looks surprised, almost angry. 'How did you know that?'

'He told me. When I came to speak to him about Neil Topham's death.'

'You don't suspect that there's any link between Dan's death and that chap at the museum,' says Romilly. 'I mean, it's preposterous to suggest—'

'I'm not suggesting anything,' says Nelson, 'but I've got two unexpected deaths in a week. I'm sure you'll agree that I need to investigate. Likely as not, your husband's death was from natural causes. I'll leave you alone now, I'm sure you've all had enough questions. My sergeant will be here in a few minutes. Could you show her any CCTV footage from last night? I believe you have CCTV?'

'Yes,' says Caroline. 'But I'd know if anyone came in. My cottage is by the gate.'

'Did you hear the doctor and the ambulance?'

'No. They came the other way. By the house.'

'So it's possible that someone could have got in that way?'

'Do you really think that someone could have got in and . . . and poisoned him or something?' asks Caroline.

Interesting assumption, thinks Nelson. Never assume, that's his motto.

'It's unlikely,' he says. 'I just want to make sure that we leave no stone unturned.'

And what do you find under stones, he reflects, as he walks back through the yard, watched by the curious horses and impassive stable lads.

Snakes.

14

As soon as Ruth meets Janet Meadows she realises why Cathbad said that she was the perfect person to ask about Bishop Augustine. Janet, a tall elegant woman in black, is clearly a male to female transsexual. She tells Ruth as much, as soon they sit down in the refectory, a striking modern building built next to the medieval cathedral.

'Think it's best to get this out of the way. I used to be Jan Tomaschewski. I published quite a lot under that name. Five years ago I became Janet. It's better to say so straight away, otherwise you'll be thinking to yourself "Isn't she tall? Hasn't she got big hands?" I used to be a man. End of story.'

Ruth, who had been looking at Janet's hands, blushes. 'Why Meadows?' is all she can think of saying.

'Well, Tomaschewski was such a mouthful and it was very patriarchal. Comes from the name Thomas. I was fed up with being named after someone called Thomas so I decided to name myself after something I liked. I live near the water meadows so I thought – meadows.'

'It's lovely,' says Ruth. 'I used to hate my name. Too plain and biblical. Maybe I should change it.'

'No,' says Janet decidedly. 'Ruth Galloway suits you. I understand you're a friend of Cathbad's? There's another one who changed his name.'

'Yes,' says Ruth. 'I can never think of him as Michael.'

'Well, Michael was an archangel,' says Janet. 'A rather ambivalent figure.'

Ambivalent in what way, thinks Ruth. Angels are famously sexually ambivalent, of course, and Lucifer was an angel before going over to the dark side. Again the line between saints and sinners is rather blurred.

'So you want to know about Bishop Augustine,' says Janet. 'He's the flavour of the month with you archae-ologists. I wanted to be at the opening of the coffin. I came to the first event but it was cancelled. They wouldn't let me come to the second, said it was private.'

'You would have enjoyed it,' says Ruth. Briefly, she tells Janet about her discovery. It goes down big. Janet gasps, putting her hand to her mouth. 'Oh my God! I can't believe it.'

'Can't you?' asks Ruth, rather disappointed.

'Well, I suppose I can,' Janet is recovering. 'Augustine is a fascinating figure but there are some gaps in his biography. Or her biography. My God! I'm the last person who should start getting stuck on personal pronouns.'

'What do we know about the bishop?' asks Ruth tact-fully, finishing her (delicious) coffee. The refectory really is a very pleasant place. It's all glass and polished wood with high soaring ceilings, rather like a cathedral itself. A cathedral of food; that's Ruth's kind of worship.

'We know a fair amount thanks to Prior Hugh. He was

the prior when Augustine was bishop. The prior would have been responsible for the day-to-day running of the cathedral and Hugh left an incredibly detailed account of his work – how many candles were used, what the monks ate, how much was given in alms – all that sort of thing. But he was also a chronicler and he wrote about prominent figures of the times, principally Bishop Augustine.'

'Do we know anything about Augustine's childhood?'

'Well he . . . I'm going to call him "he" if that's OK, it'll take some time to get used to the other . . . he came from a relatively humble background. The Smiths weren't nobility then. They made their money in the 1500s, they were one of the families that got rich from the dissolution of the monasteries, but in the 1300s they were just ordinary craftsmen, guild workers. Augustine's father was a stonemason. Augustine was an only child, something that was quite unusual then, though he may have had siblings who died in infancy. Now I'm wondering whether there was a son who died and that Augustine in some way assumed his identity.'

'We'll never know I suppose.'

'I suppose not. Hugh writes a lot about Augustine's holiness but there are no physical descriptions, no clues about his sexual inclinations.'

'Sounds as if Prior Hugh was quite a fan.'

'He's almost Augustine's hagiographer. I think he really felt that Augustine was a saint. There's a lot about his good works, his visions, his battles with the devil.'

'His battles with the devil?'

'According to Hugh, Bishop Augustine was constantly

tormented by the devil. Sometimes in the morning he was black and blue after having tussled with the devil all night. Augustine used to have terrible dreams apparently. His housekeeper used to hear him crying out with pain but no one was allowed to enter his private apartments.'

'Perhaps that was because they would find out his secret,' suggests Ruth.

'Maybe. Prior Hugh also says that Augustine refused to have a body servant. He sees it as evidence of Augustine's humility but, of course, there could have been another reason.'

'Is there anything else about Augustine's private life?'

'Not really. In his will he left money to pay for masses for his soul, nothing else. Prior Hugh mostly writes about Augustine's spiritual life – the torments, the visions – it's all quite apocalyptic at times.'

'I heard something about a great snake,' says Ruth.

'Well, his statue in the cathedral shows Bishop Augustine with his foot on a snake. It was thought to represent the devil, and during one of Augustine's many exorcisms Hugh reports seeing a huge snake, a "mighty worm", appear in the sky. Hugh thought it was the devil being vanquished.'

'Have you met Ted from the Field Team? He says there was a curse on the coffin. Whoever opened it would be destroyed by the great serpent.'

Janet nods. 'That's in Hugh's account. It was always believed that Augustine was buried in the cathedral and there's a stone with an inscription saying "vex not my bones" and a warning about the snake. But when they excavated in the 1830s they found that the vault was empty. No bones at all.'

'Because Augustine was buried in the other church? St Mary's Outside the Walls?'

'It's possible. There was a family connection with St Mary's. Augustine was christened there and it's thought that his parents were buried in the graveyard. Of course, he might have left instructions to be buried there for precisely this reason, to prevent his body being examined after death.'

'When did Augustine die?'

'In 1362, the year that the great spire was destroyed by fire. Prior Hugh, of course, thought that was another omen. The devil getting his revenge. In fact, the cathedral was in for a rough few years. There was the Peasants' Revolt in 1381 and Augustine's successor, Bishop Henry Despenser, the so-called "fighting bishop", led the troops against the peasants.'

'Very charitable.'

'Bishops weren't necessarily very charitable or even very religious in those days. They were usually the younger sons of great noblemen, only interested in power or money. That's what makes Bishop Augustine so interesting. He was genuinely spiritual. Of course, we can laugh at it now, all the visions and the battles with the devil, but Augustine was obviously rather a tormented soul. He was a true friend to the poor though. He doubled the amount of alms given by the monks and he founded schools and hospitals. Prior Hugh really thought he was a saint. There are stories of Augustine being able to heal the sick, even of bilocating, being in two places at once. Hugh recalls watching him praying by the Lady Altar at the same time that he was apparently administering last rites to some old woman in the village.'

Ruth has been listening with the kind of trance-like interest that she remembers from her best lectures at university. She has almost forgotten about the coffin, Ted's warning, the dead body of Neil Topham. Janet brings her back to earth by asking, rather abruptly, 'Why are you so interested? Apart from the gender thing.'

The gender thing, Ruth muses, that's one way of putting it. Aloud she says, 'There were a few other odd things about the coffin. The body was wrapped in silk which had been coated with beeswax. There were the remains of a ceremonial crosier and a single shoe made of leather, very intricate. Why would the Bishop be buried with a single shoe?'

Janet looks at her consideringly for a minute, then she says, 'There are two legends that might be linked to it. One is a bit like the Saint Nicholas story – Santa Claus, you know – he was a bishop too. In Turkey. Well, anyhow, in this story there are some penniless children and Bishop Augustine fills their shoes with money. Prior Hugh writes that children would leave their shoes outside their door and the Bishop would go through the town at night, filling them with coins.'

'And the second story?'

'Well, this one's about the devil. You know that the statue shows Bishop Augustine with his foot on the snake? Well, in one of Hugh's accounts, the devil in the form of a snake bites through Augustine's shoe so he stamps on him with his foot. Henceforward, Augustine often walked barefoot. A form of mortifying the flesh possibly, especially when you think of the state of the roads in those days. There's an inscription on the statue: You will tread on cubs and vipers. You will trample lions and asps.'

'Psalms,' says Ruth. 'He will order his angels to guard you wherever you go.'

Janet looks surprised.

'My parents are Born Again Christians,' Ruth explains. 'I know the Bible.'

'Do you have any faith yourself?'

Ruth shakes her head. 'There are people I respect who do believe but I don't. What about you?'

Janet laughs. 'I was brought up a Catholic. A Polish Catholic too, which is like being Catholic cubed. I'm a historian, I like evidence but ... I don't know. I think there are things that can't be proved.'

Once Ruth would have disagreed violently with this, but after the last few years she isn't so sure any more. About anything.

Janet stands up. 'Let's go and have a look at the old boy. Or girl, as the case may be.'

Judy arrives at the yard to find the gates open and Nelson nowhere in sight. She walks through the archway and comes face-to-face with a large chestnut horse whirling around on the end of a lead rope. Judy makes a wide arc round him. The stable girl is trying to get the horse into his box but he's having none of it, throwing up his head and clattering round in furious circles. As Judy watches, two lads come up to help subdue the horse. 'Steady, steady . . .' she hears one of them say. The girl is almost in tears. 'I can't . . .' she's saying. 'Don't be such a girl,' says one of the men, seemingly without irony. The horse continues to plunge and snort.

Judy makes her way towards the office where an older man is on the phone. He covers the handset and looks up enquiringly.

'Detective Sergeant Judy Johnson,' says Judy.

'Len Harris, Head Lad. Can you excuse me a moment? I'm just getting the declarations done.'

Judy nods and settles down to read the *Racing Post*. Unlike Nelson, she does not feel at all out of place in these surroundings. Her father is a bookie and she comes from a horse-loving Irish family. She used to ride as a child and once even had ambitions to be a jockey. What was it that stopped her, she wonders now. Was it discovering boys or getting boobs? Come to think of it, the two things probably happened at the same time.

'Sorry about that,' says Harris. 'Everything's a bit frantic at the moment.'

Judy looks up from the paper. 'Jumping Jack hasn't got a hope in the 2.10 at Newmarket.'

For a second, Len Harris looks angry, then he grins. 'No, but we don't want him handicapped too heavily for Cheltenham. Do him good to lose a few races.'

'What will the owners say?'

Len Harris shrugs. 'They're in Dubai. They won't know.'

Judy stands up. 'I'm sorry about your boss.'

Harris's face doesn't show emotions very easily but, for a second, he looks genuinely bereft. 'It's hard. He was a one-off, the governor. Some people thought he was stuck-up, but around the yard he was one of the lads. And he loved the horses, he really understood them.'

'What will happen with the yard now?'

Harris's face darkens. 'That's up to the kids, I suppose. Caroline would probably like to take over but she hasn't got the experience. Randolph's a waste of space. Tamsin's up in London. I suppose the yard'll be sold. Owners are already taking their horses away.'

'Already?'

'Oh yes. There's not much sentiment in racing, you know.'

Judy does know. She wonders what will happen to Len Harris if the business is sold. Plenty of racing stables in Norfolk but he looks a little old to go job hunting.

'I've been asked to look at the CCTV footage,' she says. 'Is there anywhere I can do that?'

'Yes. There's a room in Caroline's cottage. I've got the key.' He fumbles through sets of keys hanging over the desk. Not a very secure system, thinks Judy.

As they go out into the yard, there is a tremendous banging and clattering from one of the boxes in the far corner. Harris sets off at a run. Judy follows him.

Inside the box, a bay horse is sprawled awkwardly on the ground, almost sitting, front legs straight, back legs collapsed. Its eyes are rolling and it's clearly in agony. Two stable lads are struggling to get the horse on its feet, hauling on ropes, pushing at its rump. Len goes into the

box and joins in the effort, bracing his legs against the
wall to push with his back.

'What's happened?' asks Judy.

'Cast himself,' pants Len. 'Probably colic.'

Judy can see that the animal's stomach does look
distended, a symptom of colic. The horse appears in terrible
pain, almost bellowing, the white of his eyes yellow. She
looks at the laminated card on the stable door. The horse
is called Fancy, she reads, and he's a four-year-old colt.

'Shouldn't you get the vet?'

'He's coming,' says Len shortly. 'Now, please, can you
leave us to get on? The cottage is by the gates.'

Judy walks back through the yard with Fancy's tormented neighing ringing in her ears. She feels very shaken.
It's part and parcel of looking after horses, she knows,
but she can't forget the look in the poor animal's eyes.
She hopes the vet gets there soon. She'd wanted to be a
vet once too, before she'd realised that you needed three
As at A-Level.

Judy had imagined Caroline very elegant, a grown-up
version of the sort of girl who used to intimidate her in
her pony club days. But the woman who greets her at
the cottage door couldn't be further from the twin-setted
Home Counties lady of her imagination. To be frank,
Caroline looks a mess; her dark hair is unbrushed and
her eyes are red and swollen. She is wearing jeans and
her top is on inside out. She hardly seems to take in Judy's
explanation about who she is and what she wants to do.

'I thought you were my sister Tamsin,' says Caroline.
'She's coming from London.'

'I'm so sorry about your dad,' says Judy.

Caroline's eyes fill with tears. 'It just doesn't seem possible that he's gone. I keep expecting him to walk in.'

'It's hard, I know,' says Judy. Empathetic echoing, the books call it.

'I just feel so terrible . . .'

It must be awful to lose your dad, thinks Judy, however old you are. She hopes that Caroline's family gives her some support, but she doubts it somehow.

'The tapes?' she prompts gently.

'Oh, yes . . .' Caroline gives her a tremulous smile. She keeps looking towards the door, which is freaking Judy out slightly. 'This way.'

The room by the front door is full of screens. There are five cameras in different parts of the yard: one by the main gates, one by the house gates, one in each quadrangle and one at the far gates, 'where the original house once stood' Caroline explains.

Judy settles down to look, gratefully accepting the offer of coffee. Look at last night's footage, the boss said. She starts at eight p.m. It's incredibly boring. Hours of night vision camera showing empty driveways. The only distraction is when Lester the cat appears, walking delicately along the footpath, sitting to wash himself in the empty courtyard. Occasionally a horse's head looks out over one of the stable doors, but, for the most part, Lester is the only living thing to be seen. Judy's eyes start to blur. She sips her cold coffee. Outside she hears a car draw up and voices talking. This must be the famous Tamsin. She hears a woman's voice, very loud and upper-class. 'For fuck's sake have some respect, Randolph.' Happy families.

She fast-forwards to ten o'clock. At twenty past midnight, the camera by the house starts to get interesting. A car draws up and a man gets out. He's carrying a case, so Judy assumes he's the doctor. The door opens to let him in. A few minutes later, a sports car screeches to a halt by the house. A Porsche, thinks Judy. She likes cars as well as horses. Really, there's a speed demon in there somewhere trying to get out. A man gets out of the sports car. She can't see his face but she thinks it might be the son. What was his name? Randolph. The one Len Harris thinks is useless. The one who needs to have more respect. Ten minutes later and an ambulance is through the gates. Lights, running footsteps, a sense of urgency. A figure is carried out on a stretcher. A woman climbs into the ambulance and the man follows in the Porsche. Then the gates shut behind them and she's back to Lester and the empty yard. Where was Caroline when all this was going on? she wonders. More footage of silent horse boxes. What is she looking for anyway? The boss didn't seem convinced that there was anything suspicious about Danforth Smith's death. Does he really believe that someone sneaked in and shot him a poisoned dart or something? He's getting fanciful in his old age. She'll tell him so when she gets back to the station. She won't, of course.

More empty pathways. An owl hooting. Lester prowling through the long grass. A clock striking. Then — Oh my God. The main gates opening and a man appearing.

Judy peers closer. 'Bloody hell,' she says aloud. 'I don't believe it.'

15

Although Ruth has lived in Norfolk for thirteen years now, she has never before been to Norwich Cathedral. It's more the sort of thing tourists do, and one way or another she isn't really into churches, though she has a sneaking liking for vast Catholic edifices full of pictures of the end of the world. So, although she has often shopped in the lanes nearby, the evocatively named Tombland, and she has seen the cathedral's spire pointing up through the rooftops like a medieval space rocket, this is the first time she has entered the building.

They walk through the cathedral close across mani-cured green lawns. Janet Meadows has absolutely no truck with any sign saying 'Private'. At the main entrance, Janet points at two modern statues on either side of the door. One depicts a man, his finger on his lips in a rather threatening adjuration to silence, the other is a woman, head draped in a flowing scarf, holding a book.

'Who are they?' asks Ruth, peering up.

'Saint Benedict and Mother Julian. Julian of Norwich. Another fourteenth-century holy woman.'

The name rings a faint bell with Ruth. 'Who was she again?'

'She was an anchoress.'

'A what?'

'A hermit if you like. She lived on her own in a cell attached to Saint Julian's church. She spent her life praying and people used to come to her for advice. When she was about thirty she became very ill and had a series of visions of God. She wrote about them in a book called *Revelations of Divine Love*. It was the first book written in English by a woman.'

'I don't think that's on my reading list somehow.'

'There are some wonderful things in it. *All shall be well, and all shall be well, and all manner of thing shall be well.* Julian was incredibly optimistic given the times she lived in.'

'Do you think she knew Bishop Augustine?'

'I've been wondering about that. The dates just about coincide, though Prior Hugh doesn't mention Julian much.'

'Maybe Augustine pretended to be a man because her only other option was becoming an anchoress and shutting herself away from the world.'

'Maybe,' says Janet, looking up the statue. 'But Julian's name and her writing live on today. That's more than can be said for most bishops.'

They enter through the visitor's entrance, modern smoked glass fused onto ancient stone. Automatic doors glide open at their approach, and in the lobby interactive displays wink and hum. Ruth is surprised to see men busily erecting scaffolding outside.

'They're filming,' explains Janet. 'Lots of films are set in the cathedral.'

'It's all very commercial,' says Ruth disapprovingly. She may be an atheist but she likes her churches traditional.

'Wait till you get inside.'

Ruth ignores a sign asking for donations and follows Janet into the cathedral. At first she is simply struck by the height and space. The cathedral resembles the monastery it once was, long and narrow with a high gothic roof, stone pillars branching out like great trees. The air is cold and smells of candle wax. The stone floor is uneven, and with a slight jolt Ruth realises that she is walking over gravestones. 'Dearly beloved . . . Here lies . . . Rector of this parish . . . Beloved father . . .' A phrase from Ruth's churchgoing days comes back to her: Vanity of vanities, all is vanity.

The high altar is at the back of the church, flanked by pillars, but around the outside there is a sort of pathway, like an arched cloister. Ruth follows Janet past tombs and statues, tiers of candles glittering with wax. Crusaders lie in stone splendour, gruesome crucifixes run with blood, the occasional piece of modern artwork looks small and rather sad. You need centuries to achieve gravitas.

'Here's Augustine,' says Janet.

Bishop Augustine's statue is in a shadowy corner, placed on a plinth so high that Ruth has to tilt her head back. It shows a figure in flowing robes with a mitre on its head, holding a crosier. It looks like hundreds of other such statues and reminds Ruth of visiting Rome with Shona – the cool of the churches after the heat of the day, the myriad stone effigies of saints, their names and deeds forgotten.

'Look at the feet,' says Janet.

Ruth looks. In contrast to his formal clothes, the Bishop is barefoot and from under his big toe peeps the head of a snake.

'It's hardly a great serpent,' says Ruth. 'Looks like a grass snake.'

'He'd subdued it,' says Janet. 'Evil has been defeated. He was a great saint.'

Ruth squints up at the statue's face. It's rather beautiful, certainly, but she supposes that all such images are idealised. Shoulder-length curly hair flows from under the ceremonial headgear.

'He could be a woman,' she says.

'The hair doesn't prove anything,' says Janet. 'Look at all that fuss about St John in *The Last Supper*, people saying that he must be a woman because he's so beautiful with such long flowing hair. Da Vinci just liked painting beautiful men.'

Ruth thinks about *The Da Vinci Code* which, reluctantly, she rather enjoyed. Is there a clue here? Is there something she's missing? Something about a coffin, a snake and a shoe. About an anchoress and a bishop, a man who could be in two places at once. She walks on, deep in thought. A minute or so later Janet calls her back. She is standing by what appears to be a side chapel, a small altar surrounded by a few pews. Stained-glass windows turn the stones blue and green and gold.

Janet is pointing up at one of the windows.

'Look. There's Julian again.'

Ruth looks, and sees in the coloured glass a woman in nun's habit, covered by a rather grand red cloak. But what makes her look twice is the creature at Julian's feet.

'It's a cat!' she says in delight.

'Oh yes,' says Janet. 'I'd never noticed that before.'

But Ruth feels a new kinship with the fourteenth-century holy woman. Because Julian undoubtedly had a cat. A large ginger cat, just like Flint. Ruth is sure that Julian's pet must have been important to her, because otherwise why go to the trouble of depicting it in yellow and orange glass? There can't be very much wrong with anyone who loves their cat that much.

She is about to speak when her phone rings. Janet smiles but Ruth is extremely embarrassed.

It's Cathbad. This is getting to be a habit.

'Ruth, can you come? I've been arrested.'

'Do I need my solicitor?'

'Shut up, Cathbad. This is serious.'

Cathbad arranges his face in a serious expression. Judy glares at him. They are in Interview Room 1, the bigger of the two interview rooms at the station, but suddenly it seems far too small. Judy is acutely aware of Cathbad's hands, the long fingers tapping gently on the arm of his chair. He has a leather bracelet round his wrist, the kind that surfers wear. No watch. He told her once that he didn't believe in time.

'You were at Slaughter Hill last night. I saw you on the CCTV footage.'

Cathbad smiles enigmatically. Judy explodes. 'Don't you see how this looks? What the hell were you doing at Slaughter Hill at one in the morning?'

'Visiting a friend.'

'Who?'

'Caroline Smith.'

'She must be a very good friend,' says Judy coldly, 'for you to be calling on her at one in the morning.'

She thinks of the tear-stained woman she saw that morning. She supposes that under normal circumstances Caroline might be considered attractive. Does Cathbad think so?

'I was at Ruth's,' says Cathbad. 'I left at about midnight. I like walking at night so I thought I'd walk to Caroline's.'

'All the way from the Saltmarsh to Slaughter Hill?'

'I got a lift as far as Snettisham.'

'Who from?'

'A friend called Bob Woonunga.'

Another one of those people with ridiculous names, thinks Judy savagely. Why the hell can't Cathbad have ordinary friends? Why does he have to go prancing around the countryside calling on women in the middle of the night?

'Let's get back to Caroline Smith,' she says. 'Was she expecting you?'

'I'd said I might call in.'

'Why?' asks Judy. If Cathbad is having an affair with Caroline, she wants him to say it aloud.

Cathbad looks at her, a smile playing around his lips. Judy wants to hit him.

'There's nothing between us,' he says gently. 'She's a friend, that's all. And she's a member of the Elginists. That's why I was calling.'

'You just popped in to discuss Aborigine relics?'

'That's it exactly.'

Judy has had enough.

'You'll need a better story than that,' she says, 'when this comes to court.'

'When what comes to court?'

'Danforth Smith died last night. We think it was murder.'

Ruth arrives at the police station, hot and stressed from her long drive, to be met by a grinning Tom Henty. 'Come to post bail for Cathbad, have you?'

'I suppose so.'

All Ruth has in her purse is seven pounds fifty and a lottery ticket. Her bank account is not looking too healthy either, what with Kate's birthday and the cost of child-care. How much is bail, anyway?

Tom laughs even harder. 'Don't worry, Ruth. He hasn't been arrested and there's no bail been set. He's just been helping us with our enquiries, that's all.' He manages to make the phrase sound even more sinister than usual.

'Where is he?'

'Interview Room 1. Detective Sergeant Johnson's been speaking to him. I think they're still in there.'

Ruth looks over to where Tom is pointing. The King's Lynn police station is in an old Victorian house. Interview

Room 1 looks as if it might have been the downstairs cloakroom. A green light shines above the door.

'Can I go in?'

'Be my guest.'

Ruth is surprised, but not as surprised as she is when she bursts into the room to find Judy and Cathbad locked in a passionate embrace.

16

Ruth tries to back out but Judy has seen her. She breaks away, her face scarlet. Cathbad, on the other hand, turns round and says casually, 'Oh hallo Ruth. Good of you to come but it turns out I'm not under arrest after all.'

'You do seem to be in protective custody,' says Ruth drily.

'Ruth . . .' Judy starts to speak but then shrugs and sweeps out of the room. Cathbad is still completely unabashed.

'Are you going back to the university? Could I have a lift? I'm meant to be working this afternoon.'

In the lobby, Tom Henty tells them to be sure and call again soon. Cathbad laughs and says he'll be in touch. Ruth can't get out of the place quickly enough.

'Is Nelson around?' she asks as they go out through the double doors.

'No. I think he's out. They seem to be working flat out on this drugs case. Anyway, Nelson's knocking off early today. It's his birthday.'

Ruth is silent. She has never known Nelson's birthday and is slightly shaken to find out that it's so near Kate's. She remembers Cathbad guessing correctly that Nelson was a Scorpio the first time they met. Kate's a Scorpio too, hot-headed and passionate according to the books, not that Ruth believes in any of that nonsense.

It is not until they are in the car and driving towards the university that Ruth says, 'So what's going on between you and Judy?'

'Going on?' Cathbad is looking out of the window, a half smile on his face.

'For God's sake, Cathbad,' explodes Ruth. 'Just give me a straight answer for once. Are you having an affair with her?'

Cathbad sighs. 'You remember in April, when Nelson asked Judy to go over to your house and check that Kate was OK? You couldn't get home because it was snowing and Nelson wasn't sure about the babysitter?'

'Yes.'

'Well, I was there too. I got this feeling that I ought to check on Kate and you know I always trust my instincts.'

There is more that Ruth could say on this theme but she keeps quiet.

'I met Judy on the way there. It was late at night, snowing, very receptive conditions.'

'Whatever that means.'

'I'm sure you can guess. It was dark, it was cold, we felt cut off from the rest of the world. We ended up in bed together.'

In my house, thinks Ruth. Probably in my bed. Aloud

she says, 'But she's married. She only got married a few months ago.'

'I know. She loves Darren. She didn't want to hurt him by calling off the wedding. They've known each other since they were children.'

'But isn't she hurting him now?'

'We tried to break it off but the connection was too strong. We started seeing each other again in September.'

Four months after Judy's May wedding, thinks Ruth. She remembers Judy, radiant in her white dress. The perfect wedding, the couple who had known each other so long, the families already united. But, come to think of it, wasn't there something odd at the reception? Ruth had come across Judy, all on her own, in a darkened room. Ruth had said that she was sure Judy and Darren would be happy. 'Are you?' Judy had answered. 'I'm not.' Was Judy already in love with Cathbad? Did she already know that her marriage was doomed?

Ruth is surprised at how shaken she feels. She would never have imagined that Judy and Cathbad could be drawn to each other. Judy is so capable and efficient, her feelings kept well in check. Cathbad . . . well, Cathbad is a druid, a man of violent passions and opinions. She remembers him being at her house the morning after the snowstorm, but she had been so preoccupied with seeing Kate again that she had failed to notice any erotic undercurrents. She *had* thought that it was odd that Cathbad was there, and Judy had seemed particularly distant and professional. To think that only a few hours earlier . . .

And that's another thing. Though she doesn't like to admit it, even to herself, Ruth's predominant emotion is one of jealousy. She isn't attracted to Cathbad. She doesn't want to go to bed with him but she does want to go to bed with *somebody*. This particular need is not covered by the baby books. Single mothers are meant to be single *mothers*, not really women any more. A single mother with a boyfriend is something else altogether, a case for social services in fact. And Ruth feels rather aggrieved that Judy can forget her marriage vows while Nelson's are, apparently, indestructible.

There are so many things she wants to say. She wants to know what the hell Judy and Cathbad are going to do. Is Judy going to divorce Darren and marry Cathbad? She can't imagine Cathbad getting married somehow. But none of that's her business. She settles for asking about the one issue that *has* become her business. Why was Cathbad 'helping with enquiries' today? Why did he think that he might be under arrest?

'Well,' says Cathbad, settling himself more comfortably in the passenger seat. 'You know that Lord Smith is dead.'

'*What?*'

'Oh, you didn't know. Yes, he died in the night.'

'But how? I saw him yesterday, when we opened the coffin, and he seemed in perfect health.'

'They don't know. I assume there'll be tests and things.'

'How are you involved?'

'The police are investigating. Judy went to check on the CCTV footage and she saw that I'd visited Slaughter Hill Stables last night.'

'You did?' This must have been after Cathbad left her house, after the fireworks and the brandy, after Bob offered to drive him as far as Snettisham.

'I went to see Caroline,' Cathbad is saying.

'Who?'

'Smith's daughter. She's a friend of mine.'

'Why didn't you say so before?'

'No one asked. Caroline's interested in archaeology. She's even been on a few digs. She's friends with Trace.'

'Did Bob go with you?'

'Bob? No. He dropped me off on the King's Lynn road. I walked the rest of the way.'

'But why? Surely it was a bit late for a social call.'

'I wanted to talk to her about tomorrow's conference. Are you still coming?'

'Oh, the Elginist thing? I suppose so. If I can get a babysitter. So, is this Caroline one of the Elginists?'

'She's definitely interested. I thought she might like to go to the conference.'

'But why go so late?'

Cathbad smiles. 'I was following my instincts.'

They have reached the university. As soon as Ruth parks the car Cathbad jumps out, thanks Ruth, says he'll see her tomorrow and disappears through the doors of the chemistry block. Ruth realises that she's not going to get any more answers out of him. But as she gathers up her papers and her bag and heads towards Natural Sciences, her head is swirling with words and images.

Cathbad and Judy in her bed, the snow falling outside.

Lord Smith in the attic rooms at the museum, telling

her about his great-grandfather's collection. *There's some wonderful stuff. We've got some of it in the museum downstairs: snakeskins, dingo traps, branding irons . . .*

Janet Meadows telling her about Bishop Augustine. *Sometimes in the morning he was black and blue after having tussled with the devil all night.*

The statue with its stone foot on a snake.

Nelson's face when he first saw Kate. Standing in the maternity ward with Michelle beside him.

Fireworks exploding in the night sky.

Cathbad grinning at her across the table. *You should point the bone at him, Bob.*

Bob's face, so different when he isn't smiling. *He's dead now. The ancestors are powerful.*

Ted chomping his pizza. *Maybe the devil was about to have his revenge.*

The skulls, the sightless eyes.

The room full of bones.

17

Nelson is in a sauna. It's not his preferred way of spending the time. Michelle loves all the gym stuff – exercise classes, Jacuzzi, aquarobics, the lot – but he finds it all rather embarrassing. He likes a swim (as a teenager he had a holiday job as a lifeguard) but that's about it. He hates the recycled air, the recycled music, the little bottles of shampoo that smell like a Thai meal, the fluffy towels, the frothy coffee. He hates the women in their designer sportswear; they make him feel both lustful and disapproving, an uneasy combination. Why haven't they got jobs to go to, for God's sake? And the water's too hot too. At the Derby Baths you used to be blue when you got out of the water, despite being indoors. That was proper swimming in a proper Olympic-sized pool with diving boards that seemed to reach up to the sky. It was salt water, he remembers, made your eyes sting and your skin turn crusty. He'd once challenged a fellow lifeguard to a race over fifty lengths. When they'd got out, their legs had buckled. Like he said, proper swimming.

But today's visit is business not pleasure. Nelson has a

meeting with Jimmy Olson, his informant. Nelson suspects
Jimmy of choosing increasingly bizarre meeting places. Last
time it was a cinema, the time before in a seedy arcade. It's
like going on a series of terrible dates. At least today's venue,
in a health club attached to a hotel in Cromer, is relatively
upmarket. How had Jimmy, for whom the words low life
might have been invented, come up with a place like this?

'Mate of mine's a member,' he says, in answer to Nelson's
question.

Does Olson have mates? Nelson looks at the skinny
figure opposite, physique miserably exposed in a pair of
skimpy Speedos, and concedes that it must be possible,
though it seems unlikely. Olson looks back at him out of
eyes so pale blue that they look almost white. He sniffs
noisily. Nelson hopes that he doesn't catch Olson's cold,
these places must be a breeding ground for germs.

'Have you got anything for me?' he asks.

'I told you,' says Jimmy. 'There hasn't been a dicky bird
on the ground.'

'There must be something.'

A woman looks in through the glass door but decides
against entering the sauna. Nelson doesn't blame her.
They must look an odd couple, the thin, red-eyed twenty-
something and the tall, greying man in slightly too tight
swimming trunks (they only had one size for sale in the
lobby; cost a bomb too). They must look strange but they
probably do look like a couple. Jesus wept, what a way
to spend his birthday.

'There's a lot of charlie around. It's good stuff, clean,
but no one knows where it's coming from.'

'I don't believe you.'

'Honest to God.' Jimmy found God while serving time for dealing. He credits the Almighty for keeping him out of prison for the past three years but he would do better to thank Detective Chief Inspector Harry Nelson, who has got him off a number of smaller charges in return for information. And now Nelson is impatient; he is sure Olson must know something. He is close to a number of dealers, including a deeply unpleasant character known as the Vicar. Yet here's the market being flooded by cheap foreign cocaine and no one knows anything about it. Call themselves businessmen.

Jimmy gets up to put water on the hot coals. The room is filled with steam and Nelson catches a whiff of Jimmy's body odour over the smell of pine and lemongrass. He starts to feel slightly sick.

'Do you know a character called Neil Topham?' asks Nelson.

He can't see Jimmy very well but he's sure that he's looking shifty.

'Why?'

'I ask the questions.'

'I think I may have heard the name. He's a customer.'

'Of yours?'

'No! I swear to God, Inspector Nelson, I haven't dealt for years. No, a customer of a friend of mine.'

'Good customer?'

'I think so. Why? What's he done?'

'He's dead.'

Jimmy's mouth opens in a silent O.

'Would your dealer friend have anything to do with that? Has he been hanging round the Smith Museum?'

Jimmy starts violently then tries to conceal the fact by jumping to his feet.

'Getting a bit hot in here,' he says.

Nelson pushes Jimmy back down into his seat. He looms over the cringing younger man. The woman, who has reappeared in the window, beats a hasty retreat.

'What do you know about the Smith Museum?'

'Me? Nothing. What would a bloke like me know about a museum?' Olson reminds Nelson of a character in a classic TV serial, years ago. Uriah something. Always banging on about being humble, but evil through and through.

'Why did you jump like a cat on hot bricks when I mentioned it?' The simile is all too apt. Nelson feels the sweat running down his back. He feels more nauseous than ever.

Jimmy slumps forward on the slatted bench. Nelson sits opposite, breathing hard.

'It's just something the Vicar said.'

'What?'

'Well I met him one day down at the docks and I said how are you Vicar, friendly like, and he said he'd been to the Smith Museum. I thought he was joking because museums are for kids, aren't they? So I says what were you doing at a museum Vicar, and he says I went to see a lady.'

'A lady?'

'Yeah. So I says, still thinking he was joking, was she in a glass case, like she was a mummy or something, and he says no she was flesh and blood alright.'

'Nothing else?'

'No. On my mother's life.'

'Your mother's dead.'

'On her grave then.'

Nelson can't stand it anymore. He pushes open the wooden door and heads for the showers. He stands under the blissfully cold water until he is sure that Olson has gone. Then he dives into the tepid pool and swims non-stop for twenty minutes.

Nelson is drinking overpriced cappuccino in the hotel lounge when he gets the call from Clough.

'Hi boss. You home yet?'

Nelson has told the team that he's going home early so that he can have a meal out with Michelle. He knows they are taking bets on whether he'll come back to the office.

'Almost. Have you got anything for me?'

'Well, you know you said to check up on the Smith family, see if there were any convictions, anything like that?'

'Yes?'

'Well I've got one. A conviction for criminal damage. Part of an animal rights demonstration.'

Nelson thinks of a pale intense face fringed by dark hair. 'Was it the daughter? Caroline?'

'No.' Clough is savouring the moment. 'Romilly Maud Smith, aged fifty-five. Lady Smith to you.'

'The wife?'

'That's right. Looks like Lady Smith was part of a group

that broke into a pharmaceutical company to protest about animal testing.'

'Jesus! Wonder what Danforth Smith thought about that.'

'He must have known. It was in the papers. The *Evening News* described her as a "mother figure" to the group. Her code name was Big Mama.'

'What did she get?'

'Two hundred pound fine.'

'Any other convictions?'

'No, but according to the papers the group had been involved in lots of other demos. They're organised, these animal rights nutters.'

Are they nutters thinks Nelson, as he drives home at only a few miles over the speed limit. In his experience, animal rights activists are highly principled people, which makes them dangerous. Even so, he can't quite equate the elegant woman that he saw this morning with a camouflage-wearing extremist going by the name of Big Mama. What did Danforth Smith think about his wife's activities? And what was an animal rights campaigner doing married to a racehorse trainer in the first place? Danforth obviously loved his horses, but in Nelson's mind racehorses are linked to hunting and shooting and other bloodthirsty pursuits. He remembers his shock when Judy told him that she used to go hunting. 'It was a pony club thing,' she'd said. Pony club! Just when you thought you knew someone, they come out with something like that. Judy had done good work though, coming up with Cathbad on the CCTV. According to Judy, though, Cathbad had an alibi, which doesn't surprise Nelson at all. Cathbad had been visiting Caroline Smith. Are they having an affair? Caroline is rather attractive in a slightly nutty way. Nelson imagines that she would be just Cathbad's type.

So Caroline is having an affair with a druid and Romilly is a secret activist. How many other skeletons are going to tumble out of the Smith closet? Thinking of skeletons reminds him of Bishop Augustine and Ruth's amazing revelation. How coolly she had put it. 'Anything interesting?' that slimy Phil had asked. 'Rather interesting, yes,' Ruth had replied. Nelson never admires Ruth more than when he sees her doing her professional stuff. She is so sure of herself, there is none of that 'oh I don't know' nonsense that you get with some women, no trying to ingratiate herself with men by playing on their vanity. Ruth knows that she is as good as any man and she says so. It's refreshing. Nelson does not want to admit, even to himself, that he finds it sexy.

Which 'lady' had the Vicar been meeting at the museum? Caroline? Romilly, Lady Smith? It could even be Bishop Augustine, the amazing transvestite bishop, herself. But 'flesh and blood' Jimmy had said. What is the link between the museum and the stables, apart from the Smith family? And the fact that two men, in perfect health a few days ago, are now dead.

Nelson reaches the King's Lynn roundabout. After a moment's hesitation, he takes the turn for the station. He'll just pop in for a few minutes, talk to Judy and Clough about the case. He'll still be back in plenty of time to take Michelle out for a meal.

18

'And here we have oak with recessed brass handles. This one has a rather nice inlaid cross in the middle. Very popular with Catholics.'

'My husband wasn't a Catholic,' says Romilly Smith. Though the Smiths must have been Catholic once, she thinks, remembering Bishop Augustine. Dan had been so intrigued by that whole business with the coffin. It was just the sort of thing that interested him. Anything to do with the past, and especially his own ancestors, had him absolutely in thrall. Romilly was born in South Africa, and though she went to boarding school in England she still thinks of herself as a wanderer, stateless. Classless too, despite the ghastly upper-class accent that she's stuck with. Still, there's no denying that it comes in rather useful at times. She hates hearing herself braying away at assistants in shops, but when she was arrested the police treated her quite differently as soon as she opened her mouth. She despises the English class system. But Dan – Dan was an English aristocrat through and through.

'Any special songs? *My Way* is still popular, though a

lot of younger bereaved prefer *The Wind Beneath My Wings* or even *Angels*.'

Randolph said that it was too early to call in the undertakers. They don't even know when Dan's body will be released. But Romilly had been seized by a desire to do *something* – organise the funeral, sort out paperwork, sell the house, put the horses out to grass – anything rather than this ghastly sitting around, with everyone looking at her in that ridiculous way and the children either weeping or arguing. Tamsin, when she arrived, was an ally. 'It's no good *moping*,' she had snapped at Caroline. 'We've got to get organised.' 'Why?' Randolph had asked, with that vagueness which everyone except his immediate family seemed to find so endearing. 'For fuck's sake, Randolph,' Tamsin had exploded. 'There are things to *do*.'

So now Romilly and Tamsin are sitting interviewing the undertaker, a vaguely sinister man in a snowflake-patterned sweater. Randolph has roared off somewhere in the Porsche and Caroline is in the office talking to owners, who are probably interspersing condolences with demands that their horses be moved to another trainer. Romilly despises owners. None of them love their horses. They just want the kudos of swanking around the racecourse in stupid hats, going into the Owners and Trainers bar and talking about 'my horse'. Half of them wouldn't recognise 'their' horse if it bit them, which it probably would, given the chance.

At least Dan had genuinely loved the horses. That's how they had met. Romilly was working at a horse refuge near Norwich. Two horses had been brought in, unwanted and scared but otherwise completely fit. The refuge couldn't afford to keep them (they needed to save their money for sick animals) so Romilly had been given the job of ringing round local horse owners to ask if they could give them a temporary home. They had all refused. Horses are expensive and no one wanted the two unknown quantities who would guzzle their hay and probably frighten their own animals. Except Danforth Smith. He had arrived that very afternoon with a smart blue horsebox emblazoned with the words Slaughter Hill Racing Stables in gold. He had spoken gently to the frightened animals, loaded them with infinite patience, and by the time that he turned to Romilly with a courteous query about her availability for dinner that night, she was his for the asking. They were married six months later. Maybe it didn't hurt that, as well as an obvious love for animals, Danforth had limitless money and was building a large modern house which clearly needed a woman's touch. Romilly was getting tired of mud and dirt and encrusted denim; all the perks of working with horses. She wanted animals, but luxury too – a package that seemed to be offered by the tall, beaky-nosed man who knew how to talk to horses.

And now, after a lifetime of doing the conventional thing, Dan has finally surprised her. He has died, leaving her with three grown-up children, a house that is decorated to within an inch of its life, and a stable full of horses. Funny, Romilly had always thought that Dan would go on forever. Despite his diabetes he had seemed indestructible, part of an unchanging landscape. Whatever happened, Dan would always be there, getting up at five with the horses, going to bed by ten. Romilly feels unreasonably angry with him for letting her down like this. She needed him; she needed him there in the background, a soothing presence when she returned from her adventures, which are becoming more frequent of late. These days Romilly cares even less about the day-to-day business of looking after horses but even more about animal welfare in the abstract. Her activism lapsed when the children were growing up but in the last few years she has become involved again. Will the police find out about her criminal past? Will they find out about the group? She smiles, causing the undertaker to look shocked and Tamsin to lean over and ask if she's all right. 'I'm fine,' she says. She hates solicitude. From humans anyway.

'I think Dad would have liked opera,' Tamsin was saying. 'Something tasteful.'

Tasteful has become Tamsin's middle name. Her house in London is a monument to quiet good taste, her clothes are designer with just a hint of Boden, and even her dog is colour-coordinated (chocolate Lab). Romilly approves of all this (especially the Labrador) but she does wish that good taste wasn't also the abiding principle of Tamsin's personal life. It is years since Romilly has heard her elder daughter laugh or cry. Even Tamsin's children seem remarkably free from emotion. Romilly wants to love her only grandchildren but Emily and Laurence seem pallid little creatures, always doing their homework or prac-tising their violins. At their age Romilly was running a full-scale hedgehog rescue in the school grounds. She supposes that there aren't many hedgehogs in Notting Hill. They simply aren't tasteful enough.

Romilly agrees that Dan liked opera and they settle for *E lucevan le stelle* from *Tosca* for the cremation. The church organist can be relied upon to muddle through *Sheep May Safely Graze* for the church service.

'When will we know if the police want a post-mortem?' Tamsin asks, when the undertaker has bowed himself out.

'I don't know,' says Romilly. 'Detective Inspector Nelson was here this morning but the hospital don't think Dan's death was suspicious. Heart attack, they said. They've issued an interim death certificate.'

'I know.' Tamsin has already been to the hospital. She declined the invitation to view her father's body – 'I'd rather remember him alive' – though Caroline has already paid a tearful visit. Now Tamsin is keen to get on with the business of burying her father – tastefully, of course.

'Bit of a cheek, that policeman coming round,' she says. 'Can we make a complaint?'

'For goodness sake, Tammy, he was only doing his job.'

'And there was a bloody policewoman in Caroline's house going through the CCTV footage. I told her she shouldn't have let her in but Caro even made her a cup of bloody coffee. Typical.'

'Caro's very upset,' says Romilly mildly.

'Not so upset that she doesn't want to go to some barmy Aboriginal thing tomorrow,' says Tamsin, straightening her blameless little black skirt. 'I told her it was disrespectful.'

'Did you?' says Romilly. 'I thought it might make a nice change for her.'

Caroline puts down the phone, having told some faceless Russian oligarch that his horses will continue to be looked after. But who will train them? Len has a licence but he's only a few years off retirement. She knows that she would be useless. She rides out, but only on the more docile horses. Even as a child she was a bit of a wimp, dawdling along on her pony while all the other children galloped away over the horizon. She was always grateful that their mother refused to let them hunt, smugly adorning her riding helmet with anti-hunt stickers. 'It's cruel,' she would say, but really the thought of galloping hell-for-leather over the countryside scared her to death. She'd only learnt to ride to please her father, just as she'd joined Greenpeace and Friends of the Earth to please her mother.

Caroline used to be close to her father. 'A real Daddy's girl,' her mother used to say, in a tone comprising affection and derision in equal measure. Caroline always felt that she irritated her mother; she was too slow, too clumsy, not clever enough. Romilly used to play these word games, making up puns, poems, even songs, and Caroline remembers Randolph and Tamsin lounging around the kitchen table, coming up with outrageous rhymes, silly metaphors, clever little limericks. She could never think of anything fast enough and, besides, she didn't like making fun of people. 'Oh lighten up, Caro,' her mum used to say. But the world seemed a dark place to Caroline even then.

But Dad had understood. He hadn't minded that she couldn't write a haiku about Margaret Thatcher. He had been happy for her to trail around the yard after him, helping to groom the horses and polish tack. Even now, the smell of saddle soap brings back happy memories. When had it started to change? Probably when she came back from travelling, having seen the world through such different eyes. Dad had supported her when she had decided not to go to university. 'I'm sure you could get in somewhere not very competitive,' her mother had said kindly, looking at Caroline's less than impressive A Level results. But she hadn't wanted to go on studying. She knew she wasn't really stupid; it was just that sometimes it seemed to take her a long time to absorb new ideas. That was the trouble at school. By the time that Caroline had got her head round a concept, the class had moved on to something else. Anyway, at eighteen she'd had enough of trying to understand things. Now she was just going to experience them.

And she had. She has visited King's Canyon, the Lost City, the Garden of Eden. She has walked in the Valley of the Winds. She has seen the sun rise over Uluru and set over the Southern Ocean. She had penetrated the red heart of Australia and walked with the dead in the Dreaming. But back home everyone still seemed to treat her like the slightly stupid little sister. She had been full of ideas about how to revolutionise the yard. She'd created a website and organised an open day. Racing's so elitist, she'd wanted to involve the general public, get them to understand just how much trainers loved their horses. But the open day had been a total disaster. Len had refused to let anyone get near the horses, saying that they were too dangerous, and her father had strutted round all day like the worst kind of arrogant aristocrat. Afterwards they all said that Caroline should stick with what she was best at – managing the yard and keeping in the background.

Caroline had loved her dad, and right now what she wants more than anything is to see his tall, rangy figure striding across the yard, demanding to know which horses are running at Newmarket. But she remembers how angry she'd been with him, how frustrated she had felt, how she'd longed to escape, to go back to her beloved red valleys, to do something worthwhile in life. Meeting Cathbad had saved her. He had reminded her that there were bigger causes, more important things than which horse was running in which race and whether Jumping Jack would go better in blinkers. And that's why she can't just run away now, though she's sometimes tempted. She has bigger things to do . . .

'Hi Caro.' Randolph appears at the door. He looks pale and unshaven and she thinks she can smell whisky in his breath. She knows better than to ask where he's been.

'Hi Dolph.'

'Where's Tammy?'

'In the house with Mum. They're seeing the under-taker.'

Randolph collapses into the chair opposite her, pushing

back his hair with a hand that shakes slightly. 'Bit quick isn't it?' he says. 'He only died last night. A few hours ago.'

'Don't.' Caroline looks across the yard towards the house. 'I still can't believe it.'

'Nor me. I keep thinking that he's going to stroll in and tell me what an unsatisfactory son I am.'

'He loved you.' Even to herself, Caroline's voice lacks conviction.

'Yeah.' Randolph slumps further into the chair.

'What about me? The last thing I said to him was "I'll never forgive you."'

'Really?' Randolph's blue eyes flash at her. 'Why did you say that?'

'Oh, nothing important.' Caroline turns back to her files. 'Just that we've all got things to feel guilty about. I know Mum thinks that she neglected him for her business and her animal rights mates.'

'Rubbish. She always supported him.' Randolph is always on their mother's side.

'Well, we're all feeling rotten.'

'Except Tamsin. Little Miss Fix It.'

'I'm sure she's very upset about Dad,' says Caroline doubtfully.

'Are you?' says Randolph, stroking Lester who has just jumped onto his lap. 'I'll take your word for it. What did that policewoman want this morning?'

'Just to look through the CCTV footage.'

'Did she find anything?'

'I don't know.'

'You look nervous,' Randolph teases. 'What have you been getting up to in the woods?'

'Bugger off, Dolph. What about you?'

'What do you mean "what about me"?'

'What have you been doing in the woods?'

They lock gazes, blue eyes meeting brown. Then Randolph gets up and strides out of the office.

19

The Elginists' conference is held in a Quaker Meeting House in Great Yarmouth. Ruth has always rather avoided Yarmouth in the past, thinking of it as a kind of east-coast Blackpool, full of roller-coasters and drunken holidaymakers. Nelson once tried to tell her that Blackpool wasn't like that; it had some wonderful countryside nearby, he had said. But Ruth hadn't been convinced. She likes her seaside to be deserted, miles of lonely sand, not crammed with donkeys in funny hats. So she is rather surprised to find that the Meeting House is a delightful white-painted house dating back to the seventeenth century. If you have to have a religion, thinks Ruth, walking through the shady garden, you might as well be a Quaker. They're non-hierarchical, non-sexist and pacifist. But a notice in the lobby reminds her of an older, rather more bloodstained religion. The house, she reads, was built on the site of a medieval monastery, an Augustinian cell. This reminds her of Bishop Augustine and of Mother Julian, the mystic anchoress. The sign also tells her that Anna Sewell, the author of *Black Beauty*, used to attend meetings in the house. Ruth, who loves books about horses, begins to feel better disposed towards the whole day.

It has been a hassle getting there for nine. Although Kate was awake and ready for action at six, Ruth still found herself running round the house like a mad thing in order to get to Sandra's at eight. By the time she had fed Flint, changed her own clothes twice, got Kate strapped in the car with a bag full of nappies and a change of clothes, and gone back because she was convinced she'd left the gas on, it was a quarter past. After a lightning changeover at Sandra's, Ruth was finally on her way to Great Yarmouth. Now, after getting stuck behind two holiday coaches (who on earth would go to Norfolk in November?), she finally makes it to the Meeting House by nine-thirty. She hopes the seminars haven't started.

But when she enters the room signposted Refreshments, she realises that she has misjudged her colleagues. At nine-thirty, the assembled archaeologists are still tucking into coffee and Danish pastries. After agonies of indecision about her clothes, Ruth has finally settled on a black trouser suit to look professional (and slightly thinner). She is almost the only person not in jeans. The room also seems full of dyed hair – purple, red, pink, even a multi-coloured Mohican. Almost everyone has tattoos and multiple piercings. Someone has even brought their dog.

In the end, though, it's the dog that makes Ruth decide that she was right to come. As she stands uncertainly in the doorway, the animal comes bounding up to her and jumps up to lick her nose. Ruth is taken aback. She likes all animals but she is really happiest with cats and this is a particularly large and whiskery dog. Why on earth is it so pleased to see her?

'Claudia!' calls an amused and familiar voice. 'Come here.'

'Hallo Max,' says Ruth.

Max hasn't changed much in the past eighteen months. If anything he looks slightly healthier than she remembers, less haunted-looking. His face is brown, making his hair look greyer and his eyes bluer. He is grinning now, a wider grin than she ever remembers him giving but, then again, there hadn't been that much to smile about when they last met.

'Ruth. How lovely. Cathbad said you might be here.'

The druid telegraph system is as efficient as ever. Ruth can see Cathbad across the room, his purple cloak not that outlandish in this setting. Bob Woonunga is standing next to him; he's wearing a cloak as well but his looks as if it is made of fur.

'I don't really know why I'm here,' says Ruth. She can feel herself smiling back at Max. Her facial muscles feel rusty from lack of use. 'Cathbad persuaded me.'

'Ah, well, he is very persuasive. Would you like a coffee?'

'Yes, please.'

They walk over to the urns, Claudia following them.

'She's grown,' says Ruth, patting the dog's head.

'Yes,' says Max. 'She's eating me out of house and home. As you see, I've turned into one of those pathetic creatures who can't leave their dog even for a day. Actually, the dog sitter let me down.'

'It sounds worse than childcare,' says Ruth, helping herself to a pastry.

Max looks rather embarrassed, bending down to ruffle Claudia's fur. 'How's your . . . how's Kate? I'd love to meet her.'

Max had sent a card and a present when Kate was born and Ruth had expected him to follow these tokens in person, but somehow it had never happened. She told herself at the time that she was relieved. These last months have been complicated enough without Max reappearing in her life. It's good to see him now though.

'Kate's well,' she says. 'She had her first birthday last weekend.'

'Her first birthday,' Max looks startled. 'I don't believe it.'

'No,' says Ruth drily. 'It seems much longer.' But she knows what Max means. Before she had Kate, she had noticed how the years had begun to run together, nothing to distinguish one from the other except the appearance of a few more grey hairs. Now, with Kate, every week marks a new milestone. And while, on the one hand, it does seem amazing that Kate is already a year old; on the other, it seems as if she has been around forever.

Come and meet her, she is about to say. Come back to the house when we've finished discussing skulls and bones. We can walk on the beach and look at Kate and talk about life. But at that moment Cathbad claps his hands importantly.

'Let's go into the main hall now, friends. The first session is about to start.'

The first session, entitled 'Honouring Our Ancient Dead', is more interesting than Ruth had expected. She is shocked to discover that as recently as 2003 working parties were advising that human remains should not be returned to their country of origin because of doubts about their 'care and preservation'. She learns that in 2005 three hundred and eighty-five sets of Aboriginal remains were held in eighteen different institutions around Britain. 'Many of these relics,' says the speaker, a woman called Alkira Jones, 'were taken from their indigenous homelands through blatant acts of colonialism.' Ruth thinks of Danforth Smith (now deceased) . . . *the old man had the idea that the Abos were put together differently from us, that they were linked to cave men or some such. So he started collecting bones.* She learns about the Native American Graves Protection and Repatriation Act 1990, passed in an attempt to resolve conflict over the storage of Native American skeletal remains and grave goods. Israel also recently passed a reburial act which could affect the remains of some of the oldest anatomically modern humans. In Scotland there is an ancient 'right to sepulchre' – a right to be buried – a principle which may now be adopted by other countries. 'Museums hold on to these remains,' says Jones, 'because they say they add to the sum of human knowledge while, in fact, they add to the sum of human misery. Our relationship must be with the living descendants of these people. A living relationship, not a dead one.'

Ruth shifts uncomfortably in her seat. As a forensic archaeologist, many of her relationships are with the dead. Hasn't she often marvelled at how much we can learn from a bone or tooth? Should she forgo that knowledge in order to ensure that the remains receive a proper burial? Does it matter, after all? It matters to the living, Jones is saying, and that's the important thing. But is it? Ruth knows that some of the groups who have been demanding the return of Indigenous Australian relics are not in fact descended from the same tribes. The policy of the Australian Institute of Aboriginal Studies says that 'descent must be shown'. But what if it can't be proved? Can just anyone demand the return of bones which could contain valuable information for generations to come?

She remembers a Victorian painting that had fascinated her as a child. It was called *Can These Dry Bones Live?* and showed a woman, wearing a black shawl and a rather sumptuous red skirt, leaning on a gravestone and looking at some bones and a skull that have been unearthed by . . . who? What? A careless gravedigger? Animals? A very localised earthquake? The picture is sometimes said to represent Victorian doubts about the existence of an afterlife. If so, there are hints in the painting that might reassure the observer. The gravestone belongs to 'John Faithful' and bears the inscription, 'I am the Resurrection and the Life.' A nearby stone is engraved 'Resurgam.' A blue butterfly rests on the skull; elsewhere in the picture flowers are springing into bloom. But, for Ruth, the painting pointed to a different lesson. What could these bones tell us about the life that their owner lived? How can dry bones recall life in all its glorious complexity? She wonders now if the picture, like the Horniman Museum, influenced her choice of career. Or maybe she just liked the red skirt – an odd choice, surely, for a woman in mourning? But now these people are telling her that the bones should have stayed buried. It's all very confusing.

The next session, a canter through Indigenous artefacts kept in British museums, is more boring. Ruth dozes and wonders what Kate is doing. Sandra is good at making the day interesting, she'll probably take Kate to the park, maybe do some baking with her. All the same, Ruth enjoys her own Saturdays with Kate. They usually go to the beach and collect shells. There's a whole line of them in the garden like something from Mary Mary Quite Contrary. Sometimes they'll go to Blakeney to see the fishing boats and often end up having tea in Cathbad's purple caravan. Kate has her own dreamcatcher, glittering oyster shells and pink feathers. So far it hasn't succeeded in making her sleep any better. Maybe tonight Ruth will try to go straight downstairs after reading the story ...

She starts, pink feathers and oyster shells scattering. The speaker, a man called Derel Assinewai, is talking about the worst atrocities of colonial trophy hunters. 'We've heard of Aboriginal people being hunted, literally being hunted like animals. There are rumours that these skulls were then scalped. It was the British, not the Native Americans, who were the first to scalp their victims – and then keep the skin as a souvenir.'

Ruth thinks of the telltale marks on the skull in the Smith Museum. Was she right to tell Cathbad and Bob? She can't help feeling uneasy about the fact that, the day after this revelation, Lord Smith was dead. It's not that she suspects Cathbad or Bob. She looks over at Bob now and he smiles at her. He is sitting in the back row, very much at his ease, legs crossed, head back, listening to Derel's lecture. No, Danforth Smith's death can only have been coincidence, but even so it makes her feel glad that she hasn't got any Aboriginal remains lying around the house. *Think how much worse it is to take the very bones of our ancestors and keep them on the other side of the world.*

Why had Danforth Smith been so determined not to return the skulls? They weren't even on display anymore. And although he had seemed proud of the gruesome collection, Ruth could not see that he got much pleasure from the museum as a whole. That day (was it only last week?) when she had examined the bones, Lord Smith had seemed tired, almost frightened, and the museum itself had seemed a sad place, dusty and forlorn. Ruth can't see it ever opening again. Who would trek down a side street full of office blocks just to look at a few stuffed animals? No, better to let the place die with Neil Topham and Danforth Smith and quietly return the skulls to Australia. In any case, Ruth has done her bit. She has written a report, stating the bones are not being kept in appropriate conditions, and has submitted it to the Department for Culture, Media and Sport. She hopes this might encourage the authorities to put pressure on the Smith family to return them. But the truth is that, as the relics are privately owned, government has little or no influence. It's as if Lord Smith really did own them, body and soul. But who owns them now? Smith had a son, she knows. Will he be the new Lord Smith?

Lunch, from a local vegan restaurant, is absolutely delicious. It's such a lovely day that the French windows are open onto the garden and Ruth and Max sit on a stone seat with Claudia panting at their feet. It is only a few minutes before Cathbad comes up, accompanied by a dark woman in a red dress.

'Max. Good to see you. Ruth, I'd like you to meet Caroline Smith.'

Ruth jumps up, brushing crumbs off her trousers. Caroline is a good-looking woman of about thirty. There is something oddly old-fashioned about her. Just as Cathbad often looks as if he is wearing fancy dress when he isn't, Caroline somehow gives the impression of being in period clothing. Her hair is scraped up in a bun and the dress, an unfashionable ankle length, could be Edwardian or even Victorian. Funnily enough, it reminds Ruth of the skirt in *Can These Dry Bones Live?* She supposes that Caroline, like the painting's subject, is also in mourning.

'I was so sorry to hear about your father,' she says.

'Thank you,' says Caroline. She has rather a hesitant voice, at odds with her commanding presence. 'I wasn't sure whether to come today. Tam . . . my family thought I shouldn't, but Cathbad persuaded me.'

'He's very persuasive.' Ruth echoes Max.

'I'm fascinated by the Aboriginal peoples,' says Caroline.

'I once spent a year in Australia. You know that the Aborigine map of Australia is quite different? It's literally a different country.'

'The names are different aren't they,' offers Ruth. 'Ayers Rock . . .'

'Yes, Ayers Rock is a colonialist name. Its real name is Uluru. It's part of the Ulura-Kata Tjata National Park. The red heart of Australia. '

She manages the names with aplomb but there is something so intense about her that Ruth backs away a little.

'How do you know Cathbad?' she asks.

'I went to one of his archaeology courses.'

'Cathbad runs archaeology courses?' Ruth can't help but be aggrieved. She's the one who works in the archaeology department but Cathbad has never mentioned any courses to her.

'It's not conventional archaeology,' says Cathbad modestly. 'It's more about ritual and mystic symbolism.'

'Oh.' Ruth stops feeling aggrieved. Mystic symbolism's not exactly on the university curriculum.

'Of course,' says Max, 'archaeology's all about ritual and symbolism. Even people we think of as primitive buried their dead with some elements of ritual, for example. We don't always know what the symbolism means but we know that it's there.'

It could be Erik speaking, thinks Ruth. She looks at Cathbad, wondering if the same thought has occurred to him. Max was a fan of Erik's, Ruth remembers (though, in some ways, she has never really forgotten). She wonders why Max, an expert on the Romans in Britain, has come to a conference on the treatment of Aboriginal relics.

'Some museums in Sussex hold Indigenous Australian relics,' he says, as they take Claudia for a quick walk before the afternoon session. 'I've been asked to look into it. Personally, I don't think there can be any argument against returning them. They're so important in Aboriginal Australian culture.'

'I agree,' says Ruth, panting slightly (Max walks very fast). 'But I can't agree that human bones shouldn't ever be excavated. We learn so much from them.'

'Yes,' says Max. 'But what do we do with that knowledge? That's the question.'

The afternoon session, led by Bob Woonunga, turns out to be riveting. The autumn sun is low against the windows. Bob, wearing a cloak that is apparently made from possum skin, sits on the floor in the centre of the room. One by one the listeners abandon their chairs and sit in a circle around him. Ruth finds herself squashed up close to Max and Claudia. She is grateful to the dog for providing a barrier between them. As she strokes Claudia's head, her hand brushes against Max's leg. He smiles but doesn't move away.

'In the beginning is the Dreaming,' says Bob. 'And in the Dreaming lies the sacredness of the earth. It is the beginning of all things but it is not in the past. It is the past, present and the future. When we bury them in the earth the ancestors return to the Dreaming, and in this way the circle is complete. Every place and every creature belongs to the Dreaming. It is where the spirit children live before they are born and where the dead go when they leave their physical life.'

Bob tells them about souls that are buried in the sand, marked with twigs. Anjea, the fertility goddess, picks up the twigs and arranges them in a circle. She then makes new souls from mud and places them in the wombs of barren women. He tells them how the Bagadhimbri, two brother Gods in the form of dingoes, created the first sex organs from mushrooms. He tells them about Bahloo, the man in the moon, who keeps three deadly snakes as pets. He tells them about the Mimis, fairy-like creatures who live in rock crevices. He tells them about the Nargun, who abducts children by night. He tells them about cloud and rain spirits, about the Sun Goddess, and Yurlungar, the copper snake who was awoken from sleep by the smell of a woman's menstrual blood, ate the woman and was later forced to regurgitate her. In Australian Aboriginal rites-of-passage ceremonies, says Bob, the vomiting symbolises boys becoming men. Ruth thinks, considering the circumstances, that the transition from girl to woman would be more appropriate.

But Bob's greatest enthusiasm is reserved for the Rainbow Serpent, the great snake who, in the Dreaming, meandered over the land creating rivers and waterways. His body hollowed out the valleys; where he rested great lakes were formed; the stones are his droppings and his sloughed-off scales created the forests. The Snake, Bob tells them, is the totem of his tribe and he has written many poems about him. He reads some now, his words meandering over the room like the snake itself, winding themselves around its dark corners, taking shape in the last rays of the afternoon sun.

Strange, thinks Ruth dreamily, that the snake should be the big baddie in the Christian creation story. Here he seems to be both hero and villain, at once creating and destroying. One of Bob's poems describes how the snake eats a boy because he won't stop crying, but then the boy and his crying are absorbed into the Dreaming. Bishop Augustine, too, seems to have had rather an obsession with snakes. On one hand the snake was the demon to be destroyed, on the other the agent of his vengeance. Of course, the snake has another, more Freudian connection too, especially if Augustine's sexuality really is in doubt. Did the snake represent Augustine's assumed manhood? Aren't some snakes hermaphrodites?

Bob finishes by reading from from a piece by the great Aboriginal poet Ooderoo Noonuccal. It's called *The Ballad of the Totems* and is about her father and the sacred symbol of their tribe. In one place she describes it as a 'carpet snake', which sounds rather odd to Ruth. Carpet Snake sounds more cosy than the great Rainbow Serpent, almost as if it could be used as a draught excluder.

She realises that Max is holding out a hand to help her to her feet. She scrambles up without his help, embarrassed at how stiff she is.

'What's happening now?'

'I think we're having the smoke ceremony.' Max points to where Bob is leading the way out through the French windows into the garden. In the centre of the lawn Cathbad is enthusiastically building a bonfire.

'Cathbad does love fires,' says Ruth, putting on her jacket.

'Well, fire's important in ritual,' says Max. 'That was quite some session, wasn't it? Incredibly powerful poetry.'

It is almost dark now and the wood catches light quickly. Cathbad and Bob, in their cloaks, are silhouetted against the flames. Ruth can see Caroline just behind them, her long skirt billowing. Then she jumps as a loud crack reverberates in the darkness.

'It's just a clapping stick,' says a voice behind them. It's this morning's speaker, Alkira Jones. She smiles encouragingly. 'They're sometimes called singing sticks. They're traditional Aboriginal instruments.' Ruth sees that Cathbad and the other speaker, Derel Assinewai, are now armed with long, decorated rods which they bang enthusiastically together, creating a thunderous rhythm. Bob takes a burning brand from the centre of the fire. 'Fire is our gateway to the Dreaming,' he says. 'Surrender to the fire.'

Boom, boom. The relentless beat continues. Smoke fills Ruth's mouth and nose. The flames seem particularly pungent, as if they're mixed with balsam. Her head starts to swim. At Max's feet, Claudia whimpers.

Ruth turns to Max. 'Do you want to come back to my place?'

20

Nelson, too, is participating in a ritual. He is sitting on Brighton beach eating fish and chips out of a paper bag. Tasted better from newspaper, he thinks. Why don't they use newspaper anymore? He puts the question to Michelle.

'Health and safety,' she says knowledgeably. She is finishing the last of her chips, chasing the last grains of salt with a moistened finger. It is so rare for her to eat something so calorie-laden that Nelson watches her with genuine pleasure. For some reason, he isn't feeling very hungry. He throws a chip onto the pebbles and three seagulls immediately swoop down on it. It's getting colder now, though the sun is still warm on their faces. Behind them the carousel is playing its jolly, heart-breaking tune and, from the pier, they can hear the shrieks of people on the rides. A group of girls wearing bunny ears staggers past them, weaving in and out between deckchairs, falling over on the sloping shingle.

'Hen night,' says Michelle.

The day in Brighton was Michelle's idea. Friday night's meal was not a success. Nelson had got home late; Michelle had ended the evening in tears. But she woke on Saturday in a determinedly positive state of mind. Why not drive down to Brighton to see Rebecca? It's a long drive but they could take Rebecca out for lunch and celebrate Harry's birthday at the same time. And it has been a good day. Rebecca had told them firmly that she could only spare them an hour but they had taken her for lunch at Browns and bought her a number of pastel-coloured objects for her room. How many scatter cushions or strings of fairy lights could one student need, Nelson wondered. He didn't say it aloud though. Shops full of novelty mirrors and cute lower-case writing make him feel nervous.

After Rebecca had wandered off to meet friends at the cinema, Nelson and Michelle had done the tourist things. They had shopped in the Lanes, admired the Pavilion from afar and walked on the pier. In the arcade, Nelson developed an obsession with winning a cuddly toy from one of the machines. He fed in twenty pence after twenty pence, only to watch the white fluffy cat fall in slow motion from the feeble clutches of the mechanical arm.

'It's a fix,' he announced. 'Impossible.' When, later, he noticed a man carrying *three* of the fluffy cats, his indignation knew no bounds.

'Why do you want a cuddly toy anyway?' asked Michelle, slightly beadily.

'It's the principle of the thing,' Nelson had said.

Now they are sitting on the beach watching the town get ready for the evening. The families are drifting away, to be replaced by more hen nights (L-plates, novelty police uniforms that make Nelson wince), foreign students in brightly coloured sportswear, men too well dressed to be straight. Nelson and Michelle walk between the piers, past archways that have been turned into night clubs and restaurants. All that is left of the old West Pier is a rotting iron structure like a Victorian birdcage, a hundred yards out to sea. Appropriately enough, the birdcage is full of birds – hundreds and hundreds of starlings swooping and soaring in the last of the evening sun, black against the violet sky. Nelson and Michelle stop to watch for a few minutes.

'It's a bit spooky, isn't it?' says Michelle. 'Makes me think of that film, *The Birds*.'

Nelson grunts, he's never seen the attraction of birds himself.

'Are you OK, Harry?'

'I'm fine. Come on, we'd better get to the car.'

But, as they walk through the tunnel towards the underground car park, Nelson realises that's he's not fine, not really. Come to think of it, he's been feeling odd all day. He hadn't fancied his food and even walking is an effort, as if his feet are encased in lead. Once or twice he has noticed the promenade, with its Regency hotels and barley-sugar railings, swooping and swirling in the most disturbing way. It is only when he gets to the car and the ground lurches again, so violently that he has to hold on to Michelle to keep his footing, that he realises the incredible truth. He feels ill.

Kate is asleep when Ruth arrives to collect her. 'I'm sorry,' says Sandra, 'but we had a busy day. She hasn't stopped.'

Kate has certainly stopped now, her head back, mouth slightly open, fingers still gripped around a grubby lump of pastry. 'We made mince pies,' explains Sandra. 'A bit early but who cares. Do you want some?'

Ruth accepts a freezer bag full of mince pies while thanking Sandra profusely. She doesn't mind that Kate is asleep. She needs time to think about the evening ahead. Max has said he'll meet her at the cottage. 'I'll give Claudia a walk first,' he said. 'Shall I pick up a bottle of wine and a takeaway? Would that be a good idea?' Ruth said it would but, privately, she thinks things are moving a little quickly. She had imagined a cup of tea and a chat, maybe some time admiring Kate or walking on the Saltmarsh; now they are having dinner together. It's dark too and Kate is asleep. Awake, she is a distraction, almost a chaperone. Now she will snooze picturesquely in the background; they'll have to rely on Claudia and Flint for light relief. Flint! What will he think about having a dog in the house? Ruth hopes he won't go missing again. Maybe he'll run to Bob's house. She finds herself hoping that Bob will come home soon so that she isn't left alone on the Saltmarsh with Max.

What is she afraid of? Isn't this precisely what she wanted, what she has allowed herself to dream about over the stressful summer months when Nelson was out of bounds and Ruth was alone with her own anxieties? Yes it is, and Ruth knows that part of her fear is also anticipation. Her skin tingles, she is conscious of the touch of her clothes on her legs and arms. She feels slightly sick and, at the same time, extremely hungry. She hopes she will be able to have a shower before Max arrives. But will that look as if she is trying too hard, opening the door smelling of Badedas and toothpaste? Better than nappy sacks and last night's supper hardening in the saucepan though. She drives through the dark roads, worrying and hyperventilating. She starts to hope that Max won't turn up.

But when she draws up outside her cottage Max's Range Rover is already there. When he opens the door Claudia shoots out, barking wildly. Ruth sees a ginger streak as Flint disappears into the long grass. She hopes he'll come back soon. Ruth starts to lift out Kate's car seat, fumbling with the straps.

'Can I help?' asks Max. He is looking at Kate. 'She's beautiful,' he says softly.

'She's heavy,' warns Ruth, but Max lifts the laden car seat easily with one hand. As he follows Ruth along the path, she can't help thinking that they look like a parody of a nuclear family. Mum, Dad and baby returning from a day out. Not to mention the dog, currently sniffing excitedly under the blackberry bushes, and the (absent) cat. Ruth opens the door, kicking aside the post. Claudia rushes through to the kitchen and Ruth hears her drinking noisily out of Flint's water bowl.

'Shall I take Kate upstairs?' says Max.

Now this really does feel like a step too far. Max has been to the house before but never upstairs. No one goes upstairs except Nelson that one time and, it now transpires, Judy and Cathbad. Besides, she hasn't made her bed.

'I'll take her,' says Ruth. 'Make yourself at home.'

In the bedroom, Ruth takes off Kate's outer layer of clothes and lays her in her cot, which is beside Ruth's bed. There is a spare room, which is now almost clear, but Ruth finds herself curiously unwilling to move Kate. She likes hearing her breathing in the night, and it's easier when Kate wakes up just to reach over and pick her up. They often end up sleeping in the double bed together, something that is much frowned upon by the baby books.

Ruth hastily straightens her duvet and wonders about putting on some perfume. No, too obvious. She brushes her hair and peers at her reflection in the mirror. She's not used to looking at herself, really looking as opposed to checking whether or not she has something stuck in her teeth. Pale skin, pink cheeks, brown hair. She wishes she had cheekbones like Shona. In fact, she wishes she could borrow Shona's face for the evening. Ruth's been told that her best feature is her smile but she never smiles when looking in the mirror so that's not much help. She scowls now, pulling the brush through her tangled hair. She hasn't even got a hairstyle like other women, she thinks bitterly. Her hair just hangs to her shoulders, mid-brown and slightly wavy, as it has done since childhood. Over the last year she has noticed a few grey hairs appearing. Soon she'll be a white-haired old hag, living alone with her cat, frightening children on Halloween. Something to look forward to, she thinks, turning away from the mirror, smiling now.

When she gets downstairs, Max has collected the Chinese from the car and put it on the table. He has opened the bottle of wine and found glasses. Claudia is lying panting in front of the fireplace. Flint comes in through the cat flap and walks slowly past the dog, daring her to move. Claudia watches, bright-eyed.

'Is this OK?' says Max. 'I didn't get it out in case it got cold.'

And suddenly it is OK. Ruth doesn't feel self-conscious any more. They drink wine and eat crispy aromatic duck and talk about Cathbad, Aborigines, Brighton, Norfolk, Gay Pride, Dreamtime, fire rituals, university politics, the difference between cats and dogs. They don't talk about the past, the fact that they were once almost involved in a relationship, a relationship curtailed by kidnap and a long-forgotten murder. They don't talk about Nelson or Kate. Max does say once that it seems strange to see her with a baby.

'It feels odd to me too,' says Ruth. 'I still don't really feel like a mother, one of those women who can do it all. You know, have babies, bake cakes, make potato prints.'

'Potato prints?' repeats Max, laughing.

'You know,' says Ruth, rather crossly. 'Cut a potato in half and make it into a star shape or something. Sandra, my childminder, is always doing stuff like that. I did try once. I tried to make a K shape on a potato but I got it wrong, I didn't realise it had to be reversed so that it would print out the right way round. Kate wasn't interested anyway. She's too young. I just wanted to do it for myself.'

'Ruth,' says Max, still smiling. 'You don't need to make potato prints. You're brilliant and beautiful. I bet you're a great mum.'

But, just at that moment, Ruth doesn't care about being a great mum or a brilliant archaeologist. Max has called her beautiful.

'Shall I drive?' says Michelle. Nelson shakes his head. Apart from a few occasions when he has had too much to drink, he has never been driven by his wife. To him, it's a reversal of the natural order of things.

'I'll be fine,' he says. 'It's just the sun.'

Michelle looks at him doubtfully. 'It's November,' she says. 'It's not that hot.'

'It feels hot after Norfolk. Come on. Let's go.'

At first he feels OK. It's a comfort to be in the car, changing gear, looking in the mirror, not having to walk and talk. Then, as they pass the Brighton gates, the road ahead shimmers and almost disappears. For one terrifying moment, Nelson thinks he sees a lorry bearing down on them. Then the lorry turns into a skull with glowing red eyes. Suddenly he knows he's going to be sick.

'Harry! What's happening?'

Somehow Nelson makes it onto the hard shoulder. He staggers out of the car and is violently sick in the undergrowth. He feels hot and cold in rapid succession. Crouched on the scrubby grass at the side of the road, he stares at a twig as it smoothly turns into a snake.

'Harry.' Michelle puts her hand on his shoulder. She sounds scared.

'I'm OK.' Nelson forces himself to stand up. 'Must be something I ate. Those bloody chips.'

'I'll drive,' says Michelle.

This time, Nelson doesn't argue.

Kate wakes at ten-thirty. Her crying soon escalates from sad whimpers into full-blown howling. Ruth rushes upstairs and attempts long-range soothing, as recommended by the books. 'It's OK, Kate. It's OK. Go back to sleep.' Kate roars louder, arching her back and flailing her arms. The sound seems to expand to fill the little house. God knows what Max must be thinking. Ruth picks Kate up and paces the room with her. 'It's OK. It's OK.' Kate is rigid against her shoulder but the crying decreases slightly in volume. Ruth starts to sing.

'Three little men in a flying saucer . . .' Kate stops sobbing but manages to convey that she will start again if Ruth dares to try to put her down.

'Two little men . . .'

'Is she all right?'

Max is standing in the doorway. Ruth feels her face growing red, embarrassed to be caught singing, embarrassed to be failing in what the books call 'crying management', embarrassed that Max is in her bedroom with the bed stretched out, vast and smooth, between them.

'Shall I hold her for a bit?'

Ruth hands Kate over and Max strides along the landing with the baby against his shoulder. From the bottom of the stairs Claudia and Flint watch anxiously. Kate's head lolls against Max's neck. 'Dada', she says sleepily.

* * *

By the time they reach the outskirts of Norwich, Nelson is almost delirious. Strange lights and shapes blur before his eyes. When he looks at Michelle her profile is wonderfully familiar but, when she turns slightly, he sees the skull beneath the skin.

'Don't,' he mutters. 'Don't look . . .'

Michelle drives straight past the turn-off to King's Lynn and heads into Norwich. Nelson wakes from a dream of skulls and snakes and buried children.

'Where are we going?'

'To A and E,' says Michelle grimly.

21

At first Judy doesn't recognise the voice on the phone.

'DS Johnson? It's Superintendent Whitcliffe here.'

Judy sits up in bed, feeling the utter wrongness of being caught talking to the Superintendent while wearing a baby doll nightdress. Next to her, Darren stirs in his sleep.

'Morning, sir.' Judy looks around the room for something to make her feel more professional. She puts on her watch.

'Johnson. DCI Nelson has been taken ill in the night. He's in the university hospital. It looks bad. I'm making you SIO on the drugs case and the museum case.'

Senior Investigating Officer. At first that is all Judy can hear, then the rest of the sentence filters through.

'Nelson's in hospital? What happened?'

'I'm not quite sure. I've just come off the phone to his wife. It might be something viral, maybe meningitis. He's unconscious.'

'What?'

'That's all I know but it sounds serious. He's in intensive care. I'm going to need you to rally the team. They'll be in shock.'

Clough will also be madder than a snake, thinks Judy, getting out of bed. He'll think he should have been put in charge. He'll be devastated about the boss too; he worships Nelson.

'I'll call a meeting,' says Whitcliffe.

Judy looks at her watch. It's Sunday and they're meant to be having lunch with Darren's parents.

'I'm on my way,' she says.

'Good girl. I'll see you there.'

Ruth, too, is in bed. Weak sunlight is filtering through the blinds, she stretches and is instantly aware of two, no three, things. There are no blinds in her bedroom, she must be in the spare room. It's morning and Kate isn't awake yet and she's in bed with Max.

The last thing will have to wait for a moment. She pads across the landing and looks into Kate's cot, standing beside the pristine double bed. Kate is awake too, looking at the light reflected on the ceiling. Her dark eyes are wide open and she's smiling.

'Good morning darling,' whispers Ruth.

Kate's smile turns into a full-on beam. 'Mum,' she says.

Ruth picks up Kate and carries her downstairs. In the sitting room she is startled by a large furry shape hurtling towards her. Christ, she'd forgotten the dog. Claudia is friendly but she is anxious to tell Ruth that she's hungry. Ruth heats up a bottle for Kate and pours milk into instant porridge. Then she puts on the kettle and gives Claudia a piece of bread. It disappears in a second and Claudia looks at her expectantly. Feeling treacherous, she puts some cat food in a bowl and pushes it towards Claudia. There's no sign of Flint.

It's eight o'clock. Still early for normal people but afternoon as far as Kate is concerned. Ruth switches on the radio and is surprised to hear organ music blasting out. Of course, it's Sunday. She turns off the radio and puts bread in the toaster. Claudia is sitting hopefully under Kate's high chair. Kate drops porridge onto her head.

It takes two cups of tea before Ruth can think about last night. After Kate had fallen asleep in Max's arms, he had put her into her cot and opened his arms to Ruth. As simple as that. In the end, she hadn't thought about it at all. Like sleepwalkers they had moved into the spare room and made love on the narrow bed. Not one word was spoken. The whole thing had seemed natural and right, as if they really had been the married couple who had entered the house with their baby only hours before. Very different from Ruth's last sexual encounter with Nelson, when they had come together through fear and a mutual, desperate longing. In fact, the intensity of emotion had been almost unbearable. But some time during last night Ruth had vowed never to think about Nelson again.

She takes her tea and toast to the table by the window. Flint comes in and sits in a patch of sunlight, washing himself with his leg in the air. Kate plays with one of her birthday presents, a miniature garden complete with plastic flowers and vegetables that must be slotted into the correctly shaped holes. Kate is quite good at this game though she sometimes loses patience altogether and throws the plastic flowers around the room. Where does she get this temper from? Ruth is a simmerer, slow to anger and slow to forget. She bets that Nelson had tantrums as a child. In fact he probably has them now, yelling at his team, driving off in a cloud of exhaust smoke. 'Just fucking do it,' she heard him say once to Clough. Not the most tactful management style in the world. But then Ruth has never had to manage anyone but herself. And she's thinking about Nelson again.

It's a beautiful crisp winter morning. The sky is a clear pale blue, the sea, glimpsed over the miles of white grass, is a darker blue, almost grey. Occasionally a cloud of birds will rise up out of the reeds, wheeling and turning in the vast sky. Some birds will spend the winter on the mud flats, others are preparing for the long journey south. A few days ago Ruth saw a peregrine, swooping down on some unsuspecting prey in the long grass. Is that like Max, she wonders now, swooping down on her when she is alone and vulnerable? It hadn't felt like that but what does she know? She doesn't exactly have a good track record in romance.

'Morning.' Max stands in the doorway, looking less like a bird of prey than a large dog, a wolfhound maybe, hair dishevelled, rangy body at ease with itself. Claudia goes mad with delight, rushing round the room for something to bring him and coming up with one of Ruth's bras, tugged out of the laundry basket. Max looks at Ruth and they both laugh. Kate, carefully fitting vegetables into holes, laughs too.

'Tea?' says Ruth.

It isn't going to be so difficult after all.

Whitcliffe calls the team together and they sit in the briefing room, sleepy and resentful at being summoned on a Sunday morning. Whitcliffe tells them about Nelson; he pitches it just right, sympathetic yet businesslike. Judy stands behind him, feeling horribly self-conscious. She can see the faces of her colleagues as they take in the news. Clough looks stunned; he opens his mouth to speak and then shuts it again, a half-eaten chocolate bar falls to the floor. Tanya looks concerned, 'Can we send flowers or something?' Tom Henty is stolid, unmoveable, though Judy notices that, when he gathers his papers together, his hands are not altogether steady. Rocky doesn't seem to have understood a word.

Clough is in such a state of shock that he doesn't seem to take in Whitcliffe's breezy statement that Judy 'is going to take over for the time being'. It is only when she gets up and walks to the whiteboard that his head jerks up and he stares at her with something approaching hatred. Judy herself is shaking slightly as she writes the date on the board. Her writing seems schoolgirlish and unformed after Nelson's passionate scrawl. She sees Tanya watching her, her body language sliding almost comically between concern (head on one side) and resentment (narrowed eyes, tapping foot).

'Operation Octopus,' Judy writes on the board. That

is the name they are giving to the drugs case, chosen by Clough to reflect the fact that the drugs are thought to be coming by sea and that the smugglers seem to have tentacles everywhere. 'It's like the mafia,' says Clough, who loves the *Godfather* films and frequently intones 'I'm gonna make you an offer you can't refuse' when alone with a mirror. 'Possible sources,' writes Judy. 'The docks, the airport, freight.' Forensics has identified traces of straw on some of the drugs seized in the city. This may indicate that they were transported in freight packing cases. Judy says this now, making neat lines on her chart.

'But we know all this,' drawls Tanya. 'Are there any new leads?'

'Just recapping,' says Judy briskly. 'I'm going to talk to Jimmy Olson.'

'But he's the boss's source,' protests Clough. 'Only the boss talks to Jimmy. You'll blow his cover.'

'I want to talk to all the local haulage companies,' says Judy, ignoring him.

'We've done that,' says Clough.

'Well, we'll do it again,' says Judy. 'I'm sure we're missing something.'

Clough opens his mouth to speak, but before Judy's leadership skills can be tested the door opens and the duty sergeant comes in. He looks embarrassed. 'I've got a message. Someone asking for the boss.' He looks doubtfully at Judy, who bites back a temptation to say that she is the boss now.

The message is from Randolph, now Lord, Smith. He wants to talk to someone about his father's death. He has some new evidence, he says.

'I'll go and see him,' says Judy. She looks at the unco-operative faces of her fellow police officers. 'You can come with me, Dave.'

22

Judy and Clough drive to the stables in Judy's car, a showy jeep. Usually Clough has a few jokes to make at the car's expense but today he is silent, slouched in the passenger seat, biting the skin around his fingernails. Maybe, thinks Judy, when Clough has no food to eat, he starts on his own extremities. With any luck, he'll have consumed half his arm by the time they get to Slaughter Hill.

'Still can't believe it about the boss,' says Clough, as they trundle through the country lanes. 'What did Whitcliffe say? A viral infection?'

'I don't think they know what it is,' says Judy.

'Shall I ring Michelle?' says Clough, getting out his phone. Is he trying to show her that he's on speed-dialling terms with the Nelsons? Judy doesn't have Michelle's number; she's only spoken to her once or twice.

'I wouldn't,' she says. 'She might be at the hospital or trying to get some sleep.'

'I'll text then,' says Clough. 'Bloody hell. The boss hasn't had a day off sick in his life.'

'I believe you,' says Judy. Nelson famously even hates going on holiday.

'I saved his life once,' says Clough.

'I know you did,' says Judy. She feels unaccountably sorry for him.

'Bloody hell,' says Clough again. 'I can't believe it.' And they drive on in silence through the skeletal trees.

Sunday doesn't seem to be a day of rest at the racing stables. They pass a line of horses in the lane, and when Judy parks her car by Caroline's cottage they see stable lads leading more horses into a large round building with wooden doors.

'What the hell's that?' asks Clough.

'It's a horse walker,' says Judy knowledgeably, having learnt this on her previous visit. 'They put the horses in there for exercise or to calm them down.'

They watch as the horses are led into separate compartments and move forward as the machine starts working. It's rather like being stuck in a never-ending revolving door.

'Cruel, that's what I call it,' says Clough.

'The horses love it,' says Judy.

Aside from a few curious glances, the stable lads ignore them, but, when they enter the yard Len Harris is waiting for them. His stance, jodhpur'd legs wide apart, does not look particularly welcoming.

'We're here to see Randolph Smith,' says Judy, showing her ID.

'Well, he's not here,' says Harris. 'Doesn't bother himself about the horses, Mr Randolph doesn't. He'll be up at the house.'

'Can we walk through the yard?' asks Judy.

'I'd rather you didn't,' says Harris. 'There are some sensitive animals here and they might be upset.'

It didn't seem to worry them before, thinks Judy. She doesn't like having to retreat, she feels that it makes her lose face in front of Clough. Her colleague, though, is only too happy to be away from the terrifying beasts.

'The size of them,' he keeps saying, as they take the path behind the yard wall. 'They're massive. It's not right.'

'I think they're beautiful,' says Judy. 'I wanted to be a jockey once.'

Clough laughs scornfully. 'They don't have *girl* jockeys.'

'Yes they do,' retorts Judy. 'Women jockeys have competed in the Grand National.'

'You're too big.'

'Thanks a lot.'

'You know what I mean. You have to be tiny to be a jockey.'

Judy realises that he's trying to backtrack. Nevertheless, she can't help being pleased when he steps off the path and straight into a pile of horse manure.

Randolph is waiting outside the house. Somebody must have told him to expect them. Judy, who didn't meet him on her previous visit, is surprised how handsome he is. He looks just like the hero in some Regency romance, an effect heightened by his rather long black hair and by his slightly distracted manner. Clough just thinks that he looks like a tosser.

Randolph shakes Judy's hand. 'Thanks so much for coming. Where's DCI Nelson?'

'He's not available,' says Judy. 'I'm DS Johnson and this is DS Clough.' She can see Randolph looking at Clough. Probably thinks he's in charge just because he's a man.

'Let's go into the house,' says Randolph. 'It'll be easier to talk there.' *Safer*, he seems to imply.

They follow Randolph into the house, Clough surreptitiously wiping his feet. Judy, like Nelson before her, is surprised at how modern the house is. There seem to be no heirlooms or relics of the ancient house of Smith. Everything is as shiny and characterless as if it has just stepped out of a catalogue. Randolph leads the way through a gleaming modern kitchen, all brushed steel and red cabinets (no mention of coffee), and into a study crammed with trophies and pictures of horses. Is it his father's study, wonders Judy. If so, does it seem strange to be receiving visitors here so soon after the old man's death? Or is this what Randolph Smith has been waiting for all his life?

Randolph sits himself behind the desk. 'Ma's out,' he says, though neither of them has mentioned his mother's whereabouts. 'Caroline's off somewhere with her weirdo friends. So we won't be interrupted.'

'What about your other sister?' asks Judy, remembering the disembodied voice. *For fuck's sake Randolph . . .*

'Oh, Tammy's gone hot-footing it back to London. She can't stand too much of us country types. She'll be back for the funeral.'

'Do you have a date?' ventures Judy.

'Thursday,' says Randolph, looking down at his hands. 'It's on Thursday. Thursday the twelfth.'

He lapses into silence. Judy looks at Clough.

'You said something about new evidence,' she prompts.

'Yes,' says Randolph. His eyes, which Judy had thought were black, are actually very dark blue. He runs his hand through his hair, making it stand up in an Elvis quiff.

'Look. Officer. I don't know you very well and what I have to tell you might sound strange but I promise you I'm not on drugs or . . . or having a nervous breakdown or anything. It's just that some fairly odd things have been happening and I think they might be connected to Dad's death. That's all.' He blinks at them engagingly. Judy smiles at him.

'Why don't you tell us?' she says.

'Well, it all started a few weeks ago. I was coming home after a late night and I didn't want to disturb the old dears so I came in through the back gates – where the old house used to be – and drove through the park. It was about two or three in the morning, I was just coming through the wood, where the all-weather track ends, and suddenly I saw these three men. I couldn't believe it at first but they were definitely there, in a clearing between the trees.'

'What where they doing?' asks Clough.

'Well this sounds weird, but they had long sticks with sort of skulls on the end of them and they were dancing.'

'Dancing?'

'I know it sounds crazy,' says Randolph, rather miserably. 'But there was a fire and they were dancing round it. They heard my car and looked round. One of them waved his stick at me and shouted something.'

'What did you do? Did you speak to them?'

'No. I know it sounds pathetic but I just wanted to get the hell out of there. I drove off. Left my car outside Caroline's house and went to bed. But I went back in the morning and the remains of the fire were still there. And there were these weird patterns drawn in the ashes.'

'What sort of patterns?'

'I can't really describe them. Wavy lines and circles and star shapes. But they had definitely been drawn deliberately.'

'And have you ever seen these men again?' asks Judy, ignoring Clough, who is trying to exchange significant glances.

'No, but about a week later I came home late again.' He laughs. 'I'm afraid I'm rather a nocturnal animal, Detective Sergeant. I left my car outside Caroline's, and I thought I heard something in the yard. I went to check but I thought it was just a fox or maybe that infernal cat. There was no one there but the security lights were on. And then I saw it. A dead snake nailed up over one of the horse's stalls.'

'A dead snake?'

'Yes. A grass snake, I think. I took it down and threw it in the compost heap.'

'Did you tell anyone?'

'No.' He pauses. 'The thing is, my father had a particular fear of snakes. When he was little he had this ghoulish Irish nanny who used to tell him ghost stories, but she also used to tell him stories about snakes. You know that before Saint Patrick came along Ireland used to be infested with snakes? That's what she said anyway. Anyway, she told him that, one day, a great snake – as green as poison – was going to come for him.'

'Nice sort of nanny,' says Clough.

Randolph laughs again. 'She sounds a nutcase, doesn't she, but my dad adored her. Paid her a pension until the day she died. Anyway, because of this snake phobia, I decided not to tell him. But a few days later, he told me that he'd got up at night because of a noise in the yard and he'd found a dead snake on the kitchen step.'

'Did he have any idea who might have put it there?'

'He said he didn't but the night he died, when he was delirious, he kept going on about a snake. I mean, it can't be coincidence, can it?'

Can it? Judy wonders. She remembers Nelson mentioning some letters. Didn't they say something about a Great Snake? She asks Randolph. He looks blank.

'The old man used to get so much mail. Cranks asking for money, racing fans wanting tips. He didn't say anything about any particular letters.'

'What about when Neil Topham died? Did your father say anything about letters addressed to the museum?'

'Letters to Neil? No, I don't think so. DCI Nelson said that he didn't think there was any link between the two deaths.'

If Judy knows anything about Nelson, she's willing to bet that he didn't make any such assertion. 'Never assume,' that's his motto. She and Clough must have heard it a thousand times. They look at each other.

'Thank you very much,' says Judy, standing up. 'We'll investigate further and let you know.'

She means to sound bland and rather discouraging but Randolph seizes on her words as if they are a lifeline. 'Oh, thank you so much. That means such a lot. I hope you won't think I'm a loony but I really do think that something odd is going on. In the yard too. Something isn't right. Tammy thinks I'm imagining things but Caroline agrees with me. Something just isn't right.'

'What does your mother think?'

'I don't want to worry Ma just now. She's so cut up about Dad. All this stuff about snakes and mysterious dancing men, it would just upset her.'

They walk back through the house towards the front door. On the doorstep, Clough asks, 'The snake that was nailed up over one of the horse's stables. Which horse was it?'

Randolph looks surprised. 'Oh, a fellow called The Necromancer. Good sort. Bit of a devil in his own way, though.'

This time they go back through the yard. Judy wants to show Len Harris that she can't be intimidated so easily and perhaps she wants to scare Clough a little, taking him so close to the fearsome horses. The first yard seems quiet enough, stable lads are mucking out, trundling wheelbarrows about, but again they ignore Judy and Clough completely. A man in a leather apron is examining the hooves of a large grey horse.

'Farrier,' Judy says. Clough looks blank.

'Blacksmith,' she explains.

'I wouldn't want his job. That white horse is the size of an elephant.'

'Grey,' says Judy, pausing to pat the horse's neck. 'White horses are called grey. Unless they have pink eyes, that is.'

'Don't bother trying to educate me,' says Clough, giving the grey a wide berth. 'Let's just get out of here.'

A ginger cat comes bustling up and rubs itself round Judy's legs. This reminds her of something.

'Do you think we should tell Ruth? About the boss?'

Clough thinks for a moment. 'Maybe we should. It'd sound better coming from you.'

Thanks a lot, thinks Judy, though she agrees with him. After all, isn't bad news her speciality?

They are passing through into the second yard when, suddenly, there is a terrible noise from one of the stables. A dreadful clattering and banging accompanied by the spine-chilling screams of an animal in pain. Judy runs towards the sound but her way is blocked by Len Harris.

'No you don't.'

'What's going on?' demands Judy, slightly breathless.

'One of the horses has cast himself. It often happens. Especially if they've been flown over recently.'

Judy tried to look past Harris into the stable. She gets a fleeting glimpse of a horse on the ground, an anguished rolling eye.

'This happened before. When I was here a few days ago. I remember it.'

'Like I say, it's not unusual. Billy!' He shouts to a passing stable boy. 'Can you show these people out?' And he turns and shuts himself in with the horse.

Judy hesitates. Harris was undeniably rude and her detective instincts tell her to stay and discover what's going on. But Clough is already on his way out and, after all, the welfare of the horses is not her primary concern right now. Telling herself that she'll call the RSPCA, ask them to pay a discreet visit, she follows Billy out through the main yard. He's a thin lad, about sixteen, with spots and a pronounced squint.

'What happened to the horse called Fancy?' Judy asks. 'I saw him when I was here last.'

Billy's eyes shoot, alarmingly, in two opposite directions. 'I've never heard that name.'

'Fancy,' repeats Judy. 'Four-year-old colt. He had colic.'

Billy shakes his head. 'I'm sorry. I don't know all the horses. Here's the main gate now. I've got to get back to work.'

In the car, accompanied by a pungent smell of dung, Clough explains why all the Smith family are clinically insane. 'I mean Rudolph, Randolph, whatever he's called. All that crap about strange men dancing in the woods. Loco, that's what he is.'

'I thought it was quite convincing,' says Judy.

'I'm surprised at you,' says Clough. 'Never thought you'd fall for all that Hugh Grant crap. *It's just that some fairly odd things have been happening.*' He puts on an accent that's halfway between Prince Charles and Julian Clary.

'He doesn't look like Hugh Grant,' says Judy. 'More like Robert Pattinson from the *Twilight* films.'

'Never heard of 'em,' says Clough.

'They're for young people,' says Judy.

Clough grunts and continues with the attack. 'What

about the incredible reappearing snake? Someone's having a laugh here.'

Judy thinks of something Cathbad told her about a saint who was meant to appear in two places at once. That's the thing about Cathbad; you never know what he's going to say next. The opposite of Darren. Thinking of the missed family lunch, she sighs, feeling even guiltier than usual.

'Seriously,' Clough persists. 'You don't think there's anything in all this voodoo nonsense?'

'I don't know what I think,' says Judy. 'But clearly someone was trying to frighten Lord Smith. The letters, the dead snakes. Someone had a grudge against him and now he's dead. That's worth investigating.'

'It was a heart attack,' says Clough. 'The pathologist's report said so.'

'But what gave him the heart attack?' says Judy. 'That's what I want to know.'

'Have they gone?'

Randolph looks up. 'I didn't hear you come in.'

Romilly Smith sits opposite her son and smiles up at him. She is wearing jeans and an old jumper but still manages to look effortlessly elegant. Randolph, knowing that she has probably spent the night in some squalid bedsit discussing factory farming, can't help feeling reluctant admiration.

'They've gone,' he says.

'Was it Nelson? He was quite bright, I thought. Not your usual policeman.'

'No, the woman. Judy something. And another man. Rather an oaf but good-looking, if you like that sort of thing.'

'What were they doing here?'

Randolph hesitates. He hasn't told his mother about the men in the wood. Not, as he told Judy, because it would upset her. On the contrary, she would be far too interested. She'd want to go and join them, especially if they were plotting trouble of any kind.

He shrugs. 'Just routine enquiries.'

Romilly loses interest.

'Is there any coffee?' she says, yawning neatly, like a cat. 'I'm exhausted.' She sounds like a debutante complaining about flower-arranging fatigue.

'I'll make you some,' says Randolph. 'I didn't want to offer any to the Old Bill.'

'Old Bill,' Romilly smiles. 'How sweet.'

'Why, what does your lot call them?'

'The enemy.'

'Really, Mum, you sound very childish sometimes.' Randolph gets up and walks to the window. He can see a line of horses galloping up the hill, their manes and tails streaming out. That's the way to spend a Sunday morning, riding like a demon with the wind in your face. Not stuck in an office having a ridiculous conversation with your loony-leftie mother.

'What's childish about animal rights?' snaps Romilly. 'They suffer because we're too greedy and selfish to do anything about it. Universities use them for their ghastly experiments. This place,' she gestures towards the window, 'exploits them. Hundreds of horses die steeple-chasing every year but no one gives a damn because the bookies are making money.'

This place, thinks Randolph, gives you a socking great expense account, enough to finance any amount of designer direct action. He has been looking through his father's accounts, but now's not the time to mention that. He is thinking of something else his mother said.

'The university,' he says. 'Are you planning something?'

Romilly smiles. 'It's better if you don't know.'

'Be careful, Mum.'

'I'm always careful. Now make the coffee, there's a good boy.'

23

Ruth has had a perfectly lovely Sunday. After a leisurely breakfast, she and Max and Kate (and Claudia) had gone for a walk on the Saltmarsh. Claudia had rushed through the grass, putting up flocks of snipe, plunging knee deep into murky pools, barking excitedly at the sky.

'She likes it here,' said Max.

Kate had been fairly excited too. When they reached the beach, she ran towards the sea with her arms outstretched. The tide was coming in and Kate had been delighted when a wave broke over her wellingtons. 'Again! Again!' she had shouted.

'That's the thing about the sea,' said Max. 'It does it again and again.'

'The relentless tide,' said Ruth, quoting Erik. 'The unending ebb and flow.'

'That too,' grinned Max, throwing a stick for Claudia.

On the way back, Kate had been tired so Max had carried her on his shoulders. A very male way to carry a child, thought Ruth. She never does it that way, preferring to hoist Kate onto her hip, but Cathbad always does. She is sure that Nelson carried his eldest daughters like this when they were young but he has never had the chance with Kate. But she wasn't going to think about Nelson . . .

They drove to the Phoenix for lunch. The Phoenix is the pub near Max's Swaffham dig, the scene of much drinking and carousing that summer, two years ago. Max insists on going to see the site, striding up the steep hill with Kate riding like a Queen. That's the only problem with Max, Ruth remembered. He loves walking up hills. Nelson is a strider too, always in a hurry, never looking behind to check that she is following. But she wasn't going to think about Nelson.

To the untutored eye there is little evidence of a Roman settlement in the grey undulating landscape, but Max was looking at a bustling garrison town with Italianate villas, a market place and a road leading directly to the sea. Ruth, arriving breathlessly at the top of the hill, saw it too. She also saw children's bodies buried under walls, a skull in a well, the Goddess Hecate with her two spectral hounds. The Goddess of the crossroads. Luckily Claudia, distinctly unghostlike, provided a distraction by chasing a rabbit.

'Claudia!' shouted Max.

'Perfectly trained,' observed Ruth as Claudia, taking absolutely no notice of her master, disappeared over the horizon.

'I've been taking her to obedience classes,' said Max ruefully. 'We got a medal for trying hard.'

Kate laughed, tugging Max's hair.

Claudia arrived back in time for the descent to the

Phoenix. Ruth and Max ate roast beef and Yorkshire pudding and even Kate managed three roast potatoes. After lunch, in the late afternoon, they stood outside the pub, Ruth holding Kate, Max with a struggling Claudia on the lead.

'When will I see you again?' asked Max. 'What about next weekend?'

Ruth had been delighted that Max wanted to see her again, that he was making all the running, but, all the same, next weekend seemed a little too soon. 'I think my parents are coming,' she extemporised. 'Maybe the weekend after?'

'Sounds good,' Max had said, leaning forward to kiss her cheek. 'Keep in touch.'

And now, driving back through the twilight, Ruth feels free to enjoy the thought that she actually seems to be in a relationship with Max. A proper grown-up relationship with a proper grown-up man who isn't married to someone else. A weekend relationship suits her perfectly. She likes having her house to herself all week, not having to cook for another person or wear her chillier, more glamorous, nightwear. But it would be lovely to have someone to see at weekends, to go to plays or to the cinema, to walk with on the beach, to sit and watch *Antiques Roadshow* with on a Sunday evening. And to have sex with, of course.

It's nearly dark when she reaches the Saltmarsh. The clocks went back last week and now, at four-thirty, it's almost night. She has been chatting to Kate all through the journey, trying to keep her awake, and her efforts have been rewarded. Kate, though definitely sleepy, is still bright-eyed, exclaiming happily whenever Ruth starts a new verse of *The Wheels on the Bus*. What a sexist song, thinks Ruth, why do the mothers do nothing but chatter and the fathers nothing but nod? Kate won't be able to accuse her mother of chattering – sleeping with strange men perhaps but not chattering. Ruth stops outside the cottage. Bob's car isn't there. It's strange how quickly she has got used to having neighbours. Now she feels slightly nervous at being here on her own, on the edge of the world. Ridiculous, she tells herself, you were alone for nearly two years and nothing happened to you. But the wind is howling in from the sea and Ruth clutches Kate tightly as she gets her out of the car. You're getting soft, she tells herself.

Kate screams, a cry of real terror. Ruth reels round and sees a monster lurching towards her through the darkness. A hideous misshapen figure, ink black, with a giant head, like a goblin or a minotaur. Ruth shields Kate with her body, unable to move further. The creature looms nearer and nearer. Where's her phone? She has to ring Nelson. Oh God, it's still in the car. She and Kate are going to be murdered and no one will hear them scream. Nelson will investigate and then, perhaps, he'll be sorry for abandoning them. Her parents will pray for her soul. Cathbad will light a bonfire in her honour. The figure is getting nearer, making hideous squelching sounds. It has come from the sea, it's one of Erik's malevolent water spirits, come to put its slimy fingers round her throat and drag her back into the depths.

Suddenly they are flooded with light. The security light has come on and the monster has resolved itself into a young man wearing a wet suit and carrying a surfboard on his shoulders.

'Hallo,' he says. 'I hope I didn't startle you. I'm Cameron. Sammy and Ed's son.'

Sammy and Ed? Who the hell are they? Then Ruth remembers. The weekenders. Her other next-door neighbours. And this massive creature must be the little boy she remembers trekking over the marshes with his inflatable boat. Well, he obviously still likes the sea.

'Just come down for a couple of days surfing with some pals,' he says. 'Hope we won't disturb you.'

He has a very posh accent, far posher than his parents, but he seems friendly enough. Who on earth would go surfing in November? A public schoolboy called Cameron, that's who.

'No problem,' she says. 'Make as much noise as you like. You won't disturb me.'

'Dada,' says Kate.

Inside, she makes Kate some supper (though she isn't very hungry after the roast potatoes) and gives her a bath. Sitting in her cot, fluffy-haired, clutching her bottle, Kate looks angelic, the sort of baby who is going to sleep for eight hours without a murmur. What will Kate think if Max starts visiting regularly? She seems to like him but will she resent him taking up Ruth's time? What if Max and Ruth break up and Kate misses him terribly? What if Claudia savages Flint or vice versa? Stop it, she tells herself. The relationship hasn't started yet and you're worrying about it ending. From next door she can hear the soothing thump of rock music.

Maybe it's *Guns 'n' Roses* or Ruth's minor key version of *Wheels on the Bus* but Kate is soon fast asleep. Ruth tiptoes out of the room. Six o'clock, just time to catch the end of *Time Team*. Maybe she can have a glass of wine too. She realises that she is smiling.

The phone rings. Ruth answers, still smiling.

'Ruth. It's Judy. It's about the boss. About Nelson.'

She isn't sure when she stopped smiling. She just knows she isn't smiling now.

'What about him?'

'He's ill. In hospital. It looks pretty serious. I thought you'd want to know.'

Why, Ruth wonders. Why did Judy think she'd want to know? As far as Judy knows, Ruth and Nelson are just acquaintances, professional colleagues who've worked together on a couple of cases. Why this urgent phone call on a Sunday night? But, of course, she does want to know.

'What's wrong with him?' Her voice comes out in a whisper.

'No one really knows. Cloughie's just spoken to Michelle. They think it could be a virus, one of those that's resistant to antibiotics.'

'Is he—' Ruth stops, afraid to go on. Judy's voice is kind, professionally concerned.

'He's in a coma but his internal organs seem to be shutting down. It doesn't look good. Michelle and the girls are with him.'

Michelle and the girls. From a long way off, Ruth hears her voice saying, 'Thanks for telling me Judy. I've got to go now. Bye.'

Ruth puts the phone down and realises that she is shaking. In all her worst fears, in all her most fevered 'what ifs', she has never imagined this. She had thought that Michelle and Nelson might move away, even that Nelson might be killed in the line of duty, never that he would succumb to something as prosaic as a virus. It's like Hercules dying of a common cold. It just can't happen. She sits down, stands up again, switches on the TV, switches it off again. What can she do? She can't exactly ring Michelle or turn up at the hospital. She tries to remember the last thing that she said to Nelson. It was at the museum, wasn't it? Nelson had just been winding up their interview when Danforth Smith had barged in. 'We've finished, haven't we?' she'd said to Nelson. And he'd answered, 'Yes. We've finished.' So is that it? Finished. Over. Can there really be a world without Nelson? She thinks of her daughter sleeping upstairs. Now Kate may never have a chance to get to know her father. Ruth realises that she is crying.

The phone rings and she snatches it up. She steels herself to hear Judy saying, compassionately, 'It's over, he's gone' or any of the hundreds of platitudinous things people say to avoid telling you that someone is dead. But it's Shona. Ruth feels quite weak with relief.

'Hi Ruth! What are you doing?'

'Nothing much. Watching TV.' Not for anything in the world is she going to tell Shona about Nelson.

'Cool. Can I come over? Phil's got the flu and he's being such a man about it. I'm so bored. I haven't been out of the house all day. It's hell being pregnant.'

But to Ruth now it seems like heaven. When she'd been pregnant, Nelson had been alive and well and Kate had been safe, safe inside Ruth.

'I'm sorry,' she hears herself saying, 'but I've got a lot of work to do.'

'OK. Not to worry.' Shona sounds disappointed, then her voice picks up again. 'Did you go to that Aborigine conference? Phil was invited but he thought it would be too weird.'

'It was weird. Weird but interesting.'

'Are you sure you're not free for a quick chat?'

'Sorry Shona, I'd love to see you but I've got a ton of essays to mark.'

'All right then. See you soon.'

'Bye. Hope Phil feels better.'

Outside, the wind continues to blow. The front door rattles and she hears her dustbin falling over. She remembers the time when she was lost on the Saltmarsh and Nelson came to save her. He had found his way along the hidden paths, the secret crossing places, and he had come to rescue her. She remembers the time when he had thrown himself into a freezing river for her sake. She'd taken him for granted, Nelson and his lunatic bravery. What would it be like not to have that presence in her life, that massive, exasperating presence? Although she has only known Nelson for a few years, she just can't imagine it.

The knock on the door freezes her with terror. She thinks of other unexpected summonses: Erik, Cathbad, David, even Nelson himself, that dreadful night when they found Scarlet's body. Who is it this time? The reaper whose name is death? The nameless creature from *The Monkey's Paw*? Maybe it's Cameron, come to invite her for a spliff and a talk about the meaning of life.

She opens the door.

It's Michelle.

24

'Can I come in?' says Michelle.

She looks terrible – unmade-up, hair lank, clothes crumpled – but she is also, mysteriously, more beautiful than ever. Ruth thinks that she looks other-worldly, a creature of the night, an ageless picture of feminine grief.

'Of course.' Ruth stands back.

'Have you heard?' asks Michelle. 'About Harry?'

'Yes,' says Ruth.

Michelle comes in and sits on the sofa. Flint appears from nowhere and tries to sit on her lap. Ruth shoos him away.

'Can I get you some tea or coffee?' Ruth is aware of how ridiculous she sounds, but Michelle must have come straight from the hospital. Maybe she hasn't eaten all day.

'No thank you,' says Michelle. She looks down at her hands, long elegant fingers with a huge diamond on the wedding finger. How had the young PC Nelson ever afforded a ring like that?

Ruth sits opposite, waiting. There's nothing else she can do.

'Harry's in a coma,' says Michelle at last. 'Did you hear that?'

'Yes,' says Ruth. 'Judy rang me.'

'Judy? Oh, the policewoman. What else did she say?'

'Just that Nelson ... Harry ... was very ill and no one knew what it was.'

'Yes. They think it might be a virus but they're not sure. He's not responding to anything at the moment. It's terrible, they're nursing him in masks because they don't know if it's contagious or not.' She stops and takes a deep breath. 'He doesn't recognise anyone, not me or the girls. It's as if we can't get through to him.'

'I'm sorry,' says Ruth, inadequately.

Michelle looks at her. Ruth thinks it might be the first time that they have been alone together. She is struck again both by the classical purity of Michelle's face and by the expression in her eyes. Something about Michelle's expression makes Ruth feel very scared indeed.

'Do you know why I've come?' asks Michelle.

Ruth shakes her head.

'I want you to go to him.'

'What?'

Michelle looks at Ruth and her eyes are huge, wet with tears.

'I want you to go to see Harry,' she says. 'He misses you.'

Ruth's voice sounds as if it's coming from a long way away. 'He doesn't,' she says.

Once again Michelle looks at her with that awful shining simplicity, 'Oh, he's not in love with you, I know that. But he does care about you. He hates not being able to see you. He's . . . he's used to me. I thought . . . if he saw you . . .'

Ruth's eyes also fill with tears but she says nothing.

'I thought, if he could just see you, hear your voice . . .'

Ruth looks at Michelle, who is watching her with those big, strangely innocent, eyes. At this moment she really feels that she loves Michelle, loves her more than she ever loved Nelson. But it doesn't change her answer.

'I can't. I'm sorry.'

'Why not?'

'I'm afraid. Nelson's ill, no one knows what it is. I'm afraid of carrying the infection back to Kate.'

Michelle stands up. She is taller than Ruth but now she seems ten foot high, a vision of implacable justice.

'I was wrong about you, Ruth. I thought you loved him.'

Ruth says nothing.

'All the things I've thought about you, I never thought that you didn't love him. It's funny, it didn't make me hate you. It made me think that we had something in common. I love him. I love him more than anything.'

That summer, the long cold summer when Nelson finally chose Michelle over her, had been one of the hardest times of Ruth's life. She was on her own, everyone seemed to be on holiday: Shona and Phil in Tuscany, the Nelsons (she'd heard) in Florida, Cathbad in a monastery on Iona. Ruth had resisted an invitation from her parents to join them at a Christian camp on the Isle of Wight. She had spent her time going for long walks with Kate in her buggy, down the shingle paths of the Saltmarsh, along the seafront at Cromer, through the streets of King's Lynn. She would have lost weight if she hadn't spent the evenings eating chocolate biscuits.

But through the grey lonely days and endless nights, Ruth was stalked by fear. She let herself be consumed by this fear, surrender to it, almost seemed to revel in it, spending hours searching the internet, seeking out information that could feed the fear. And the fear was illness, specifically Kate becoming ill. In the early part of the summer, the news had been full of the swine flu scare. Ruth, feverishly searching websites at night, kept coming upon stories of healthy babies, happily playing one minute, critically ill in hospital the next. Some of the babies died. Ruth, slightly unhinged by solitude, did not take in the fact that the children who had died usually had some existing medical condition. All she knew was that Kate might be taken away from her. She felt Kate's forehead constantly, invested in a thermometer that went in the ear and used it so often that Kate developed an ear infection and howled all night. Ruth, pacing the floors with her sick child, felt herself to be literally on the edge. She wasn't sure that she could cope any more. She thought about walking into the sea with Kate in her arms, surrendering to Erik's relentless tide. She would have prayed if she'd known how.

But things got better. Friends returned from holiday, swine flu disappeared from the news, Ruth let whole days go by without taking Kate's temperature. Term started and she was able to immerse herself in work. A beautiful autumn succeeded the dreary summer. But when she had heard Judy's words, 'They think it could be a virus, one of those that's resistant to antibiotics,' it had all come flooding back. Nelson is dying of a mystery virus and now Michelle wants her to expose Kate to this danger. If it was only her own safety, Ruth thinks that she would sacrifice it willingly for Nelson. After all, he has risked his life to save her. But she has Kate to think about and she is all Kate has.

'I'm sorry,' she says again.

Michelle sweeps to the door. 'Goodbye Ruth. I hope you won't feel too guilty.'

A forlorn hope. As the sound of Michelle's car disappears into the night, Ruth wonders if it is actually possible to die of guilt.

25

Ruth is relieved when morning comes. She doesn't think that she slept for more than a few minutes all night. But those few minutes were enough for terrible dreams: Nelson drowning, his hand stretched out to her, Erik's voice calling from the sea, Cathbad turning into a snake, hissing 'sleep little three eyes,' and Kate, always Kate: Kate burning with fever, Kate lying dead in her cot, Kate lost in the dark, searching for her. When Kate's imperious crying wakes her at six, Ruth is only too glad to get up. She showers with Kate in her arms and goes downstairs to get on with the day. She is so tired that her feet seem to be stuck to the floor and every step feels like uprooting them. Coffee briefly gives her enough energy to collect her rucksack and Kate's nappy bag and get them both in the car, but by the time she reaches Sandra's, great waves of weariness are breaking over her.

'You don't look too good,' says Sandra. 'Got the flu?'

The flu. People like Sandra make illness sound so normal, an irritation, something to be coped with and got over. But to Ruth, the slightest sniffle from Kate is the sound of impending death. Why does she feel like this? Is it because of her parents who, after they found God, also lost all faith in contemporary medicine? 'God will provide,' became their mantra. Ruth blames her parents bitterly for not having her vaccinated against measles, resulting in a nightmare few weeks at university. Her parents' imaginations also became markedly more apocalyptic, their conversation littered with references to death, judgement, heaven and hell. The devil became a regular correspondent. Is this why Ruth sometimes feels that some terrible catastrophe is just around the corner, or is this just normal paranoia?

More coffee gets her through her first lecture and tutorial, but by lunchtime she is flagging. She breaks her own rule and keeps her phone on when she's with her students. Every second she expects to hear Judy's voice, 'I'm sorry . . .' Or perhaps she won't ring at all. Perhaps she'll just send a text massage. *N dead* ☹. Maybe no one will bother to tell her and Ruth will have to struggle through this day and the next not knowing whether Nelson is alive or dead. She buys a sandwich from the canteen but can't be bothered to eat it. She sits at her desk staring at her poster of Harrison Ford, the archaeologist's pin up. She feels as if she's in an Indiana Jones movie, running desperately through traps and obstacles, each one more cunning and improbable than the last. Should she go to see Nelson? On one level, her fear is completely irrational. Kate could easily catch a virus at Sandra's, or at the doctor's, or at one of the soft play areas that Ruth resorts to on rainy Saturdays.

But that is different from Ruth herself passing on the infection, giving her child up to the danger, like Abraham taking Isaac to be sacrificed. Oh, bugger her parents and their Bible stories. She puts her head down on the desk.

'Ruth!'

Ruth jerks her head up. It's Cathbad.

'I've just heard,' he says.

Like Michelle – disconcertingly like Michelle – Cathbad looks stunned, as if he's been involved in a car crash. This, and the fact that he's dressed in ordinary clothes, has the effect of making him look diminished. Cathbad's not a large man but he usually dominates any room he's in; now he sinks into Ruth's visitor's chair looking almost like a *student*.

'Who told you?' asks Ruth.

'Judy.'

That figures. 'Is there any news?' Ruth asks.

'No. He's still in a coma. The doctors are completely baffled.'

Ruth allows herself to relax very slightly. He's not dead. Nelson's still alive, and while he's alive he'll be fighting, whatever the doctors say.

'I don't think anyone knows what it is,' she says.

Cathbad looks up, his eyes wide. 'I do,' he says.

Ruth almost laughs. 'What do you mean?'

'I know what's wrong with Nelson,' says Cathbad. 'And, if you think about it, I think you do too.'

Ruth stares. Perhaps tiredness is making her stupider than usual but she really has no idea what Cathbad is talking about. Since when has he been a medical expert?

'What's wrong with him then?'

'He's been cursed,' says Cathbad.

Ruth does laugh now, but inwardly she feels angry with Cathbad. This isn't the time for his mystical new age nonsense. Nelson is ill. He's in hospital. Nothing else matters. Then she looks at Cathbad and her anger fades. He really does look very upset. She supposes that, in his way, he's trying to help.

'Do you mean cursed by the bishop?' she asks, thinking of Ted. 'Vex not my bones and all that?'

'No,' says Cathbad, as if this is a ridiculous idea. 'I think he's been cursed by Bob.'

'By *Bob*?'

'Yes. Do you remember the evening at your house? Fireworks night? I said that Bob ought to point the bone at Lord Smith. Well, I think he did. That night, Lord Smith died.'

And you were nearby, thinks Ruth, visiting his daughter. Caroline who loves Uluru Rock and the red heart of Australia. 'But why would Bob curse Nelson?' she asks.

Cathbad frowns. 'I don't know. Maybe he was angry because the police hadn't been able to get his ancestors back. Maybe Nelson was just near Smith at the time of the curse. Maybe it backfired on him.'

'Backfired on him?'

'That can happen,' says Cathbad, 'with a very powerful curse, and Bob is a proper shaman, a Wirinun they're called. He has pretty devastating powers. Maybe he's cursed everyone to do with the museum.'

'What about me?' says Ruth. 'I was at the museum. I actually handled the bones.'

'Oh, he's put a circle of protection round you,' said Cathbad. 'He told me so.'

Ruth supposes that she should be grateful but she just feels disorientated, as if she is still in one of her livid dreams. How can she be sitting here with Cathbad, discussing curses and witch doctors as if they are everyday things? She realises that Cathbad is still speaking, '... Bob cursed Danforth Smith and he died. I don't know how but Nelson somehow got involved in that curse, but he's not dead. He's lost. He's wandering. He's lost in the Dreaming.'

Ruth remembers the dark, the fire, the sound of the singing sticks. *Fire is our gateway to the Dreaming.* Was it really only two days ago?

'Well, what can we do about it?' she asks. 'If Nelson's stuck in Dreamtime or whatever?'

'I'm going to go and get him back,' says Cathbad.

'What do you mean "go and get him back"?' Irritation – and fear – makes Ruth's voice sharp.

'Just that. I'm going to enter the Dreaming.'

'How?'

'You don't need to know the details. I'm going to take drugs, hallucogens, I'm going to burn eucalyptus leaves, I'm going to chant, I'm going to chew certain herbs. Then, I believe, I will enter the Dreaming and I'll find Nelson.'

'What if you don't? What if you die of a bloody drugs overdose?'

'Ruth,' Cathbad looks at her kindly. 'I know you're scared but it's OK. I know what I'm doing.'

This, Ruth considers, is the single least reassuring state-ment she has ever heard.

'Cathbad.' She, in her turn, tries to sound soothing, tries to channel Judy's professional voice. 'You're upset. We're all upset. Jesus, I still can't believe it. Nelson's the last person in the world I thought would ever get ill like this. But he's in hospital. He's in the best place. And he's tough. He'll pull through.' Say it enough times, she tells herself, and you'll begin to believe it.

'There's nothing the hospital can do,' says Cathbad. 'This is beyond modern medicine.'

'Listen to yourself!' shouts Ruth. 'Do you know how insane you sound? This isn't about curses or . . . or . . . Dreaming. Nelson is *sick*. He's caught something. Can't you, for once in your life, realise that it's *nothing to do with you*.'

There is a silence. Ruth wonders if Phil, in the next-door office, heard her yelling. He'll be round in a second, if so. But Phil does not materialise.

'I want to do it at your house,' says Cathbad.

'What?'

'I think the energy would be better on the Saltmarsh. And it's near Bob, I might absorb some of his power.'

'Are you saying that you want to come over to my house to have a drugs trip? In front of my daughter? What if you die? It'll traumatise her for life.'

'It'd traumatise me too,' says Cathbad reasonably. Then he smiles. He has a singularly disarming smile.

'Please Ruth. I know you'd do anything to help Harry.'

* * *

Nelson is in the dark. He can hear the sea. Is it Brighton or Blackpool? The present or the past? There are voices in the water, in the surf and the backwash, but he can't hear what they're saying yet. There are lights too, objects just out of his reach. He hears singing and thinks it might be his mother, her Irish voice full of sadness. Dolores of the sorrows. The black coach pulled by six black horses. The coachman knocks three times on your door. Does this mean that he's dying? It doesn't hurt if so, but something's wrong. He can't die yet. He's got things to do. His children. He struggles to remember their names. There was once a king and he had three daughters. Rebecca, Laura. Rapunzel, Rapunzel, let down your hair. Kate. Kiss me Kate. When you hear the banshee, you know your time is up.

And then, through the darkness, he sees a boat coming towards him. A boat that looks as if it is made of stone. And there's a man on the boat, a man with long silvery hair. He has a band around his head almost like a crown. His eyes are blue, terrifyingly blue.

'Nelson,' he says, in a strange sing-song accent that is like the sea itself. 'Raise up your hand to me and I will save you.'

But the black tide carries him away again.

As soon as she finishes her last tutorial, Ruth packs up her bag and makes for the door. Cathbad has told her that he'll be round at nine, 'with all that's necessary'. Is she really going to let Cathbad do this ridiculous thing? Is she going to let him dance round a bonfire, then go upstairs and take drugs? Under her roof? What if Cathbad dies and she'll be known forever as the university lecturer whose colleague died in her house after a drug-fuelled orgy? What if he dies and she never sees him again? What if Cathbad and Nelson both die and Kate is left without a father figure of any kind, apart from Flint and the postman?

But she can't just sit around and do nothing. She may have refused to help Nelson but she can't stand in the way of Cathbad's efforts, however lunatic they may be. Is it because, over the years, she has absorbed enough of Cathbad's mumbo-jumbo to think that it's possible for there actually to be a dream world where souls wander between life and death? She hears Erik's voice. *One step the wrong way and you're dead, straight to hell. Keep on the path and it'll lead you to heaven.*

'Ruth! You look like you're in another world.'

It's Shona, glowing and beautiful in a purple smock over white jeans. Her hair, almost orange in the afternoon sunlight, clashes brilliantly with the Imperial purple. She looks like a stained-glass window come to life.

'I just came in to get some books for Phil. He's still suffering with this flu, poor darling.'

So that was why Phil didn't come charging in earlier. Still struck down with terminal man flu.

'Are you OK, Ruth? You look awfully pale.'

Perhaps because Shona looks so vibrant and full of life while she feels so low, Ruth has a sudden desire to tell Shona everything.

'It's Nelson . . .' she begins.

She tells Shona about Nelson's illness and Michelle's visit. When she gets to the part about seeing Nelson, Shona says, as Ruth knew she would.

'But why would Michelle want you to go to see Nelson?'

Ruth says nothing. She knows Shona will work it out sooner or later.

'Ruth! Nelson's not . . .?'

Ruth nods.

'Bloody hell.' Shona sits down heavily on Ruth's visitor's chair.

'Nelson's Kate's father?'

'Yes.'

'And his wife knows?'

'She found out at the christening.'

'How?'

Funny, Ruth has never asked this question. 'I don't know.'

'God, Ruth,' Shona is staring at her now, half-resentfully, half almost admiringly. 'Nelson. I'd never have guessed. I thought you didn't like him much.'

'He has his moments,' says Ruth drily.

'Did you have an affair with him?'

'It was just one night,' says Ruth. 'That's all it takes.'

'One night? Jesus, Ruth, why didn't you tell me?'

'I didn't want to tell anyone.'

'Does Cathbad know?'

'I think he suspects.'

'What about Phil?'

'Please don't tell Phil!'

It comes out almost as a scream. Ruth realises that she is very near tears.

'All right,' says Shona soothingly. 'I won't tell Phil. So now Nelson's wife wants you to visit him. Bloody hell, that's big of her.'

Ruth lowers her eyes. 'I know.'

'She must really love him.'

'She does.'

Shona looks at her curiously. 'Why did you say no?'

'It's Kate,' says Ruth. 'I'm scared of her getting sick.'

'But she wasn't asking you to take Kate, was she? Babies aren't allowed in hospitals. I know that because Phil's boys won't be allowed in to see me when I have the baby. It's a bit harsh, I think.'

'I know but I might carry some germs back to her, infect her. No one knows what's wrong with Nelson.'

Ruth looks almost timidly at her friend. She half wants Shona to tell her that she's doing the right thing. Ruth has slept with another woman's husband and is now refusing to move a muscle to save that man's life but she's still doing the right thing. The other half of her wants Shona to say that she's being ridiculous and to order her a minicab to the hospital.

But Shona is still looking at her as if she has never seen her before.

'Michelle must really love him,' she says again.

Judy is sitting at Nelson's desk. Dead man's shoes, she thinks morbidly. But Nelson's still alive and where there's life there's hope and all those other irritating, but none the less oddly reassuring, clichés. It's darkest before dawn. Where did she hear that one recently? Got to get worse before it gets better, she tells herself savagely, looking at the transcript of her interview with Randolph Smith. Does she really think that there's anything suspicious about Danforth Smith's death? She has requested a copy of the death certificate. Cause of death: I Myocardial infarction II diabetes mellitus. Seems straightforward enough, heart attack complicated by an existing medical condition, but what about all that spooky stuff with the snakes? Did something happen that night that literally scared Lord Smith to death?

She thinks about Randolph. She did find him attractive, in a theoretical way, though she would never admit as much to Clough. He's not really her type though; she's never been one for posh men. But then Cathbad's not exactly Judy's type either, which doesn't explain why she can't keep away from him; why, within seconds of meeting, they are ripping each other's clothes off despite promising each other solemnly that it's never going to happen again. Judy can't explain it and she doesn't try. For the past few months she's been wandering around in an erotic trance, knowing that she's headed for disaster. And now this news about Nelson ... Cathbad had been devastated when she told him, unlike Ruth, who had seemed strangely cold. She wonders, fearfully, whether Nelson's illness will be the final catalyst that will send the whole edifice of her life tumbling to the ground. The last straw, the last nail in the coffin, and various other clichés.

She ought to have another team meeting but she can't face it just yet. Clough and Tanya are trudging round the haulage yards, Rocky is out on a course designed to turn him (not before time) into a 'twenty-first-century police professional'. Only Tom Henty is in the building and Judy is rather afraid of Tom, having been told once too often how he was out on the beat before she was even born. Maybe she should go back to the yard and confront Len Harris. It would be easier without Clough cringing at the horses and putting his flat foot in the horse muck. She allows herself a slight smile, reliving the episode. Then she stops, smile frozen on her face. She sees the offending pile of manure, hears Clough's furious cursing and she sees something else too, sees it for the first time.

She knows what's going on at Slaughter Hill Stables.

26

Night. Michelle sits at Nelson's bedside. Rebecca and Laura have gone home, exhausted by their late-night summons and the emotion of the day. But Michelle sits on, watching the red and green lights of the machines, looking at a cobweb high on the corniced ceiling. A few miles away, on the very edge of the coast, Kate, too, is asleep, unaware of her father's epic struggle. She has had a fairly epic struggle herself, as she hadn't wanted to go to bed while Cathbad was in the house and available for fun. But Ruth had, for once, insisted, and Kate now sleeps fretfully in her white cot with the oyster shell dreamcatcher over-head. And in the garden, watched from an upstairs window by a frightened and sceptical Ruth, Cathbad burns branches and walks slowly round the flames.

Nelson's eyes move under his closed eyelids. What is he seeing, Michelle wonders. Nelson has always been so impatient, so incapable of staying still, it seems impossible that he can just be lying there, tied down by wires and drips and monitors. Michelle doesn't know when she last watched him sleep. It has always been Nelson who gets up first, who goes downstairs to make her a cup of tea. He likes the early mornings, he always says. On Sunday mornings he used to watch the early edition of *Match of the Day*. Michelle remembers the theme music, that wonderfully nostalgic jaunty tune filtering upstairs to where she lay in bed, comfortably conscious of the hot tea by her side and the sun streaming in through the curtains. When they were young, the girls used to watch *Match of the Day* too; both had been enthusiastic Blackpool fans for a while. In recent years, though, they had slept in, leaving Nelson in solitary splendour with the TV, the *Mail on Sunday* and a mug of strong tea. He probably liked it better that way.

She hums the *Match of the Day* theme softly. What will it take to make him open his eyes? A guest appearance by the Blackpool first team? Michelle resolves to ring the manager tomorrow. Nelson's mother is on her way down from Blackpool. A visit from Maureen is enough to wake anyone up. Michelle likes her mother-in-law but she's rather dreading spending any time in her company, both of them eaten up with worry over their beloved Harry. Maureen is always forthright with her opinions, telling Laura that she's too thin and Michelle that she spends too much on clothes. Michelle is not looking forward to Maureen's first meeting with the masked nursing staff.

'Wake up Harry,' whispers Michelle. 'Your mum's on the way.' Do Nelson's eyelids flicker slightly? He loves his mum but a few days in her company are usually enough for him. They've had some monumental rows over the years. Michelle always used to try to act as the peace-maker but Grainne, Nelson's sister, once pointed out that as Harry and his mother both obviously enjoyed the arguments, why spoil their fun? After that Michelle tended to ignore the shouting and accusations of ingratitude (her) and terminal interfering (him). She herself is usually in her mother-in-law's good books (spending habits aside) and Maureen often calls on God to witness that Harry does not deserve such a wife. Maureen and God are on very good terms and the Almighty can always be called upon to take Maureen's side in any disagreement.

Should Michelle call in a priest for Harry? He was brought up a Catholic but has hardly been near a church for years. There's Father Hennessey, whom Nelson befriended on an earlier case, but Michelle has no idea how to get hold of him. Still, if it helps, she is prepared to call on the Pope himself. She wonders if Maureen will appear with a priest in tow, she usually has a tame one somewhere. Michelle knows that it is really fear that is stopping her from ringing the nearest Catholic church. A priest would mean that Nelson is really ill, perhaps dying. 'It could go either way,' a doctor had said to her earlier. But Michelle can only conceive of one way. She won't let herself think about the alternative.

The fire is out. Cathbad walks slowly towards the house. He is wearing his cloak and it swishes gently over the dead leaves. His face is intent, his eyes almost closed. Has he already taken the drugs wonders Ruth, watching him from above, unwilling to come closer. She hears him coming upstairs, footsteps heavy on the uneven boards. Ruth, who has been watching from the bathroom window, comes out onto the landing. Cathbad walks straight past her into the spare room. She hears the door shut. The house seems heavy with silence. Far away, she can hear a fox barking and, further away still, the sea. Is that it? Will she have to wait until morning before she knows if he's still alive? And what about Nelson? She listens to the sound of the sea in the dark and thinks about another night, that terrible and wonderful night when Kate was conceived. What had Nelson said to her then? *Thanks for being there.* Well, she's not going to be there for him tonight. She walks slowly back into her own room.

Romilly Smith is checking her bag: phone, hairbrush, scent (*Après l'Ondée*), Smythson notebook, spare keys, plastic gloves. A sudden sound makes her go to the window and look out but all is quiet in the yard. Caroline is at the pub, bonding with the servants. Randolph is probably visiting some underground gay bar, though now that his father is dead surely there's no need for him to go on denying his sexuality. Romilly would be delighted if Randolph brought some nice young chap home. Far better than another dreary girlfriend. That poor Clary, hanging on for years, hoping that Randolph would propose. Too tragic. No, Romilly would welcome a suitable boyfriend with open arms. He would have to be suitable though. She would go to any lengths to protect him from someone she considered unsuitable.

Slinging her bag over her shoulder and slipping on a

pair of flat pumps, she makes for the door. Half-past ten. Rendezvous is at eleven. Romilly is smiling to herself as she gets into her car. She does enjoy a late-night rendezvous.

Judy is still in Nelson's office, poring over reports from the drugs squad. Every bit of information they have ever pieced together about Operation Octopus lies scattered somewhere about the room. Nelson would have a fit. Judy is normally fairly methodical too, but today she feels almost desperate in her desire to get to the bottom of this case. In some odd way, it seems tied in with everything else: Nelson, Darren, Cathbad, everything. She hunts frantically through forensics reports, witness statements, reports from other forces. It must be here somewhere.

When her phone vibrates she doesn't notice at first because it is buried under a pile of paper. It is only when the papers start moving about as if they are auditioning for a séance that she retrieves her trusty Blackberry.

Text message. *Meet me by the old gates at 11. Important. Randolph.*

27

Nelson fights like a madman when he sees the tunnel approaching. He knows what this means and he's not going to take it lying down, in bed or not. The long journey, the bright light, the departed loved ones – not this time, thank you very much. Sorry and all that, Dad. He struggles, desperately trying to stop the inexorable progress towards the light. I'm not ready, he says, fingers sliding on a surface that seems at hard yet, at the same time, liquid, like black water. I don't want to ... He makes one last effort, flailing at nothingness. He is in the tunnel.

Michelle watches in horror as Nelson writhes on the bed, fighting for breath. 'Nurse!' she cries, her voice croaky with fear. 'Nurse!'

Very quietly, Ruth opens the door to the spare room. Cathbad lies on the bed, on his back, very still. The blinds are up and moonlight shines on the floor. Ruth tiptoes closer and touches Cathbad's hand. His skin is cold but she can feel a pulse. Cathbad's eyes are closed and his long hair lies over his shoulders, like an effigy. He is smiling. If he survives this, thinks Ruth, I'll kill him.

She goes back into her own bedroom and lies on the bed. In her cot, Kate is sleeping peacefully. It is only half-past ten. What on earth is she going to do with all the hours until morning? She thinks that she'd even welcome Kate waking up screaming. But Kate sleeps on. Ruth goes downstairs and tries to watch television but *Newsnight* has a feature on drugs in schools and the film on Channel 4 is *Picnic at Hanging Rock*. Ruth feels that she has had enough of drugs and mysterious happenings in Australia to last her a lifetime. She wants a drink but supposes she should stay sober in case she has to rush Cathbad to hospital. Oh God, what if he dies, there in the single bed where only two nights ago she and Max ... She goes upstairs again. Cathbad and Kate are still sleeping, though both seem restless. The wind is getting up. A sudden squall of rain batters the windows. Her letterbox bangs as if some ghostly postman is outside. Eleven o'clock.

She has a bath and gets into bed, listening to Radio 4 on her headphones. Against the soothing murmur of *Book at Bedtime* she sees other, less cosy, images. Another night, another storm, a child's hand reaching up to her. A madman with a knife. A child's body. Then Nelson, turning towards her with troubled eyes. *I don't want to go home. You don't have to.*

Ruth sighs and pulls the covers over her head. If this night ever ends, tomorrow she is going to see Nelson. She will even take Kate with her.

* * *

It's karaoke night again at the Newmarket Arms. Caroline sits alone at the back of the saloon bar, wondering where the hell she's got to. Eleven o'clock, she'd said. It's not like her to be late, just as it's not like Caroline to be on time. It's a horrible night as well. She can hear the rain outside even above the noise of the stable hands singing *Don't Stop Me Now*. Her glass is almost empty but she's embarrassed to go to the bar through the knots of people laughing and talking. Funny, she has backpacked alone through the Outback but she's scared to order a drink in a country pub. She fiddles with her phone to avoid making eye contact with anyone. She wishes she'd arranged to meet Cathbad later but he seems to have vanished. She must have left two or three messages on his phone today. She hopes he won't think she's stalking him. But it would be a comfort to have him here now, wearing his cloak and talking about ley lines. And at least if he were here she'd have someone to have a bloody drink with.

Sod it. Caroline puts her phone away. She might as well go to the bar.

Judy, driving past the brightly lit pub with her windscreen wipers on double time, thinks it looks like an ocean-going liner sailing through a midnight sea, the ship's band playing on, the captain blissfully oblivious of impending icebergs. The car park is full; with any luck, all the stable hands will be in the pub belting out *Take That* numbers and she'll be able to talk to Randolph in peace. She can't help a slight shiver, though, as she leaves the light and noise behind and enters the woods. She remembers her father telling her about the stagecoach accident. 'On dark nights you can hear the screams of the passengers and see the ghost horses running through the trees.' She remembers Danforth Smith and the great snake 'as green as poison'. What is it about Irish people and scary stories? Well, she's not afraid of ghosts. Even so she grips the wheel tighter, the last thing she wants is to go off the road and it's so dark amongst the trees, her headlights show only a few hazy feet in front of her. The wind moans and branches lash to and fro. Where's the entrance to the stables? Surely she should be there now.

The high wall appears almost out of nowhere. The old gates, Randolph had said. She drives around the park, following the wall. Why did Randolph choose such an inconvenient meeting place? He must be trying to avoid someone. His mother? His sister? Judy wonders just how much Randolph knows about what's going on at the stables. She's only just worked it out herself. But if Randolph had been involved, surely he wouldn't have asked for a meeting with Judy and Clough? Surely he wouldn't have told them about the dead snake and the men in the woods? Unless it was a clever diversionary tactic. But she doesn't have Randolph down as clever exactly. There are lots of other words that spring to mind, but not clever.

Here are the gates at last, looming up out of the darkness. And they do look old, in fact they look as if they haven't been opened for a hundred years. But didn't

Randolph say that he came this way the other night, when he saw the sinister figures dancing round the fire? Judy parks her jeep and turns off the lights. It's still pouring with rain. She'd better get her cagoule out of the boot. A torch too. She struggles into the cagoule; it's bright yellow, which means she should present a nice target for any possible assassins. But there aren't going to be any assassins. This is Norfolk, not Sicily, whatever Clough might say. She has, however, taken the precaution of texting Clough and telling him what's she's doing. She's pretty sure that he won't check his messages tonight though; she knows he's out with Trace.

Head bowed against the rain, Judy makes her way towards the wall, torch in hand. The wind is really strong now, forcing her to bend almost double. The gates are padlocked together, with a heavy stone pushed in front of them. How is she ever going to get in? But as she gets nearer she sees that the padlock is unlocked, the chain hanging free. When she pushes at the great iron gates they move easily. Clearly this entrance has been used recently. She shines her torch in a wide arc. All she can see are bare trees, blowing wildly in the wind. Beyond the trees there seem to be some low walls. Didn't Randolph say this was where the old house used to be? Great, now she's stuck with the ruined mansion and probably the Smith family ghost as well. Where the hell is Randolph?

She is just wondering if she should go back to the car when, through the trees, she sees a figure approaching. A man, she thinks. Despite herself, she's relieved. The whole haunted castle scenario is starting to get to her. 'Randolph?' she calls.

'Not exactly,' says a voice. Judy turns towards the sound, not really scared. She is not even really frightened when she sees that the figure is Len Harris, with a gun in his hand.

28

Nelson is bracing himself for his contact with the light, but before he can reach it he feels a jolt, as if he has fallen through the air. His feet, he realises, are on the ground. Shingle, like a beach. It is a beach but the stones are black. The sea is black too, breaking in smooth round waves, like oil. Nelson doesn't stop to wonder where he is or what he is doing; he starts to walk along the shore. He knows that it's very important to move quickly. He mustn't wait, he mustn't look behind him. It is some minutes before he realises that someone is walking next to him. He sees the man's shadow before he sees his face, a cloak flying up like great wings.

'Hallo Harry,' says Cathbad.

'What are you doing?' asks Judy, trying to keep her voice steady. Trying, in fact, to sound like a twenty-first-century police professional.

'Setting a trap,' says Len, breezily, coming closer. At this distance, the gun looks disconcertingly real. 'And I must say, Detective Sergeant, you're remarkably easy to trap. One text purporting to be from brainless Randolph and you turn up, without any back-up even! Were you wanting to rescue the damsel in distress? How very macho of you.'

'Why did you send me the text?' asks Judy, trying to back towards the gates. She's only a few metres from her car, from safety, from back-up.

'Stand still,' barks Harris, in a voice that has no doubt subdued many a rampaging horse. Judy stands still. She puts her hand in her pocket, trying to find her phone. But it's in her jeans pocket, impossible to find under the folds of the cagoule. Really, she's made a complete mess of everything. She's not fit to be the Senior Investigating Officer. If she dies, will the obituaries be kind to her? Will Darren be given her uniform and a folded union jack? What about Cathbad? Will anyone even tell him? Or will he know, with his famous druid's sixth sense?

'Such a shame,' Harris is saying. 'A tragic accident. Shot, no doubt, by those mysterious intruders spotted by Mr Randolph. I knew his drug trips would come in useful one day. What a brave policewoman. So young, too. So pretty.' He leers at her.

'I know everything,' says Judy desperately. 'About the drug smuggling, everything. I know you're smuggling the drugs inside those poor horses. They're *literally* mules aren't they? You force them to swallow the drugs and sometimes they get terribly ill, like the horses I saw. Fancy and the other one. But you don't care, do you? They're not living creatures to you. They're just tools.'

'Very eloquent,' says Harris, who sounds as if he's smiling. 'But who's going to believe such a fairy tale? Poor Detective Sergeant, it sounds like you've been sniffing some of Randolph's magic powder.'

'I've written it all down in a report,' lies Judy. 'I've got proof. They found straw in some of the drugs; it can be traced back to the stables. I saw a condom in some horse manure. That can be traced too.'

But Judy hadn't, at the time, realised the significance of the piece of rubber in the crap that had found its way onto Clough's shoe. Realisation had come later. The horses had been forced to swallow drugs wrapped inside condoms. What had Clough said? Kinder Egg. Surprise every time.

'Bullshit,' says Harris. 'Or should I say horse shit? You've got nothing on me.'

Judy lunges at him, meaning to knock the gun out of his hand. But Len Harris is too quick for her, he sidesteps and she falls sprawling in the mud. The next moment, she feels the cold muzzle of the gun pressed against her cheek. This is it. She closes her eyes, wondering why she isn't thinking of Darren, Cathbad or her parents, but of Ranger, her old pony. Then, instead of the explosion, the nothingness, the triumphant entry into heaven (she isn't sure which she is expecting), Len Harris is pushed aside by a force that comes from nowhere. Judy crouches on the floor, afraid to move.

'For Christ's sake Johnson,' yells the force. 'Run!'

It's Clough.

* * *

The nurses and doctors swarm around Nelson's bed. Michelle is pushed to the back. She can't see anything except white coats. Someone brings a machine and it is clamped to Nelson's chest.

'We're losing him,' says one of the doctors.

Michelle stands pressed against the wall. She feels as if her own heart has left her body.

'What are you doing here?' Nelson asks.

'Trying to save you,' says Cathbad.

The black waves break against the beach. Black birds fill the sky.

'It's called a murmuration,' says Cathbad.

'What is?'

'The birds gathering like that. Murmuration.'

'What's happening to me?' asks Nelson.

'I don't know. Interesting isn't it?'

The waves continue to break against the stones. The relentless tide.

Clough hauls Judy to her feet and they run, blindly, in the darkness. Judy has dropped her torch and has no idea which way they're going. But Clough seems to know and that is enough for her. She runs behind him, the wind pummelling her face. Somewhere close by she can hear Len Harris staggering about. Please God, let them reach the gates before he does. It seems that God is listening; the huge gates loom up in front of them. Judy hears the gates rattle as Clough pulls at them.

'Shit,' she hears him say. 'Shit.'

'What is it?'

'They're locked.'

How can they be locked, thinks Judy. But Clough is pulling at her arm again. 'Come on!' They turn and run back towards the park and the trees and the ruins of the Smith mansion. Len Harris is nowhere to be seen. They run on, through the seemingly endless trees.

Romilly watches the Vicar carefully lift the creature from its plastic container. Terry used to be called the Vet because of his encyclopaedic knowledge of animals (and of drugs) but then the group decided that vets, though infinitely preferable to doctors, were not entirely blameless in regard to the animal kingdom. Didn't vets attend horse races and support hunting? Well, they do round here at any rate. No one is quite sure how they came up with the priesthood instead, but it's undoubtedly true that the name suits Terry who, in his pressed jeans and neat v-necked jumper, could be a trendy vicar on his day off. He even has little round glasses which he now takes off to rub his eyes.

'It's beautiful,' says Romilly, looking at the snake in Terry's gloved hands.

'Yes,' says Terry. '*Vipera berus*. Note the distinctive diamond patterning.'

'And it's properly poisonous?'

'It's not aggressive,' says Terry, 'but it's poisonous all right. Could give someone a pretty nasty bite.'

Gently, Terry takes a padded envelope and places the snake inside. The parcel bugles obscenely.

'That won't hurt it,' asks Romilly, 'being wrapped up like that?'

Terry shakes his head. 'They can survive for up to three days without food.'

'Whose name is on the envelope?'

'Michael Malone. He's a lab technician. I got him from the website.'

The name means nothing to Romilly. She nods approvingly. A properly addressed parcel is more likely to reach its target. The plan is to drop the parcel through the door of the science block at midnight. They'll be seen on CCTV but so much the better. They'll be wearing masks and ski-jackets with 'Animal Action' written on the back. Romilly designed them herself.

'My husband was terrified of snakes,' she says now.

'Lots of people are,' says Terry, carefully sealing the envelope.

'Could it kill someone?' she asks.

Terry looks at her. 'Are you hoping someone will die?'

'Of course not! We just want to make our point.'

'Yes,' says Terry. 'It could kill someone.'

Ruth feels Cathbad's pulse. It's very slow. Should she call a doctor? What about Cameron next door? Surely he and his public school chums know a few things about drugs. Ruth goes to the window. In the back garden the fire is still smouldering, an eerie orange glow in the darkness. She looks again, pressing her face against the glass. Someone is standing in her garden, looking down at the embers. A tall figure wearing a cloak and carrying a long staff. The figure moves and seems almost to vanish into the blackness, cloak swirling in the wind, covering its face. Ruth's blood runs cold. It's Bob Woonunga.

Judy and Clough run wildly, falling over branches, slipping on wet leaves. Judy has no idea where they are heading. She fixes her eyes on Clough's black jacket with its reassuring reflective stripe. She falls and twists her ankle but Clough doesn't look round. 'Come on!' he shouts. She hobbles after him. How big can the grounds be? Surely they should have reached a road or a track by now? Somewhere nearby there is a splintering crack like a tree falling. It's crazy to be in the woods in the middle of the storm. But then the whole thing's crazy, and somewhere, not far away, there's a man with a gun. She stumbles on, a stitch burning in her side. She's not sure if she can go on much longer.

Then, suddenly, the black jacket disappears. Where the hell is Clough? She stops, hearing her gasping breath even above the noise of the wind. She takes a few steps forward and then she's falling, going head-over-heels in a chaos of loose stones and broken branches.

'Come on Johnson,' yells a familiar voice. 'Get up.' Judy lies on the ground, panting. She knows Clough saved her life and she'll be forever grateful but, right now, she almost hates him. 'Where are we?' she says.

'I think we're on the racing track,' says Clough. Judy realises that she's lying on something soft. The all-weather track. And, very far off, she can see some lights.

'Come on,' says Clough again and, like two exhausted

horses, they set off along the all-weather track. Behind them, the wind roars through the trees.

'Where are we going?' asks Nelson again.

'I don't know,' says Cathbad again. He hums quietly to himself. Everything remains the same: sky, sea, beach. Is this a dream? wonders Nelson. But he can feel the stones beneath his feet, smell the sea, even the faint herbal scent emanating from Cathbad.

'The flow,' Cathbad is saying. 'You have to trust to the flow.'

But Nelson has never been one to trust what he can't see. He trudges along the beach, looking for a way out.

Bob is walking round the bonfire, occasionally raising his stick to the skies. What is he doing? Is he ill-wishing Cathbad? Is he pointing the bone? Or is he trying to save him? What about Nelson? Is Bob too trying to enter the Dreaming? Will he fight with Cathbad over Nelson's life-less body? It's all nonsense, Ruth knows, but, somehow, here in the darkness with the wind roaring around the house, it doesn't seem like nonsense.

Bob stops and looks up at the house. Ruth doesn't know how visible she is, standing in the dark bedroom. She shrinks back against the wall. Bob continues his pacing, moving in and out of the light. Then he stops and is looking at something on the ground. What is it? Ruth presses her face against the window again. Oh God, it's Flint. The ginger cat has appeared from nowhere and is rubbing around Bob's ankles. Get away from him, Flint!

She sends up a prayer to Mother Julian and her cat. Protect Flint. Don't let him become one of Bob's sinister Dreamtime creatures.

Cathbad stirs in his sleep. This is all your fault, Ruth wants to tell him. I should be sleeping peacefully with my baby in her cot and my cat on my feet. Instead she has entered some ghastly dream world where snakes and sacred animals prowl in the darkness and two of Ruth's best friends lie between life and death. She crosses the landing to check on Kate. As she does so, she hears a noise downstairs. What is it? Has Bob broken in? Did Cathbad even lock the door? She stands frozen, prepared to defend her baby with her life. Cathbad will have to fend for himself. Then thunderous paws sound on the stairs and a reproachful meow greets her. Thank God. It was only Flint coming through the cat flap. Ruth picks up her cat and hugs him tightly.

The lights are getting brighter now. Judy can see the walls of the yard, the house rising up in the distance. Thank God. They've made it. Her ankle hurts, she's wet through and she feels as if her heart is about to explode, but she's curiously elated. They've made it through the dark woods and there, a few yards away, is shelter, a telephone, backup. The wind is still roaring but the rain seems to have stopped. She's just about to turn to Clough to congratulate him, thank him, when the most terrifying noise fills the night. A kind of drawn-out moan, guttural and agonised. Judy stops, petrified. She hadn't thought it possible to be any more frightened but now she feels as if her hair is standing straight up on end.

'What the hell was that?' she whispers.

'Sounds like a donkey,' says Clough briskly.

'A donkey?'

'Yeah, a donkey braying. Come on. We've got to keep moving.'

Why would there be a donkey at a racing stables, thinks Judy, but she jogs to keep up with Clough. She's not about to let him out of her sight for a second. They are near the stable wall now and she can see the clock tower and the horse walker, monstrous in the moonlight. The light is coming from the cottage by the main gates.

'Caroline's cottage,' pants Judy.

'She's a mate of Trace's,' says Clough. 'She'll help us.'

Judy is still not very well disposed towards Caroline but right now she'd trust anyone who isn't actually pointing a gun at her. She thinks of warm houses, lights, telephones. She starts to run.

As their feet touch the tarmac, the security lights come on, almost blinding them. The terrible noise reverberates again. It's only a donkey, Judy tells herself, but it gives her the horrors all the same. Surely the noise must have roused someone up at the house. Randolph? The mysterious Lady Smith? Surely, any moment now, Len Harris will appear and shoot them down like vermin. But no one appears. They run through the car park, past sports cars and jeeps (Judy is now sure that the blue Ferrari belongs to Len Harris), and seconds later they're pressing the bell marked 'Visitors Please Report Here'.

Caroline takes some time to come to the door but, when she does, she is fully dressed in outdoor clothes.

She looks different, Judy thinks. Perhaps it's because she has her hair up.

'Police,' gasps Judy. 'Need to use your phone.'

'The lines are down,' says Caroline. 'It's the storm.'

'I've got my phone,' says Clough. 'Can we come in?'

She ushers them into the sitting room. Clough stabs away at his phone but can't get a signal; Judy has lost hers. She collapses in a chair, feeling that nothing much matters any more.

'How did you find me?' she asks Clough.

He looks up. 'You sent me a text, didn't you? I was checking my phone every few minutes. Thought there might be news about the boss. I never thought you'd come down here on your own like Nancy bloody Drew. Jesus, Johnson, how could you be so stupid?'

'I don't know,' says Judy. 'I thought I'd solved the case. I thought I could do it all myself.' She tells him about the mules. Clough whistles silently. 'Of course, half the horses come from the Middle East. The perfect cover. Brilliant.'

'Glad you think so,' says a voice from the doorway. Len Harris is standing there, next to Caroline. Both are holding guns.

The voices have started. Voices coming from the sea. Nelson knows that he mustn't listen to them. If you listen, you are lost. If you answer the knock at the door, you are lost. He sets his mind against the soft, beguiling whispers from the deep. Michelle, Ruth, Laura, Rebecca, his mother.

Always women's voices. He mustn't give way to them. He must keep walking along the beach, walking beside Cathbad. One foot in front of the other. But it's hard, the hardest thing he has ever had to do.

'This way,' says Caroline politely. An effect slightly ruined by the gun, which she is pointing directly at Judy's chest.

'You're making a big mistake,' says Clough, blusteringly, to Len Harris.

'No, you've made the mistake,' says Harris. He doesn't sound out of breath at all. Has he just run through the woods or did he have a car waiting outside the gates? It must have been Caroline, Caroline who locked the gates and then opened them again for Harris, driving him round to her house as calmly and efficiently as a taxi. Caroline, Trace's friend, whom Clough said they could trust.

Harris is smiling now, his leathery gnome's face transformed into something far less benign. A goblin or a troll perhaps. 'You wandered into the yard,' he is saying, 'and, sadly, became the victim of a tragic accident.'

He looks at Caroline. 'The walker?' she says.

'Perfect.'

'This way,' he points the gun. Judy and Clough have no choice but to follow. Clough considers turning on Harris and trying to force the gun out of his hand, but the trouble is, if it works, Caroline will probably shoot Judy. If it doesn't work, Harris will definitely kill him. Both of them look like people who know how to handle guns. He curses himself for not arranging back-up. He curses Judy even more.

They cross the yard, silent except for the sound of the wind. Judy thinks about shouting for help but who would hear her? The horses? The cat? The donkey? She wonders where Randolph and Romilly are, not that they'd be much help. Their feet squelch in the mud as they approach the horse walker. What is Harris planning to do to them? Surely if he wanted to kill them he'd have done it by now. Or does he have something more exciting in mind?

Harris kicks open the door of the horse walker and Judy and Clough are pushed into one of the compartments. They hear the door being locked and footsteps going away. They look at each other. They are shut in a triangular wooden box, just wide enough, at its widest, for two people standing abreast. Clough hurls himself against the door. The wood creaks but holds.

'Have you still got your phone?' asks Judy.

'No. That bastard took it.'

'What are they going to do to us?'

'I don't know,' says Clough grimly.

'I can't believe Caroline's in it too.'

'Nor can I. Trace told me that she was a real airy-fairy type, loved all the birds and the little animals, that sort of thing. Wait till I tell her.'

They are both silent, both thinking the same thing. Will Clough ever have the chance to tell his girlfriend about Caroline's perfidy? Funnily enough, Judy finds it harder to imagine Clough being killed than it is to imagine her own death. Is this because she feels so guilty that, in some way, she thinks she deserves to die?

The sound of hoof-beats recalls Judy to life. She looks

at Clough, who tightens his lips and clenches his fists. He looks quite formidable. All these years Judy has deplored her colleague's Neanderthal tendencies; now she's glad of them. The hooves come closer. Then the door is unlocked and Len Harris stands in front of them, gun in hand. Next to him is Caroline, holding a large black horse by the halter. The horse arches his neck and paws the ground, reminding Judy of Nelson.

'We've brought The Necromancer to keep you company,' says Harris. 'So sad. Two policemen, sorry police *people*, trampled to death by a wild horse. And, believe me, he is wild.'

Judy believes him. Close up, The Necromancer looks huge and very frightening. His eyes roll and he stamps his great hooves. In a few seconds they will be trapped in a tiny space with him. Clough looks terrified, all his swagger gone. He flattens himself against the side of the compartment. Harris sends the horse forward with a slap on his rump. Caroline drops the halter and the massive animal is inches away from Judy. She can see his red nostrils and rolling, hysterical eye. She smells his woody animal smell, the scent she remembers from her own pony and which, oddly enough, still has the power to comfort her.

'Have fun!' shouts Harris. The walker starts to move forward. Judy falls to the floor. The great horse looms over her.

29

The stairs are suddenly just there, white stairs leading up from the black beach. And he's climbing them, Cathbad just in front, purple cloak flapping. And even in this dream state or whatever the hell state he's in, he knows that stairs have got to be a good sign. Going up has to be good. It's not like the tunnel. Every fibre of his being told him that the tunnel was a bad idea. But stairs – *white* stairs – that's got to mean progress, surely? And then, without warning, a great wave breaks over him. He staggers, losing his footing and then he's drowning in the black water and there's no one to save him.

Michelle thought the frenzied activity was bad but this sudden silence is worse. 'What's going on?' she shouts, but no one answers her.

Judy struggles to her feet. Beside her Clough is panicking, battering at the wooden sides of the horse walker. The Necromancer turns on him, teeth bared, ears back.

'Clough!' shouts Judy. 'For God's sake, stay still. You'll scare the horse.'

'*I'm* scaring *him*?' But Clough stops flailing about. He edges next to Judy, breathing hard. The Necromancer twists his head, snake-like, and tries to bite him.

'Jesus Christ!'

'Stay still.'

Judy tries to call on all her old horse whispering skills. 'It's OK horse,' she says. 'It's OK.' The Necromancer puts one ear forward but he still looks furious. The walker lurches forward. The horse kicks out angrily and they hear wood splintering.

'It's OK,' says Judy but with less conviction. The Necromancer is trying to turn in the small space, getting angrier and angrier. Judy and Clough find themselves pressed into the apex of the triangle. A hoof flashes out, catching Clough's leg. He yells and falls to the floor. The Necromancer kicks again and Judy only just pulls Clough out of his reach. But the horse is turning, getting closer. All they can see in the darkness is the white stripe on his face and the whites of his rolling eyes. Judy thinks of the other horses that she saw writhing in agony. Has The Necromancer been drugged? He is certainly more vicious than any horse ought to be. Now, fatally, he turns his back on them, preparing to kick out with those powerful quarters. Judy and Clough huddle together, trying to protect their faces. It's all they can do.

They are both flung forward as the walker stops. The Necromancer staggers too, momentarily distracted. Then the door is opened and a voice is saying, with much more authority than Judy could manage, 'It's OK, boy. It's OK.' Instantly the horse's ears go forward and he drops his head. Judy, cowering in the corner, is only aware of the sudden space and silence as the horse is led away. She straightens up. Randolph Smith stands by the open door, stroking The Necromancer's nose.

'Are you all right?' he asks.

'Never better,' answers Clough, who is limping badly. They stagger out of the walker into the cold night air where the wind is still blowing through the trees. Randolph's black hair and The Necromancer's mane both stream out behind them.

'Did Harris shut you in there?' asks Randolph.

'Harris and Caroline,' says Judy. 'They're in it together.'

'Caroline's here,' says Randolph. Judy is suddenly aware that a woman is standing in the background, a tall woman with long dark hair. Judy squints at her in the darkness.

'Then who . . .?'

'Tamsin,' says Caroline. 'You saw Tamsin. She looks very like me.'

Is it possible? Judy thought she recognised Caroline but she'd only seen her once before. And because she was expecting Caroline, she'd hardly looked at the dark-haired woman who'd opened the door. Clough, by his own admission, had never met her before.

'Tamsin,' Judy repeats.

'I was due to meet her at the pub this evening,' says Caroline. 'But she never turned up.'

'She and Harris are both tied up in this drugs thing,'

says Randolph. 'We've suspected for some time, haven't we, Caro?'

'We suspected something,' says Caroline, 'but we weren't sure . . .' Her voice dies away.

'Where are they now?' says Judy. 'They're both armed. We've got to call for back-up.'

'They're not at the big house,' says Randolph. 'We've just come from there.'

'Can we stop chatting and call for back-up,' says Clough. His voice sounds strained, as if he's in pain.

'Come to my house,' says Caroline. 'I can give you something for that leg.'

'I'm going to search the park,' says Randolph. 'They won't be far away. They must have been planning to come back and check on you.' And without another word he vaults onto the back of the great seventeen-hand horse. The Necromancer cavorts like a charger, arching his neck and swinging his quarters round. Randolph just laughs. The horse has no bridle, only a halter. A few seconds ago he was a raging mass of muscle and fury. Now he looks like the perfect mount, spirited but in complete control. 'See you later,' says Randolph, and with a clatter of hooves he and The Necromancer gallop off into the night.

Judy watches, open-mouthed. 'I thought that Randolph didn't know anything about horses.'

'Who told you that?' says Caroline indignantly. 'He's a wonderful rider.'

Ruth watches from her bedroom now, still holding Flint. The wind is louder than ever, the stunted trees in the garden blown into a frenzy. Bob finishes another circuit of the embers, then he pauses and, unmistakably, raises his staff in her direction. Is it a salute or a threat? Ruth doesn't know, because Bob turns and forces his way back through the low bushes into his own garden. The fire is almost out. Ruth looks at the clock by her bed. Nearly two o'clock. She thinks of the hospital, miles away across the storm-tossed night. What's happening to Nelson? Is he alive or dead? Isn't three a.m. the low point for the human soul, the hour when most people die? Flint meows and she puts him down. She can hear him wandering crossly around the room as she gets into bed. She thinks that she will lie awake for hours, but when she closes her eyes sleep comes instantly.

Judy rings for an armed response unit from Caroline's mobile phone. Tamsin was right about one thing; the telephone lines are down. Judy also rings Whitcliffe, who asks a million awkward questions ('How did you come to be there in the first place?') and says he'll be on his way. Judy also sends a unit to Len Harris's flat and a Met patrol car to Tamsin's house.

'But her children . . .' says Caroline, her face crumpling.

Tamsin should have thought of that before she started drug smuggling, thinks Judy. But aloud she says, 'They'll be very discreet.' How discreet can a knock on the door at two a.m. be? She sees the time on Caroline's mantelpiece clock, a strange chrome contraption resembling Dali's famous floppy timepiece. It fits with the surreal nature of the night. Has she really been threatened at gunpoint, rescued by Clough and trapped in a confined space with a mad horse? But it must be true. Clough is here now, having his leg bandaged by Caroline. The Necromancer's hoof took a chunk out of his shin and it's bleeding copiously. Caroline says he'll need a tetanus jab, Clough grunts sceptically. Judy thinks that Caroline is pleased to have something practical to do. She seems quite calm and organised, looking round for antiseptic cream and cotton wool, but as soon as the bandaging is done she collapses in a chair and buries her face in her hands. Judy pats her shoulder.

'It's OK.' But this is as unsuccessful with Caroline as it was with The Necromancer because it's not OK, is it?

The sound of hooves outside adds to the unreal atmosphere. The Highwayman came riding, up to the old inn door. Judy learnt that poem at school. It ends badly, she seems to remember. The door is flung open and Randolph strides in, looking rather highwayman-ish in his jeans and white shirt, soaked to the skin, his black hair wild.

'No sign of them.'

'Len's car's still outside,' says Caroline.

'Which is his car?' Judy can't help asking.

'The Ferrari.'

Bingo.

'I couldn't see Tammy's car anywhere. The back gates are padlocked shut.'

'She locked us in,' says Judy. 'Tamsin locked us in so that Harris could finish us off. He sent me a text message pretending to be from you asking me to meet him by the old gates. When I got there he pulled a gun on me.'

Randolph looks at her curiously for a minute. 'How did you suspect about the drugs?' he asks.

Judy tells him about the mules and the condom in the horse manure. Clough laughs out loud at this point but Randolph and Caroline are still looking stricken. Randolph starts to shiver and Caroline gives him a blanket which he wraps round his shoulders.

'But what about the other stuff?' says Randolph. 'The snakes and the men in the woods? I didn't make that up, you know.'

Caroline makes an odd noise that is halfway between a laugh and a wail. 'That was me.'

'*What?*'

'I put the snakes over The Necromancer's door and on the kitchen step. I wanted Dad to give the skulls back. It was outrageous that he should keep them. A crime against humanity. I used snakes because I knew he was scared of them and because of the Great Snake, the Rainbow Serpent. But then he died and I felt so guilty . . .' She collapses in tears again.

'Did Cathbad know about this?' asks Judy sharply.

'Oh yes,' says Caroline, looking up with swimming eyes. 'We performed a smoke ceremony in the woods, me and Cathbad and Bob. It was meant to make Dad give the skulls back, not kill him.'

'You were one of the men?' asks Randolph incredulously.

'Well, I'm quite tall,' says Caroline with dignity. 'I expect you just thought I was a man. You were probably drunk or stoned anyway.'

Randolph doesn't deny this and Judy remembers Len's comments about Randolph's 'magic powder'. She is absolutely furious with Cathbad. How dare he cavort in the woods with Caroline and not mention it to her when he knew she was conducting an investigation? He's made a complete fool of her.

'That does it,' says Randolph suddenly. With a plaid blanket round his shoulders, he should seem ridiculous but instead he looks rather impressive, like an Indian chief. Watched by a bandaged Clough and a still sobbing Caroline, he goes to the writing desk in the corner of the room and starts scribbling. Then he turns and thrusts a piece of paper at Judy:

I, Randolph, Lord Smith, hereby return the skulls of the ancestors to the Noonuccal people.

It is dated 10 November 2009, 2.30 a.m.

Judy is about to speak when flashing blue lights illuminate the room. Back-up has come at last.

Nelson is floundering in the sea. There are lights and voices but they are too far off now. The waters close over his head – black, stifling waters. He fights and fights for breath but knows that sometime soon even his battling spirit will give up and he will be content to drift, lying back on the outgoing tide. He makes a last titanic effort and, raising his head, sees the boat again, its stone sides lit by some inner radiance. If he can just raise up his hand to the boat. The water is as solid as glass. He can't break through it. Then, with one last despairing thrust, his hand is above the waves and, miraculously, it is clasped in a strong hold.

'It's OK, Nelson. I've got you.'

'Cathbad. Don't let go.'

'I won't.'

30

Ruth wakes up to Radio 4 telling her about fallen trees and blocked roads and villages without power. It is still dark outside. Six o'clock. In the garden, she can just see the faint outline of the bonfire. Kate is still asleep; though Ruth doesn't realise it yet, it is the first time since early babyhood that she has slept through the night. But right now Ruth has other priorities. Pulling on a dressing gown, she crosses the landing to the spare room. Cathbad too is asleep, lying on his side with his arm stretched out, touching the floor.

Ruth shakes him roughly. 'Cathbad! Cathbad!'

Cathbad opens his eyes. 'Hallo Ruth. Is it morning?'

Ruth doesn't bother to answer. Cathbad is alive. That's enough for her. She runs back into her room where Kate is just starting to squawk. She changes Kate's nappy and dresses her in warm clothes. Kate is so surprised by this turn of events that she is quiet, watching Ruth out of her great, dark eyes. Then Ruth gets herself dressed, throwing on clothes at random. She goes downstairs, feeds Flint (who is also surprised, though not displeased, at the early start) and makes some porridge for Kate and a black coffee for herself. Then, just as dawn is breaking over the Saltmarsh, she carries Kate out to the car. She doesn't know when visiting starts but she's determined to be at the hospital as early as possible.

In the car she switches on the local radio and learns that last night's storm caused devastation around Norfolk. A tree fell on a car outside Swaffham, caravans in Cromer were destroyed and trains in and out of Norwich are delayed. But there seems to be nothing in the way of Ruth reaching the university hospital. She drives carefully, avoiding fallen branches and waterlogged gutters. As she reaches the King's Lynn road she drives through water that is several inches deep; she skids slightly but the little car holds the road well. As she reaches the suburbs she sees rubbish bins strewn across the road and fallen hoardings extolling the beauties of Norfolk. Ruth drives on, unheeding. After a while she switches from the local channel back to Radio 4 and is, as ever, soothed by the familiar voices telling her about war, disaster and financial collapse. It is nearly seven o'clock.

She pays an extortionate amount to park in the hospital car park and carries Kate to the main entrance. It is some minutes before she finds the way to Intensive Care. She doesn't want to ask for directions in case they tell her that babies aren't allowed. But Kate is going to see her father, no matter what. Kate enjoys the adventure, trotting along beside Ruth through endless swing doors, up and down stairs, into lifts, across a glass walkway. This last transfixes her. Sky is all around them and pigeons are actually flying under their feet. 'Bird!' she shouts joyously. 'Bird!' 'Come on, Kate.' Ruth picks her up. They must, they must get there in time.

But the entrance to the Intensive Care ward is barred by an avenging angel. A nurse is actually standing in her path, arms akimbo.

'You can't bring a baby in here.'

'But we've got to see Harry Nelson,' pants Ruth. 'It's urgent.'

'He's not here.'

Ruth feels her legs giving way underneath her. She's too late. Nelson is dead and she will always know that she failed him. As she struggles to frame the fateful question, a voice behind her says, 'Ruth?'

Michelle is standing by the sign telling visitors to wash their hands. She is putting away her phone. Is she ringing her daughters to tell them ... what? There's no clue in Michelle's pale, closed face. Ruth runs towards her, bouncing Kate against her hip.

'So you've come, have you?' says Michelle.

'Is he ...' Ruth stops. She is a coward, even at the last.

Michelle stares at her for a long moment then she says, with the faintest trace of a smile, 'He's regained consciousness. They've moved him onto a ward.'

'What? Oh my God.' Suddenly Ruth's feet can't hold her any longer and she and Kate collapse onto a nearby chair.

'Yes. At about three o'clock this morning,' says Michelle, almost as if she's talking to herself. 'He's very weak but they think he's going to make a full recovery.'

'Oh God.' Ruth leans forward, tears spilling from her eyes. Kate touches them experimentally. 'Mum?'

'I'm going home to get some sleep,' says Michelle. 'I've just rung the girls. Neither of them slept a wink either.'

But I did, thinks Ruth, and so did Kate. She feels as if they have failed some important test. She stands up. 'Thank you,' she says. 'Thank you for telling me.' And she turns to follow Michelle back out of the swing doors.

Michelle stops her with an imperious hand. 'Don't you want to see him?'

'Yes . . . I . . . I didn't think . . .'

Michelle gestures towards a door on their left. 'He's in there. They'll probably let you in. Go on. Take Kate to see him.'

Judy is mopping up. She has just finished an exhaustive debrief with Whitcliffe and feels as if she has been awake for several years. Len Harris was apprehended at King's Lynn airport, where he kept a private plane. He must have come back to the yard, seen the police cars and made a run for it. He is in the process of singing to the rooftops. Tamsin, on the other hand, drove calmly back to London, where she attempted to resume her life as a blameless solicitor and mother of two. 'You should have seen the house,' one of the London PCs tells Judy over the phone. 'It was like something out of a magazine, everything perfect, a Range Rover and a BMW in the garage, two kids at private school. Poor little sods. I felt for them, setting off for school in their boaters while their mum was on her way to prison.'

Was this why Tamsin had masterminded the drugs smuggling operation, just so that she could send her children to private schools wearing boaters? It doesn't seem enough to Judy. Tamsin was born into a wealthy family; she had obviously worked hard and established herself in her career. Her husband is a successful banker. (Does he know about it, Judy wonders, or does he think that the Range Rover and the BMW came from the Top Gear fairy?) Surely Tamsin had enough of everything without turning to crime? Maybe the more you have, the more you want. Maybe it was the adventure that appealed to her, the idea of carrying on a complicated illegal operation under the noses of her father and sister. Or maybe she just resented all the time spent on the horses. Because Tamsin, according to Caroline, was the one who really couldn't stand horses. Randolph had been an amateur jockey, Caroline toiled away in the yard for little reward or appreciation but Tamsin really hated the animals.

Tamsin had got as far as possible from the world of mucking out, dawn rides and endless backbreaking work, only to be drawn back in at the suggestion of Len Harris, a man with vast experience, both of horseflesh and drugs. But Harris says that it was all Tamsin, right down to the idea of using the horses themselves to smuggle the drugs. 'She got a real kick out of that.' Harris claims that Tamsin forced him to comply, he was only obeying orders. Judy, when she has heard more about the actual process involved, feels absolutely no sympathy for Harris. Sometimes the drugs were fed into the horses' stomachs through a tube (hence the condom in the manure) but more often they were inserted vaginally into mares and sutured to keep them in place. Apparently stud mares routinely have vulval sutures so, even if the procedure had been discovered, it wouldn't have seemed unduly suspicious. The whole thing makes Judy feel sick. Tamsin is currently denying everything.

Romilly Smith, who arrived home on Tuesday morning to find her driveway full of police cars, was even more interesting. She didn't seem in the least surprised to find out that her eldest daughter had been drug smuggling or that she and her accomplice had tried to murder two members of the police.

'Poor Tammy,' she had said, sinking into a chair. 'I never gave her enough attention.'

'Rubbish,' said Randolph, who was still charging around like Ben Hur. 'She was just greedy. And she wanted to pull a fast one over us. Show how stupid we are.'

What Judy thought strangest of all was that no one enquired where Romilly had been all night. She was wearing jeans and a black jumper and looked, to Judy's critical eye, rather dishevelled. Where had she been all night? With a boyfriend? Caroline had apparently been in the Newmarket Arms. When Tamsin hadn't turned up she'd been unexpectedly joined by Trace, probably still seething at Clough's desertion. Judy thought of the shabby little pub, lights blazing, music blaring, a beacon in the dark woods. She couldn't quite imagine Caroline and Trace at the microphone, belting out *I Will Survive*. Well, maybe she could. Randolph had been at a 'private' club in King's Lynn. Witnesses? Plenty, apparently.

When Judy got back to the station, she found, to her slight annoyance, that Operation Octopus had not been the only excitement of the night. Head office received a call at one o'clock in the morning, informing them that a suspicious device had been sent to the University of North Norfolk. A special squad had been dispatched and had discovered not a bomb but a poisonous snake in a jiffy bag. Who would send a snake to a university (apparently it was addressed to someone in the science department)? Animal rights nutters, says a laconic Tom Henty, this sort of thing has happened before. Judy feels that she would give a lot to know what Romilly Smith had been doing at one a.m.

Judy makes her report, skating over certain aspects such as her lack of judgment in going to the yard on her own in the first place. She does, though, give Clough full credit for rescuing her. Whitcliffe keeps trying to send Clough home to rest but he insists on hanging around, limping like Long John Silver and eating a vast McDonald's breakfast. 'Could be a commendation in this,' Whitcliffe tells him. Clough grins at Judy, wiping ketchup from his chin. Typical. She cracks the case and Clough gets all the glory.

Forensics teams are currently swarming all over Slaughter Hill Stables and have unearthed enough drugs 'to float the QE2', though why an ocean liner would want to float on pure Colombian cocaine is a mystery to Judy. The Drugs Squad thinks that the cocaine came via Dubai. Presumably, whenever a batch of horses was flown over from the Middle East, one or two were carrying the drugs inside them. She wonders how many of the stable lads were involved. She remembers Billy's anxious squint, the studied nonchalance of the jockeys. Quite a few of them would have had to be in on it, given the regularity with which the 'mules' were collapsing. Judy believes, though, that Randolph and Caroline were completely in the dark. Randolph might have a recreational drugs habit but Tamsin was the professional. Nelson told her about the mysterious 'lady' that the Vicar was meeting at the museum. Was that Tamsin? The museum, deserted and almost invisible in its colourless back street, might have been the scene for many such meetings. Neil Topham, another man with an expensive habit, was probably in on it too. And Danforth Smith, the man who apparently loved and understood his horses. Had he known?

Tanya Fuller has interviewed Randolph and has texted Judy to say 'phwoar'. Very well put, thinks Judy, remembering Randolph in his white shirt, riding off into the night. The Highwayman. *He'd a French cocked hat on his forehead, a bunch of lace at his chin.* She would fancy him herself if she had the energy.

At half-past nine, Judy has finally finished writing reports and is just tidying Nelson's office when Clough puts his head round the door. He's still chewing, she notices.

'I've just heard from Michelle. The boss is on the mend.'

'Really?'

'Yeah. He regained consciousness at about three this morning, apparently. The docs think he's going to be OK.'

Three in the morning, thinks Judy. Half an hour after Randolph agreed to return the skulls to their ancestors. Not that she believes in any of that rubbish.

'Are you going home now?' she asks.

'Think so. I need my beauty sleep.'

Judy does not make the obvious retort. Nor does she mention that Clough is now limping with the wrong leg. She owes Clough; she's going to have to be nice to him for about a year. It'll be tough, though.

She is just putting the Operation Octopus files in the Case Closed cupboard when her phone rings. Cathbad. She has been expecting this call, she realises, all night. She suddenly feels desperately tired, as if she could lie down on the dirty carpet tiles and sleep for a week.

'Hallo Cathbad.'

'Hallo Judy.'

'Have you heard about Nelson?'

'No. What?'

'He's regained consciousness. They think he's going to be all right.'

'I'm glad.' Cathbad doesn't sound surprised, she notices. But then he doesn't really do surprise.

'Where are you?' she asks.

Cathbad laughs. 'I'm at Ruth's. It's a long story.'

Isn't everything, thinks Judy, straightening the pens on Nelson's blotter.

'Can I see you later?' asks Cathbad. 'I've got a lot to tell you.'

'I'm sorry,' says Judy. 'There isn't going to be any later.'

Ruth approaches the bed. Nelson lies with his eyes shut, his chin dark with stubble. He has surprisingly long eyelashes, thinks Ruth, as she has thought before. A wire extends from a clip on his finger and a nurse is fiddling with a blood pressure cuff. She looks up.

'I'm afraid you can't bring the baby in here.'

'Just for a minute,' pleads Ruth. 'She's his daughter.'

The nurse looks at her sceptically, obviously remembering Michelle, and Nelson's other, older, daughters. At that moment, Nelson opens his eyes.

'Hi Ruth.'

'Hi Nelson.'

'Is that Katie?'

Ruth holds the baby up so he can see her. Kate claps her hands and, right on cue, announces, 'Dada.'

'Just for a few minutes then,' says the nurse. Nelson's eyes are full of tears. 'She called me Dad.'

Ruth doesn't tell him that Kate has said it to every male within a twenty-mile radius. She is perilously close to tears herself.

'How are you?'

Nelson frowns. 'I don't know. Last thing I remember we were driving home from Brighton.'

'You've been in a coma. Everyone's been worried sick.'

'Michelle told me.'

'She's been incredible,' says Ruth softly. 'She's hardly left your side.'

'I know,' says Nelson. 'The nurses say she willed me back to life.'

'Do they know what was wrong with you?'

'No. I'm a medical miracle.' He closes his eyes.

'Are you still feeling bad?' Ruth looks around nervously for a nurse but they are all standing by the door talking about *The X Factor*.

'A bit odd. I had all these weird dreams. Cathbad was in them.'

'Cathbad?'

Ruth must have spoken sharply because Kate, fretful after her early start, begins to cry. Ruth tries to distract her with her black cat key-ring. The nurses are looking over now.

Nelson is gazing at Kate. 'She's got so big.'

'She can say sixteen words.'

'That's more than me.'

They smile at each other and suddenly the atmosphere becomes charged with something more than goodwill. Ruth looks at Nelson's hair, now quite grey around the temples. She has an insane desire to stroke it.

Suddenly, though, sexual attraction is blown away as if by a whirlwind. A large woman wearing a purple coat erupts into the ward.

'Harry! How's my boy?'

Nelson winces. 'Hallo Mum.'

Maureen Nelson advances on her son, her black eyes taking in every detail of his appearance and that of the ward. 'You should have water by your bed,' she says. 'It's a basic human right.'

'I'm OK, Mum.'

'OK? Michelle says you nearly died. She's been out of her mind with worry. How could you do this to her?'

'I didn't do it on purpose,' says Nelson, rather sulkily.

Maureen's laser-beam gaze now takes in Ruth and Kate, who is chewing furiously at the key-ring.

'Who's this?'

'This is Ruth. A . . . a friend.'

'What a lovely baby,' says Maureen. She pronounces it 'babby'. She has a distinct Irish accent, something Ruth did not expect.

'Better take the baby home,' says Maureen, settling herself at Nelson's bedside. 'These places are full of germs, you know.'

31

Ruth doesn't want to go home. She rings Sandra to say she won't be bringing Kate in today, then she and Kate have breakfast in the hospital canteen, a dreamlike world of patients with drips attached and nurses coming off the nightshift. Ruth drinks black coffee and consumes eggs and bacon, Kate eats a piece of toast. Then Ruth drives to the university, taking Kate with her. She finds the place in uproar.

The science buildings have been sealed off and the grounds are full of students and lecturers standing around looking scared and intrigued in equal measure. Ruth hears talk of parcel bombs, of anthrax spores, of masked men scaling the walls at night. The students are all on their phones, updating their Facebook statuses. *Bomb scare at the uni!!!*

Phil, who is sitting under a tree eating a banana, tells Ruth a different story.

'A *snake*?'

Ruth's head feels like Medusa's, swarming with snakes. She thinks of Bob Woonunga. *The Snake's my tribal emblem.*

She thinks of the poems about the Rainbow Serpent, of the stone grass-snake crushed under Bishop Augustine's foot.

'An adder, apparently,' says Phil. 'Just posted in a padded envelope. They think some animal rights group sent it.'

Kate points at the banana. 'Want.' Phil laughs and breaks off a piece. He is in high spirits and seems completely recovered from yesterday's flu. Ruth is rather embarrassed by Kate's forceful tendencies but impressed at her success with Phil. Ruth has never once succeeded in making her own wishes so clear to her head of department.

'You'll never guess who it was addressed to,' says Phil.

The awful thing is that Ruth thinks she can guess.

'Not Cathbad?'

'Yes. The police have been trying to trace him all morning. Have you any idea where he is?'

'No,' says Ruth. She has no intention of telling Phil that Cathbad is currently in her spare room, sleeping off a drugs trip. 'I expect he'll turn up.'

'He always does, doesn't he?' says Phil, standing up and brushing grass from his trousers. 'Looks as if they've opened the doors at last.'

Lectures have been cancelled so Ruth takes Kate up to her office to collect some exam scripts. She has so far resisted the temptation to bring her daughter into the university. When Kate was born there were numerous invitations from female members of staff (and from Phil, of course) but Ruth had been wary about letting the two sides of her life overlap. But now, watching Kate toddle around her office, pulling books from the shelves, it feels oddly right to have her here. Because, whether she likes it or not, Ruth is both things now, archaeologist and mother. She smiles, moving a flint hand-axe out of Kate's reach.

Debbie, the department secretary, offers to take Kate to the canteen. Ruth privately feels that Kate has had enough stimulation for one day but everyone is being so *nice* that she can't refuse. There's a febrile, unreal atmosphere about the university today. No one is doing any work; they are all just standing around talking about the poisonous snakes and parcel bombs. Elderly professors whom Ruth hasn't seen for years have crawled out of the woodwork to enjoy pleasurable discussions about death, murder and mayhem. Phil is in his element, pressing shoulders reassuringly and talking about his contacts in the police force.

After Debbie has disappeared, carrying a thoroughly over-excited Kate, Ruth rifles through her desk collecting scripts and lecture notes. There, under a dissertation on *Syphilis, Yaws and Diseases in Dry Bones*, Ruth finds an article on Bishop Augustine, sent to her by Janet Meadows. She glances at the first lines and instantly is transported back to that Halloween afternoon: the empty room, the open window, the pages turning in the breeze.

She picks up her phone. 'Hallo,' she says. 'It's Ruth Galloway. Could we meet up? Yes, that would be fine.'

Ruth drives to a park in the centre of King's Lynn, called The Walks. It's very old and contains a fifteenth-century chapel, said to be haunted. There's also a children's play-ground and a river with ducks on it. It's a bright after-noon so there are a few people wandering about, the sort of people who don't have to be at work at two in the afternoon. Pensioners, mothers with pre-school children, a bird-watcher whom Ruth eyes with distrust. Predictably, Kate ignores the more picturesque birds in favour of stag-gering about after a mangy pigeon and is soon joined by two other yelling toddlers. Ruth watches them with pleasure, until it becomes too cold to stand still and she persuades Kate to move on. They pass Red Mount Chapel, a strange hexagonal building said to contain a relic of the Virgin Mary. Ruth thinks of Bishop Augustine and her visions. Really, religion is so strange – virgin births, the devil disguised as a snake, bread turning into flesh – if you believe all that you can believe anything. And maybe that's the attraction.

They cross the bridge and walk, through streets that become increasingly less green and pleasant, to the Smith Museum. To Ruth's surprise, a woman is by the front steps, sweeping up leaves. Getting closer she sees that it's Caroline Smith. She doesn't think that Caroline will recog-nise her, but in answer to Ruth's hesitant hallo, the other woman says, 'It's Ruth, isn't it? Cathbad's friend?'

Ruth cautiously admits that she's Cathbad's friend.

'Have you heard?' asks Caroline, pushing her dark hair back behind her ears. She seems very friendly, almost manic.

'Heard what?'

'The skulls are going back,' says Caroline. 'Randolph

agreed last night. We're going to have a repatriation ceremony. It'll be wonderful. Bob's here now.'

Ruth doesn't quite know how she feels about seeing
Bob. She doesn't believe that Bob was responsible for Lord
Smith's death and Nelson's illness but, all the same,
thinking of the mysterious figure in her garden last night,
she still doesn't quite trust him. She remembers his face
when he told her about the fate of the man with a skull
on his mantelpiece. *He's dead now. The ancestors are powerful.*

'You must be pleased about the skulls,' she says to
Caroline.

'Oh yes,' Caroline grins at her. 'The wrong will be
righted. Mother Earth will be satisfied. Everything will
be all right now.'

Ruth thinks of Mother Julian's adage: *All shall be well
and all shall be well and all manner of thing shall be well.* Why
is it so hard to believe this?

'What's going to happen to the museum?' she asks.

'Oh, I'm going to manage it,' says Caroline, with
another wide smile. 'I've got great plans. It'll be a different
place.'

'What about the stables?'

'Well, after that drugs business . . .'

'What drugs business?' Ruth wants to scream, but she
carries on standing there smiling, holding Kate by the
hand. There's too much going on here that she doesn't
understand.

Caroline switches the smile back on. 'If the stables stay
in business, Randolph will be in charge. It's what he's
always wanted. He's a genius with horses. And I'm going

to make the museum a real success. We're going to have proper local history exhibitions starting with "Augustine: the first woman bishop."

'Sounds great,' says Ruth. 'I'm meeting someone. Is it OK to go inside?'

'Of course! She's waiting for you. '

The museum seems deserted but benign in the afternoon light. There's a room by the entrance lobby which Ruth hadn't noticed before but which is full of butterflies, impaled upon pins and labelled with spidery Victorian writing. Kate loves the butterflies but her real enthusiasm is reserved for the stuffed animals. She runs delightedly from case to case shouting 'Fox!' 'Dog!' 'Cat!' Her range of animals may be limited but her enjoyment is not. Ruth finds herself looking at them all, even the murderous gulls, with a kinder eye.

Eventually Kate allows herself to be led through the study of Lord Percival Smith ('Man!') and into the long gallery. In the Local History Room, Janet Meadows is looking out of the window.

'Hallo Ruth,' says Janet.

'Hi. Thanks for meeting me.'

'No problem. Is this your little girl?'

'Yes, this is Kate.'

'Hallo Kate.'

'Fox,' says Kate.

Ruth looks at Janet and remembers her comment when Ruth had remarked flippantly that Augustine's snake didn't look very terrifying:

He'd subdued it. Evil has been defeated. He was a great saint.

She thinks of the room as she saw it that day: coffin, guidebook, grass snake and a single shoe.

'You were here, weren't you,' she says, 'the day Neil was found dead.'

Janet suddenly looks wary. 'I told you I was. I came to see the opening of the coffin but the place was closed off.'

'But you came earlier, didn't you? You put the snake in here and a single shoe, to remind people about Augustine.'

Janet either brought a spare pair of shoes or she walked home barefoot. Ruth bets on the latter. Janet would have walked barefoot to emulate the man she called a 'great saint'.

'They had no right to desecrate his grave,' says Janet. 'He . . . she didn't want anyone to open the coffin. That's why it was buried where it was. So I put a snake there, a grass snake in a glass case, to remind them of Augustine's warning. The shoe too. It was one of Jan's shoes . . .' For a second Ruth wonders who Jan is but then she remembers. Jan is, or was, Janet. Her old self, Jan Tomaschewski. 'I dressed as Jan too,' Janet is saying now, 'in one of my old suits. The museum was deserted. I got the snake from the Natural History Room and carried it in here. The coffin was on a trestle in the middle of the room – open.'

'Open?'

'Yes, slightly open. I think the curator must have prised it open. I could hear him moving about in his office. So I put the snake and the shoe on the floor. I left the guidebook too, with a few words highlighted, just as a warning.

Then I heard someone coming so I climbed out of the window. I don't think anyone saw me and, if they did, they saw a man in a suit and a hat. Not a woman.' She turns and does a mock twirl.

It must have been only seconds later that I came in and found Neil Topham dead, or nearly dead, thinks Ruth. Why on earth had he opened the coffin? But it was closed when she saw it. She remembers how easy it was for Phil to prise up the nails, far easier than it should have been. The coffin had already been opened, just days before.

Why would Neil open the coffin?' asks Ruth.

Janet shrugs. 'Search me. Perhaps he just wanted a look. Perhaps he just got impatient. Either way, it did for him, poor guy. Bishop Augustine had his – her – revenge.'

By afternoon Nelson is well enough to be moved to another ward. He enjoys the trip. It's good to see a different view and, as the porters seem determined to take the longest route possible, he gets to see quite a lot of the hospital. Also, the move gave him an excuse to suggest to his mother that she go back to his house and get some rest. She agreed reluctantly, saying that she'd be back in the evening with a proper meal for him. 'The muck they serve in these places is enough to kill you, so it is.' As Michelle has also promised to bring him some food, Nelson fore-sees a clash of wills over the shepherd's pie. Perhaps Michelle will be so tired that she'll be happy to let Maureen do the honours. She's good with his mum. Better than he is, anyway.

The new ward is much more relaxed. Nelson's bed is

by the window and the nurses' station is right at the other end of the room. He guesses, correctly, that this means that he is considered to be out of danger. His recovery really has been remarkable. He has been able to eat, drink and have a pee – the three measures of achievement in a patient. No one really knows why he has got better so quickly or what was wrong with him in the first place. 'Last night we thought you were a goner,' one of the doctors tells him cheerfully. Nelson smiles faintly. He likes a near-death experience as much as the next man but it worries him that so much could have happened while he was out of the picture, asleep, unconscious. He has thought about the prospect of death, all policemen have, but he'd always thought that he'd have a leading role in the drama: negotiating the release of hostages, foiling a terrorist plot, saving children from a burning house. He never thought, when the Grim Reaper came knocking, that he'd be fast asleep.

Nelson's first visitor of the afternoon is Clough. He comes bearing a bunch of flowers which he is told to leave in the lobby 'due to health and safety regulations'. Nelson doesn't know where to look. Cloughie bringing him flowers! He'll be making him a friendship bracelet next. Still, he appreciates the chance to catch up. Clough tells him all about Operation Octopus, dwelling on his own heroism, and Nelson is suitably impressed. He always knew that there was something funny about the stables but he never thought that it would turn out to be the centre of an international drugs ring. That was smart detective work from Judy. Less smart, of course, to go skipping off in the middle of the night, alone, as a result of a text message. She was lucky that the whole thing turned out so well. Nelson particularly enjoys the bit about The Necromancer and the horse walker.

'Honestly, boss, he was as big as an elephant. And his teeth! He attacked me but I managed to hold him off. I'm pretty strong when I'm roused. Bastard took a chunk out of my leg though. Do you want a look?'

'No thanks.'

'I think Johnson was pretty shaken by the whole thing.'

'I bet she was.'

'Some people thought I should have been put in charge but I don't know . . .' Clough trails off modestly. Nelson says nothing, though he would have put Clough in charge. Judy may be the better detective but Clough is senior and that counts for something. Nelson is a great believer in fairness; it comes of being the youngest of three.

No sooner has Clough disappeared through the swing doors than another figure appears, a figure wearing a rather crumpled purple cloak.

'Hallo Cathbad.'

'Hi Nelson. You're looking better.'

'You didn't see me when I was ill. At death's door I was, wasn't I love?' Nelson appeals to a passing nurse.

'So I hear,' she says, straightening his sheet. 'They'd given him up for dead in ICU.'

'Quite an experience,' says Cathbad, when the nurse has gone.

'I can't remember any of it,' says Nelson. 'I had these weird dreams though. You were in some of them.'

'I know,' says Cathbad.

'What do you mean you know?' says Nelson. He'd forgotten how infuriating Cathbad could be.

Cathbad leans forward. He looks tired, Nelson realises, and rather unhappy, but still has plenty of his old force.

'I know what was wrong with you, Nelson. You were cursed. You got in the way of a curse meant for Danforth Smith. It killed him but you were too strong for it. You were lost in the Dreaming, between life and death. So I came to rescue you.'

'You . . . came to . . .' Nelson is speechless. He has always known that Cathbad is more or less mad but this? This seems to be pure delusion. He wonders if Cathbad is on drugs.

Cathbad's next words don't exactly put him at his ease. 'I prepared a libation and took certain substances. I entered a dream state and I came to rescue you.' He smiles kindly at Nelson.

'Well I'm very grateful,' says Nelson sarcastically. 'I hope I said thank you at the time?'

'You think you don't remember,' says Cathbad, 'but you do. You remember the water and the darkness and Erik guarding the portal to the afterlife.'

Cathbad doesn't seem to expect any answer to this, which is lucky because Nelson shows no sign of giving one. Instead, Cathbad leans over and takes a handful of the grapes that he has brought with him.

'Did you know someone tried to kill me last night?' he says chattily.

'Is this something else that happened in your bloody dream world?'

'No. Someone sent me a poisonous snake.'

'What?' Nelson struggles to sit up. 'What are you talking about?'

'A venomous snake was sent to the university, addressed to me. I got a call from the police as I was on my way here. I told them I was a friend of yours.'

Nelson groans inwardly. That's all he needs. Head office thinking that he's best mates with a warlock in a purple cloak. And what the hell's this about another bloody snake? He thinks of the warnings in the letters about the Great Snake. Could this be the work of the Elginists? But Cathbad's one of them, isn't he?

'Do they know who sent it?'

'They think it's some animal rights group but I have my doubts. I have a lot of enemies. The snake's fine,' he adds. 'They've sent it to a zoo near Great Yarmouth.'

There's not a lot Nelson can say to that. He looks at Cathbad, who is calmly finishing off the last of the grapes. The ward is quiet; all the other patients seem asleep. The afternoon sun makes squares on the worn lino floor. A very old woman is pushing a trolley laden with tea, coffee and squares of cake. Is Cathbad mad or is he?

One thing is certain: Nelson will never tell a living soul that he did see Erik.

Kate wants to see the stuffed animals again so Ruth is forced to run the gamut of the glass eyes. Kate stands for ages, breathing heavily on the glass, watching the foxes looking into their *trompe l'oeil* den. A squirrel teeters precariously on the branch above.

'Fox,' says Kate in ecstasy.

'Yes, fox,' says Ruth, who wants to get home. 'Like Fantastic Mr Fox. Say goodbye to the fox, Kate. We've got to get home to Flint.'

'Fox,' says Kate, ignoring her. 'Fox, box.'

'She's a poet,' says a voice behind them. Ruth can see Bob Woonunga's smile reflected in the cabinet doors. Ruth, instinctively, moves between him and Kate. Behind her, Kate starts making the didgeridoo sound.

'Don't be scared, Ruth.' Bob sounds amused. 'I'm your friend. Your friendly neighbour.'

Is he her friend? He has certainly always been friendly towards her. Didn't he find Flint that first night? In fact, both Flint and Kate seem entranced by him. And Cathbad likes him, though Cathbad also seems believe that he was capable of casting a spell that killed a man.

'I heard that the skulls are going back,' says Ruth. 'You must be pleased.'

Bob is playing peek-a-boo with Kate, but when he looks up to meet Ruth's eyes his face isn't playful in the least. 'I'm pleased, of course,' he says. 'But I've just been down to the cellars. The way those bones were kept! There's no respect, no reverence, not even an acknowledgement that they're human. I tell you, Ruth, it turned my stomach.'

'I did say in my report that they weren't kept in appropriate conditions,' says Ruth weakly.

'I know you did,' says Bob, his voice softening. 'I knew all along that you were on our side.'

Is that why you put me under a circle of protection, thinks Ruth. But she doesn't believe in the curse, does she? Surreptitiously, she takes Kate's hand.

'We'd better be going.'

'I hope you'll come to the repatriation ceremony. It'll be something else, I promise you.'

'I'd like to come. Thank you.'

'Bye Ruth,' Bob stands aside. 'Bye Kate.'

As they go out of the room, Ruth sees the case containing the grass snake, its glass eyes winking in the afternoon sunlight.

Up next is Judy. She hasn't brought flowers or grapes. Instead she dumps a couple of lurid-looking paperbacks on his locker.

'Thought you might want something to read.'

Nelson isn't much of a reader. One of the books has a skull on the cover, the other a swastika. He squints at the blurbs: conspiracy ... war ... torture ... blackmail ... death. Judy really has him down as the sensitive type, doesn't she?

'I heard all about last night,' he says.

'Who from? Oh, Clough's been in has he? What did he tell you?'

'Just that you solved Operation Octopus.'

Judy seems to relax slightly. 'It was a lucky guess. A series of lucky guesses.'

'Sounded like good police work to me.'

Judy looks away. 'I messed up. Clough had to save me.'

'He saved me once,' says Nelson. 'Don't worry about it.'

'I should never have gone there without back-up but I wanted to solve it on my own.'

'Policing's about teamwork,' says Nelson, who has never waited for back-up in his life.

'You're right,' says Judy, fiddling with a hand sanitiser. 'Clough's a better team player than me.'

'I hear he wrestled a mad horse to the ground.'

Judy laughs. 'He was scared stiff. Did he tell you that? Mind you, it was terrifying, shut in a small space with a horse like that. I like horses but I'm not sure I ever want to see one again.'

'So you're not going to go back and see Randolph Smith?'

'Did Clough tell you I fancied him? I don't. He was brilliant last night though. I don't know what would have happened if he hadn't turned up when he did.'

'So the older sister turned out to be the black sheep?'

'Yes. She was the clever one, despised the other two. Hated the dad too, by all accounts. Mind you, Caroline, the younger sister, is a bit mad too.'

She tells Nelson about the dead snakes and the men dancing in the woods.

'Snakes again,' says Nelson.

'Yes, turns out that Danforth Smith was terrified of them.'

With reason, thinks Nelson. Aloud he says, 'And this Caroline's a friend of Cathbad's? Figures.'

'She wanted her father to give back the Aborigine bones. It sounds like she was obsessed with them.'

'Do you think she wrote the letters to the curator? And

there was a snake found in the room with the body. Maybe that was her too.'

'I don't know. She didn't mention the curator. It seemed to be all about her dad. Like it was all his fault.'

'It's always the dad's fault,' says Nelson.

Judy thinks of her own genial, horse-loving father. 'I think dads are OK,' she says.

She sounds so like her old self that Nelson begins to hope that the silent, withdrawn Judy has gone for good. Maybe now they can get back to police work. He'll give her some more responsibility. She didn't do so badly with Operation Octopus, after all. Then she spoils everything by telling him that she's pregnant.

Flint is delighted to see Ruth and Kate. He has been alone all day, he tells them, purring sinuously about their ankles, starving and neglected. He has, in fact, been asleep in the airing cupboard. Ruth feeds her cat and starts making some pasta. It's only five o'clock but it's dark outside. Kate must be tired, she has only had a tiny sleep in the car. Maybe last night will herald a wonderful new era of sleeping through the night. They'll have supper at six, Kate will be in bed at seven and Ruth can have all evening watching television and drinking white wine. Heaven.

She has almost forgotten Cathbad and the horrors of last night. Nelson is going to be all right. Michelle let her see him, perhaps she might even allow Nelson to have regular contact with Kate. She admitted that he wants to see her. Ruth knows how much that admission cost Michelle, how much it cost Michelle to come to her house and beg her to visit her husband. She would do anything for him, she said. Ruth doesn't know if she's ever loved anyone that much. Except Kate, of course.

She half expects Max to ring but he doesn't. After the last few days, it seems strange to have no one knocking on the door demanding help or babbling about the Dreaming. After supper, Ruth tries to read a Percy the Park-Keeper book to Kate but she's more interested in charging around the room with her plastic vegetables. Ruth is determined not to switch on the TV but Kate does it for her (she loves the remote) and soon they are both dozing in front of *In the Night Garden*. Ruth forces herself to her feet. She's got to keep Kate awake for a little longer. Routine, she tells herself sternly, it's all about routine. She puts Kate in her cot while she runs the bath and they both have a strenuous half-hour playing with water. Kate's eyes start drooping as soon as Ruth puts her into bed. She is asleep before Ruth has read two pages of *After the Storm*. Ruth finishes the book anyway. She loves it that all the animals find a home in the big tree. She doubts that Norfolk Social Services will be so efficient after last night's high winds.

Ruth tiptoes out onto the landing. All evening she has avoided looking into the spare room but now she opens the door quietly. The bed is neatly made but lying on the cover is a single feather, long and beautiful, a pheasant's perhaps. Ruth stays looking at it for a long time.

Nelson's last visitor is the most surprising. Chris Stephenson, swaggering through the doors as if he's paying a state visit. Disappointingly, two of the nurses recognise him and flutter around calling him 'Doctor' Stephenson. They even offer to get him a cup of tea, although the old woman with the trolley is long gone.

'Hi Nelson,' Stephenson greets him. 'Not dead yet?'

'Not yet.'

'Bet you can't guess why I'm here.'

'Was it to bring me flowers?'

'Not allowed. Health and safety.' Stephenson hasn't brought any sort of present, not even grapes. Nelson guesses that this call is about business rather than concern for his well-being.

The nurses bring tea in chipped green cups. Stephenson makes a big thing about not needing sugar because he's sweet enough already. For the first time that day, Nelson feels sick.

'Your friend Ruth Galloway,' says Stephenson by way of introduction, slurping his tea.

'What about her?' asks Nelson cautiously. He doesn't know how much his colleagues know about his relationship with Ruth. He thinks that Judy has suspicions about Kate's parentage; Clough has probably never given it a thought.

'Remember the bishop? The one that turned out to be a tranny? Well, Ruth sent off some of the material to be analysed. The silk stuff that was wrapped round the bones. Results came back today and guess what they found?'

'Surprise me.'

'Traces of a fungus called aspergillus.'

He leans back as if expecting a reaction. Nelson looks at him coldly. 'That doesn't mean a lot to me, Chris.'

'They're spores, incredibly toxic. They can stay alive for hundreds, thousands, of years. As soon as the spores come into contact with the air, they enter the nose, mouth and mucous membranes. They can cause headaches, vomiting and fever. In people with a weakened immune system, it can result in organ failure and death.'

Nelson looks at him, 'Danforth Smith.'

'Yes. He was diabetic, you say. That would have compromised his immune system. He died from heart failure. Could have been brought on by contact with these spores. If we'd done an autopsy, we'd have known.' He sounds regretful.

'And the curator,' says Nelson, 'Neil Topham. If he'd opened the coffin ...' He thinks of the DIY tools in Topham's office, of the open window and the curtains blowing. If the spores had got into the air and into Topham's mouth and nose ...

'He was a druggy,' says Stephenson, with his usual sensitivity. 'Immune system would have been shot to pieces. One whiff of aspergillus and he'd have been out like a light. Cause of death was lung failure. Spores would have gone straight onto the lungs.'

'Is this asperthing, this spore, what made me ill?'

'I think so. You were next to Lord Smith when the coffin was opened. You would have got a direct hit but you're healthy, you were able to fight it off.'

Only just, thinks Nelson. Another thought strikes him. 'What about Ruth? She was right there too.'

Stephenson laughs. 'I've been thinking about that. She was about to look into the coffin when she got a phone call. She moved away and you and Lord Smith were the first to look inside. Whoever phoned Ruth probably saved her life.'

Nelson would be willing to place a large bet on the identity of Ruth's caller. There's only one person it could have been. Cathbad to the rescue again.

'Would these spores . . . could they give you nightmares, delusions?'

Stephenson looks at him curiously. 'I suppose so. One of the symptoms is a high fever. Why do you ask?'

'Lord Smith's wife mentioned that he had a terrible fever before he died, was seeing things, shouting out in his sleep.'

'That was probably the aspergillus. Of course, we'll never really know.'

Did the poison spores give Danforth Smith nightmares about snakes and ghostly horsemen? Did they plunge Nelson into a shadow world of sea and sky and a man calling from a stone boat? As Stephenson says, he'll probably never know. But it seems that the Aborigines are innocent; it was the bishop who did it, after all.

'I'm going to ask the docs to do a chest radiograph on you,' says Stephenson cheerily. 'Something might show up.'

'Thanks a lot.'

'Why should you worry? It's a rest cure in here.'

Rest? This feels like the busiest day Nelson has ever had in his life. And as Stephenson saunters out of the ward, he sees Michelle and Maureen on their way in, both carrying covered bowls full of nourishing food.

32

The Necromancer comes galloping around the corner of the all-weather track, the black earth flying up behind him. At the top of the hill, by the trees, a woman is standing. The horse starts violently at the unfamiliar figure, standing on his hind legs, nostrils wide with fear. But the horse's rider just laughs and shifts his weight slightly in the saddle.

'I'm sorry,' says Romilly Smith. 'Did I scare him?'

Randolph laughs. 'He's just playing silly buggers.' He pats the animal's shuddering neck. 'Calm down horse.'

'I'd forgotten what a good rider you are,' says Romilly, falling into step beside the horse.

'I'd forgotten too,' says Randolph, loosening the reins so that The Necromancer can stretch his neck. 'Not that I could ride but how much I enjoyed it. I was devastated when I got too tall to be a jockey. '

'You wouldn't want to be a jockey, darling. All that dieting plays havoc with your skin.'

Randolph laughs and turns the horse towards the stables. Romilly again falls into step beside them. There is still frost on the ground and her smart boots crackle over the grass.

'Are you really going to run the yard?' she asks.

'I'm going to give it a go,' says Randolph. 'Do you mind?'

'Not at all. I think I'm going to move out. Give you some space.' Romilly looks up at her son, sitting so loosely on the great black horse. He really is lovely, she thinks. I'm glad I don't have to share him with another woman.

'Are you still involved with them? The group?'

Romilly pauses with her hand on The Necromancer's neck. 'Well, the group's rather gone into hiding . . . after that tip-off last night.'

For a few minutes they walk in silence. Both know that it was Randolph who told the police. Eventually, Randolph says, almost apologetically, 'You just can't go round doing things like that, you know. Sending poisonous snakes to people.'

'I know,' Romilly sighs. 'It would have shaken things up a bit though. Make people take notice.'

'Do you think the police suspect you?'

'Oh, I'm sure they suspect – I've got a record after all – but we've all got alibis for last night. Pity it didn't come off. We'd been planning it for ages.'

'An innocent man could have been killed.'

'Innocent animals die every day,' Romilly counters. But she says it without real heat, as if her mind is elsewhere.

'And that Vicar person,' continues Randolph. 'He's a psychopath.'

'That's where you're wrong,' says Romilly triumphantly. 'He absolutely refused to kill Neil.'

Randolph reins in so sharply that the horse stumbles. 'What?'

'I asked him to give Neil some contaminated drugs but he refused. You see, he's quite moral really. For a drug dealer.'

'You asked him to kill Neil? Why?'

Romilly looks up at him. 'Because Neil got you into drugs. I'll never forgive him for that.'

'He didn't. We spent a couple of nights together, that was all. I'd started taking drugs at school, for God's sake. Neil was just a supplier. Like your mate the Vicar.'

'I don't care,' says Romilly calmly. 'He was a bad influence. I was glad he died. I tried to scare him off before. That's why I wrote him those letters.'

Randolph looks at his mother, her silvery hair blowing back in the wind. She looks beautiful but somehow frightening, as if he doesn't really know her at all.

'Which letters? The ones the police kept going on about?'

'Oh, did the police find them? Yes. I wrote Neil some letters about the skulls, trying to scare him. I got the idea from the letter that was sent to Dan by those Elginist people. I wanted Neil to leave, to go back home. He wasn't worthy of you.'

'But you can't just . . .' Randolph's voice fades away. They have reached the yard and The Necromancer's hooves clatter on the tarmac. Randolph pulls him to halt.

'I'm off drugs,' he says. 'You can't combine running a yard with taking drugs. Too many bloody early mornings. Human beings can only take so much.'

Romilly smiles up at him. 'Humans are horrible. They're not nearly as nice as animals.'

Randolph takes this in, realising that this philosophy has been the guiding force of his mother's life. Is this why they are all so mixed up – him and Caroline and Tamsin? Because, deep down, their mother preferred animals to them?

'Are you going to go on with the animal rights stuff?' he asks. 'If the group ever reforms?'

'Oh, I'm going to start a new group. Strictly non-violent. Demonstrating at hunts etcetera. I'm going to buy a little cottage somewhere and really devote myself to it.'

Great, thinks Randolph. He hasn't told his mother that he's decided to join the hunt. He has always loved hunting (he used to sneak off to go cubbing as a child) and it's excellent exercise for the horses. He looks forward to seeing her at the barricades. He's not sure he believes the non-violence either.

'Do you think Dan knew?' Romilly asks suddenly. 'About the other men?'

Randolph dismounts and loosens The Necromancer's girth. Steam rises up from the horse's hot body.

'No,' he lies. 'I don't think Dad knew a thing.'

'I hope not,' says Romilly, moving out of the way as a stable boy comes past leading two horses towards the walker. 'I never wanted to hurt him. I was just . . . bored.'

'Yeah,' says Randolph, lifting off the saddle. 'Boredom has a lot to answer for.'

'But you won't be bored now, will you? You've got the

stable to run and Caroline's got the museum. I've never seen her so happy. Not since she came back from Australia.'

Not that you ever did anything about Caroline's unhappiness, thinks Randolph, because she's not a beagle or a laboratory rat. The Necromancer rubs his head against his shoulder and suddenly Randolph, too, feels a great surge of love towards all animals. The Necromancer doesn't care if he's gay or straight, on drugs or clean. As long as Randolph feeds him and takes him out on long gallops, it's all the same to him. Randolph rubs the horse's ear affectionately and turns to his mother.

'There's going to be a big party at the museum,' he says. 'Caroline's organising it. To celebrate the skulls going back. Will you come?'

Romilly reaches up a gloved hand to touch his cheek. 'No darling. I think I'll give it a miss. One way or another I've rather had enough of the museum.'

33

The repatriation ceremony is held on the fifteenth of December. Ruth has, that morning, opened the fifteenth window on Kate's advent calendar. She ate the chocolate herself to save Kate's teeth. What a good mother. Christmas suddenly seems to be uncomfortably close. It is the last week of term and the department noticeboard is groaning with parties and carol concerts. Phil and Shona are having a party on Christmas Eve ('our last fling before the baby's here') and Ruth is already thinking of ways to avoid it. She is wondering whether she has the nerve to invite Max for Christmas. They have had one weekend together since the Elginist conference, and even to Ruth's over-critical eye it seemed to go rather well. She knows that Max has no family left alive and, as for her, she'd do anything to avoid Christmas with her parents and brother.

Driving from the university to the Smith Museum, she allows herself to think about Christmas on the Saltmarsh with Max and Kate. She could buy a tree. She's forty-one years old and she's never bought her own Christmas tree.

How pathetic is that? She has a vision of herself and Kate decorating the tree. They could make the decorations out of salt dough (something which, like potato prints, seems to Ruth the very pinnacle of mothering). They could go into town to see Father Christmas, though she loathes shopping malls – and Father Christmas too for that matter. She remembers the time, two years ago, that she saw Nelson Christmas shopping with his wife and children. It had been her first glimpse of Michelle and Ruth had disliked her on sight. So much has changed since then. Ruth herself has changed, she thinks, almost beyond recognition.

Michelle has agreed that Nelson should see Kate once a month and the first meeting, on the bouncy, neutral ground of a soft play area, had been predictably awkward. Nelson had played with Kate while Michelle and Ruth drank coffee and talked about Christmas and families and aren't home-made mince pies nicer than shop-bought ones. When Kate is used to him Ruth is going to let Nelson have her on his own. That should be easier all round. Maybe Kate will gain a much-needed aunt figure in Michelle. She'll need someone to take her shopping when she's a teenager.

Will Kate gain a father figure in Max? That remains to be seen. Even in Ruth's festive fantasies, Max is relegated to the background, mulling wine and roasting chestnuts. Despite everything, she doesn't seem to want a man around all the time. Still, Max will be there today and maybe she can broach the subject of the holidays. Nothing like an Indigenous Australian Repatriation ceremony to remind you of Christmas.

Ruth parks in the museum car park, remembering the day, just over a month ago, when she came here to find Neil Topham lying dead in the Local History Room. The curator has not been forgotten by the Smith family. The Local History collection will be renamed The Neil Topham Collection, and, according to Cathbad Randolph is talking about sponsoring a Topham history prize at the university.

Cathbad is the first person that Ruth sees as she walks into the entrance hall. He is standing looking at the stuffed figure of the Great Auk. The moth-eaten bird is the only survivor of Caroline's enthusiastic modernisation. The lobby has been freshly painted, the map of King's Lynn and the oil painting of Lord Percival Smith have been replaced by computer screens asking visitors to rank their experience from 'Awesome' to 'Disappointing.' Instead of the dusty chandelier, modern light fittings snake across the ceiling and, in honour of the Indigenous Australian guests, the Aboriginal flag, bands of black and red intersected by a glowing yellow sun, covers one wall.

Ruth blinks. 'Blimey. This is all a bit different.'

Cathbad turns and smiles. 'I know. These days, if you stand still long enough, Caroline either paints you or plugs you in.'

Cathbad is looking impressive in a fur-lined cloak with his long hair loose. Ruth is pleased to see him dressed up. The last few times they have met it has been in the university canteen and Cathbad was in his ordinary clothes and white coat. He looked like any other middle-aged lab technician and there was something in his eyes, something sad and rather defeated, that made Ruth in turn feel sad. Cathbad told her that Judy had ended their relationship. 'She said that she wanted to give her marriage a proper chance. I supported her, of course. The spirits are strong within her.' Judy certainly seems strong these days. Maybe it's because she was in charge when Nelson was ill, because on the couple of occasions that Ruth has seen her recently, Judy has been in full-on police professional mode. She wonders if Judy will be here today. She knows that Nelson and Superintendent Whitcliffe are expected. Whitcliffe is making a speech complete with references, according to Nelson, to Mother Earth and the mystic unity of the nations.

Ruth and Cathbad walk through the Natural History gallery. The stuffed animals are still here, red in tooth and claw, and Ruth realises that she would be quite sad to see them go. The only concession to modernity is an interactive display showing endangered species, the world pulsing with red, amber and green lights. Ruth presses on Australia and an icon of a koala fills the screen. Surely koalas aren't endangered? They're in all the ads.

Cathbad is staring at a case labelled 'Wandering Albatross'.

'That's a great name, isn't it?' he says. 'Wandering Albatross.'

'Do me a favour and don't name your next child Albatross.'

'I won't have another child,' says Cathbad.

They walk into the replica study where the stag still gazes down from the red-painted wall. Ruth looks at the waxwork figure of Lord Percival Smith, the man who thought it would be a good idea to collect human bones and keep them in boxes. She notices that the label describing him as 'adventurer and taxidermist' is missing. Ruth is sure that Bob and Caroline will find a better phrase to describe him.

This time they take the door not into the Local History Room but into a space marked New World Collection. And it *is* a new world: a long light room painted white, with doors opening onto a patio. The rainbow serpent forms splashes of colour on the walls along with hugely magnified words from Bob's poems. There is a display of children's artwork and a papier-mâché model of a kangaroo. Where are Lord Smith's branding irons and dingo traps, wonders Ruth. If they are present, they are buried somewhere under the red and yellow flags. This is a land of primary colours; darkness has no place here.

At the end of the room Caroline Smith, resplendent in a gold dress decorated with vaguely Aboriginal patterns, is pouring glasses of champagne. There is a table laden with food and drink and decorated with pine branches. The smell reminds Ruth of her fantasy Christmas tree. Clough is already getting stuck into the buffet and various local reporters wander round clutching glasses. A handsome man in a black suit stands beside Caroline, dispensing bonhomie.

'Have you met my brother Randolph?' says Caroline.

So this is the man Judy referred to as the highwayman. He's certainly very dashing, like a Georgette Heyer hero. Cathbad and Ruth shake his hand and Randolph offers some pleasantries on the day and the weather (bright but cold).

'Be a bit different in Australia.'

Bob Woonunga has told Ruth that he is going back to Australia for the winter. 'I need warmth in December.' Ruth thinks of her friend and the cards with the sun-bathing Santas. A hot Christmas still doesn't seem right to her. She has to admit though that this whole business has given her a new interest in Australia. She sees herself walking across red sand, watching the sun go down on Ayers Rock, or Uluru as Caroline would call it. She imagines blue seas and vast deserts, formed by the Great Rainbow Serpent himself. She thinks about souls made from mud, about cloud and rain spirits and the demons who hunt children by night. Really, her imagination has come on a long way since *Neighbours* and maybe this is due to *her* friendly neighbour. On balance, she's glad that Bob's coming back for the new term.

She agrees with Randolph that things are, indeed, different in Australia, and after a few further pleasantries he turns away to greet some new arrivals. Ruth grabs a handful of crisps and looks for someone to talk to. She wants to be talking to someone when Max arrives, not standing on her own by the buffet like a saddo.

'Hi Ruth.' It's Clough. The other person guaranteed to be found near the food. Ruth greets him with enthusiasm. She wonders if Nelson has arrived.

'Hi Clough. How are you?'

'Surviving.' Clough gives a brave smile. He has been recommended for a bravery award and still limps sometimes – when he remembers. 'How are you? How's that baby of yours?'

'Fine. Not really a baby anymore.'

'Bet she's excited about Christmas.'

'She is.' Kate can now say Christmas and Santa and, worryingly, Baby Jesus. Who taught her that one? Ruth wonders.

'Christmas isn't Christmas without kids.'

Ruth looks at him with interest. She wonders if he and Trace are thinking of having children. She's heard rumours that they've bought a dog. She asks, and is rewarded by seemingly endless photographs of a labradoodle puppy.

'It's the only breed that Trace isn't allergic to.'

'He's lovely,' says Ruth truthfully.

'Do you want to see pictures of my dog?' Max is leaning over her shoulder. Ruth turns and smiles.

'Hi.'

'Hi Ruth.'

Clough, who has been watching this greeting curiously, wanders away, trailing crumbs.

'How is Claudia?' asks Ruth.

'Fine. She sends her love to Flint.'

'Would she ... would you ...' But, before Ruth can finish, Bob Woonunga, glorious in an even bigger and furrier cloak than Cathbad's, appears in the doorway and asks them to step outside.

In the tiny museum garden, overshadowed by office blocks and the flats managed by Stanley, the scourge of dog owners, Bob has built a bonfire. 'It's called a coolamon,' says Max. He tells Ruth that he's hoping to have his own repatriation ceremony in Sussex soon. As eucalyptus branches are in short supply, the pyre is comprised of pine branches and their scent is like expensive bath oil.

'Crack!' Ruth jumps but it's only Cathbad and his friends with their clapping sticks. A strange procession starts to form. Bob, in his cloak and now a feathered headdress, chanting, and occasionally shouting out strange staccato cries that echo in the cold air. Then Caroline and Randolph, carrying what looks like a rectangular box but which, Ruth supposes, is actually the coffin containing the skulls and bones of the ancestors. Then Alkira Jones and Derel Assinewai carrying a second box. They are followed by a little girl, as solemn as a bridesmaid, carrying a large feather, just like the one Ruth found on the spare-room bed.

Caroline and Randolph place their box in front of the fire. Alkira and Derel follow suit. Randolph carefully unwraps an Aboriginal flag and places it over the coffins. Judy, watching from the back, thinks of the time when she imagined her funeral, the last post, the folded union jack. Next to her, Darren smiles and takes her hand. He's so excited about the baby that he hardly likes to let her out of his sight. Judy squints through the smoke so that she can see Cathbad. He should look ridiculous in that cloak, but to Judy he looks wonderful, like an ancient warrior. Darren squeezes her hand. 'Tired?' Judy shakes her head.

Randolph clears his throat and takes a piece of paper

from his pocket. 'On behalf of the Smith family, alive and dead . . .' he begins. Ruth thinks of Bishop Augustine who was also, of course, a member of the Smith family. There is already a battle royal over his (or her) remains. Randolph wants them to be buried in the cathedral, near the statue with the warning about the great snake, but Janet Meadows and the other local historians want a private burial in accordance, they say, with the Bishop's own wishes. The coffin will find a home in the Smith museum, though Ruth, who has heard about the poisoned spores from Nelson, thinks that she will probably give visiting it a miss. She looks at Phil, standing proudly beside Shona. Was his flu also courtesy of the Bishop? Trust Phil to come into contact with a deadly virus and still only suffer from man flu.

'On behalf of the Smith family alive and dead,' says Randolph, Lord Smith, 'I would like to apologise, here and now, for the actions of my ancestor in removing these bones from their sacred place of rest.' He pauses and looks at Caroline. 'Our ancestor was wrong to remove the bones and my father was wrong to keep them here, in the museum, when they should have been returned to the fields of their fathers.' That's a nice phrase, thinks Ruth. Did he get it from Bob, who is smiling encouragingly, or from Caroline, who is gazing fiercely into the middle distance? Is she thinking that she is the one who should have made the speech? She was the one, after all, who lobbied for the return of the relics. Why should Randolph take centre stage, just because he's a man? That much, at least, hasn't changed since Bishop Augustine's time.

'We return the ancestors to Mother Earth and to the arms of their people. We remember those who have died, especially my father Lord Danforth Smith.' He falters slightly and looks at Caroline again. Then his voice strengthens. 'We also remember Neil Topham, who loved the museum and who, in his own way, honoured the ancient dead.' He looks straight ahead, as proud as a French aristocrat making a speech at the foot of the guillotine. 'We ask,' he says, 'that our family, the Smith family, should be free from the curse brought down upon the head of our father. We ask that we be free, as the ancestors are now free.'

There is some applause, faint and tinny in the open air, but most people seem rather baffled by the mention of the curse. Ruth sees Phil laughing with Shona behind his hand and some of the reporters smiling as they think of an amusing new slant to give their articles. But Caroline squeezes her brother's hand with what looks like genuine gratitude and Bob Woonunga smiles at them benevolently.

Whitcliffe now begins an interminable speech about understanding between nations. Nelson, who has to stand at his side looking supportive, wishes that an Aboriginal thunderbolt would fall from the sky and transform his boss into a toad. He looks for Ruth in the crowd and sees her next to that other archaeologist, the one who gave him so much trouble a few years ago. Are they together now? He supposes he should wish them well; Ruth could do with some company and, after all, he's married, more married than ever it seems, after his illness and miraculous recovery. Michelle seems to have moved on from jealousy and resentment; now she is almost terrifyingly strong and optimistic. She has even agreed to let him see Katie. At the thought of Katie, Nelson's face softens.

Whitcliffe finally draws to a close. Bob make a brief but poetic speech, welcoming the ancestors back to the sacred land. Of course, strictly speaking they are not repatriated yet. Their journey will not end until the Qantas Airbus delivers them to Brisbane airport in two days time. Even then, the relics face another journey by road and sea to Minjerribah, the islands in the bay. But to all intents and purposes the handover is now complete. Bob shakes hands with Randolph and Caroline, Derel raises the didgeridoo to his lips, and a new tune breaks out – a happier, more joyful sound. Cathbad lights the fire and the smoke reaches up into the winter sky (Stanley rings later to complain). The little girl, who turns out to be Alkira's daughter, carefully places the feather on the bonfire.

Perhaps because of the smoke, starlings roosting on the nearby rooftops rise into the air in their own inky cloud. Murmuration, thinks Nelson. Now why does he know that word? As the crowd disperses, he finds himself next to Randolph Smith.

'How's everything at the stables?' he asks.

Tamsin Smith and Len Harris have both been remanded in custody pending trial. Tamsin is denying everything and, as she has employed an expensive and unscrupulous QC, it promises to be quite a battle. Nelson's looking forward to it; he hasn't had a good fight for ages.

'Not too bad,' says Randolph. 'Some owners have taken

their horses away but we've got some who're loyal to us. And we've got the horses that Dad owned, like The Necromancer. He's a terrific prospect. I'm going to enter him for next year's National.'

'Did you hear that?' says Nelson to Clough, who is hovering nearby, eating crisps. 'Your favourite horse is going to run in the National. You must have a bet.'

'I never want to see that horse again,' says Clough with dignity.

Randolph laughs. 'He's a reformed character, Sergeant. You should see him. I've been riding him out twice a day and he's a lamb.'

'I'll take your word for it,' says Clough.

Ruth and Max are watching the birds wheel and turn in the darkening sky. Ruth thinks of the Saltmarsh, of the lonely, beloved landscape, of walking with Kate and Max on the beach.

'Do you want to come for Christmas?' she blurts out. 'It'll be quiet, just me and Kate, but we could get a tree, roast some chestnuts.'

Max's face breaks into a smile worthy of Bob Woonunga himself. 'I'd love to,' he says.

He reaches out and takes her hand. Ruth is rather taken aback. It's been so long since she's been in a relationship that she's forgotten how couples behave. Do they really hold hands like this? It feels rather odd but she's willing to try anything once. She lets her hand rest in his.

'Hallo Ruth.'

'Hi Nelson.' She tries to remove her hand but Max's hold tightens. 'Do you remember Max Grey?'

'Yes,' says Nelson, without enthusiasm. 'How are you? You're a long way from ... Brighton, isn't it?'

'I've come for the ceremony' says Max. 'And to see Ruth of course.'

'Well, I don't blame you for giving Norfolk a miss,' says Nelson. 'Not much of a place is it?'

'On the contrary,' says Max, smiling warmly at Ruth. 'I like Norfolk very much. I have a feeling I'm going to be spending a lot more time here. In fact, I'm coming to Ruth for Christmas.'

It ought to be easy, thinks Ruth, watching Nelson disappear into the crowds and the smoke. Nelson is happily married, Ruth is about to start a relationship with a man she really likes. Nelson can see Kate; perhaps, in time, all four adults can become friends.

It ought to be easy. But it isn't.

ACKNOWLEDGEMENTS

The Smith family and the Slaughter Hill Stables are completely fictitious. However, in order to see how a racing stable operates, I spent some time at the incredible Cisswood Racing Stables in Lower Beeding and would like to thank Jayne and Gary Moore for their hospitality and help. Special thanks to Lucy Moore for showing me round and answering all my questions. I need hardly say that Jayne and her wonderfully talented family have absolutely nothing in common with Danforth Smith and co.

Similarly, the Smith Museum has no counterpart in real life, though many British museums do hold human remains, and there are pressure groups demanding their return. For details of one such repatriation, I am indebted to John Danilis's marvellous book *Riding the Black Cockatoo* (Allen and Unwin).

Bishop Augustine is fictitious although Pope Joan apparently did exist.

Thank you to Michael Whitehead for the Blackpool background and apologies to Sarah Whitehead (who looks lovely in tangerine) for the football joke. Thanks to Andrew Maxted and Dr Matt Pope for their archaeological expertise and to Keith Jones, equine vet extraordinaire, for the information about horses. However, in all these cases, I have taken the experts' advice only as far as it suits the plot, and any resulting mistakes or inaccuracies are mine alone.

I didn't get his name but thanks to the lovely guide at Norwich Cathedral who showed me Mother Julian's cat. Thanks to Becki Walker for her help with proof-reading.

I'm very grateful, as ever, to my editor Jane Wood, my agent Tim Glister, and all at Quercus and Janklow and Nesbit, for their continued faith in me. Heartfelt thanks to all the publishers around the world who have taken a chance with Ruth.

Love and thanks always to my husband Andrew and our children, Alex and Juliet.

This book is for my friends Nancy and Anita, with whom I shared so much of my childhood, and in memory of their mother, Sheila Woodman, who was always so encouraging about my writing.

E.G. January 2012

JUN - - 2012